Legacy of the Ripper

The Sequel to *A Study in Red*
The Secret Journal of Jack the Ripper

Brian L. Porter

To David & Ann
With love.

11/7/09

龍

Double Dragon Publishing

Legacy of the Ripper
Copyright © 2009 Brian L. Porter

Double Dragon Press

Published by
Double Dragon Publishing, Inc.
PO Box 54016
1-5762 Highway 7 East
Markham, Ontario L3P 7Y4 Canada
http://www.double-dragon-ebooks.com
http://www.double-dragon-publishing.com

ISBN-10: 1-55404-690-4
ISBN-13: 978-1-55404-690-4

A DDP First Edition June 29th, 2009
Book Layout and
Cover Art by Deron Douglas
http://www.derondouglas.com

Also from Brian L Porter
and Double Dragon Publishing

A Study in Red – The Secret Journal of Jack the Ripper *(Winner of The Preditors and Editors Best Thriller Novel of 2008 Award, and coming soon in Motion Picture from Thunderball Films LLC)*

Dedication

'Legacy of the Ripper' is dedicated to the memory of Enid Ann Porter, (1914 – 2004). Her belief in me and my work never wavered even though she never lived to see the first book in publication, and to Juliet, who provides the help and support without which none of my books would ever be completed.

Acknowledgements

This sequel to 'A Study in Red – The Secret Journal of Jack the Ripper' owes much to a number of people whose invaluable help and support went into creation the final manuscript. My thanks are due to Frogg Moody and the members of the committee of The Whitechapel Society 1888. Not only have I learned much from my membership of this august organisation, but the committee generously gave their permission for me to use the name of the society within the book, when I could just as easily have used a fictitious organisation with which to link the character of Alice Nickels. Their generosity has helped lend a greater realism to 'Legacy of the Ripper' than I could have hoped for.

To my friends and fellow Ripperologists at www.jtrforums.com, I also add my thanks, in particular to Howard Brown and Mike Covell. As a source of information and support to anyone with an interest in the Whitechapel murders, their pages are a goldmine of information. Special thanks go to Howard and Mike, for their continued support and encouragement.

I owe a great deal of thanks to Deron at Double Dragon Publishing for his confidence in my work and for his wonderfully innovative cover design, and to Lea Schizas, my editor, who does a superb job of 'tightening up' and I'm sure, improving my manuscripts.

Mario Domina of Thunderball Films LLC, producer of the movie version of 'A Study in Red' was a wonderful source of encouragement as the novel drew to a close, as I found it hard going to complete the final chapters, as was my great friend Graeme S Houston.

A word of thank goes to Brian Gallagher for his occasional and priceless insights in the field of criminal psychology, and for providing me with reams of reading material on the subject.

My gratitude also goes to all those readers who purchased 'A Study in Red – The Secret Journal of Jack the Ripper' and made it the success story it has become.

Finally, it would be impossible for me to say thank you without including my wife in these acknowledgments. Over the course of my creating 'A Study in Red' and 'Legacy of the Ripper' she has now 'lived' with Jack the Ripper and his crimes for over four years. Her patience and her fortitude in reading every at times harrowing chapter as they've been created is worthy of praise I can never rightly bestow. Her help, opinions and advice have been invaluable.

In the Beginning

In the year 1888, in what became known as 'The Autumn of Terror' a series of killings took place in the East End of London, which shook not only the people of the capital of the greatest empire the modern world has known, but reached into the lives of the population of the whole country as the murderer prowled at will through the dark, crime-ridden streets of Whitechapel, where he murdered and mutilated his victims, seemingly at will. The police appeared helpless in their search for this brazen and sadistic killer who history has recorded forever under the name by which he soon became known, *Jack the Ripper!*

As the body count grew, more and more police officers were assigned to the case and the largest manhunt England had ever seen was launched in a bid to bring the murderer to justice. Despite such action, and the questioning of dozens of potential suspects, no arrests were made in the case, and the speculation as to the identity of the Ripper began, and has continued to this day. Was he a single man, a loner, or could he have been a married man with a family of his own. Did he have children? Could his genes have been passed down by the heredity of birth through the years, thus allowing his descendants to walk among us, unknown and unknowing of their own ghastly and murderous heritage?

Many theories have been propounded over the years. Was he a doctor, a lunatic, a woman-hating member of the Jewish community, or was 'Jack the Ripper' a convenient cover name for a group of two or more killers operating as part of some great Masonic plot, or, perhaps the most outlandish theory of all, a member of the Royal family?

It's likely that the identity of the world's first officially recognised serial killer will remain a hidden secret, never to be revealed, and the only thing we can say for certain is that Jack the Ripper died a very long time ago, and thus his reign of terror ended with his passing...or did it?

My Name is Jack, A Statement by the Patient.

When did it start? That's what they all want to know. Doctor Ruth is always asking me:

"When did it start? What are your earliest recollections of these feelings?"

I keep telling her the same as I'm telling you all now. It's hard to put a time or a place on when it began, though I was young, very young, maybe four or five years old when I first realised I was 'different' to other children of my age. Even then I knew that my life was mapped out ahead of me, that I had a destiny to fulfil. At such a tender age, of course, it was impossible for me to comprehend what that destiny was. Only much later did I realise that I was being guided by a hand far more powerful than mine, one whose intelligence and guile was such that I had no doubts, when the time came, of the course of action I must take.

I was different you see, different from all of those children who made my life a misery, the ones who called me names because I didn't want to join in their silly games, or take part in stupid group activities after school. When I was very young, I didn't know that I held the power and the means within me to put an end to their taunting and name calling. Only when I reached the age of nine did I suddenly make a stand against those silly, laughing, taunting voices. That was the day when a group of children cornered me in the school playground, out of sight of the watchful teachers and playground assistants. Somehow, they'd heard about my regular visits to the child psychologist. My going in itself wasn't a secret of course. They all knew that I had to attend regular doctor's appointments, but, as happens from time to time, word spread around the school about the real reason for my appointments.

"Bloodsucker, Dracula, do you eat your meat raw, Jack Reid?" they shouted in a cacophony of screeching, childish screams.

"He's a vampire, he sucks the blood from living cats, that's what I've heard," screeched Andrew Denning, one of the ringleaders of the haranguing group.

"You're a weirdo, Reid, that's what you are," Camilla Hunt shouted in my face.

I'd had enough. As Denning came closer to scream in my face once again, I waited until he was within touching distance, and, quick as a flash, I grabbed my tormentor with both hands, one either side of his face, and pulled him close to me. He struggled as I bent my head to the side and the others screamed in panic, but no-one came to his aid as my teeth sunk deeply into his flesh, biting hard on the tender mass of sinews and muscle that made up his ear. That was when the loudest scream of all erupted, this time from Andrew Denning himself, as I pulled my head back from his to reveal a large chunk of his ear still stuck between my teeth. Blood pumped from the side of the boy's head and the other children stood screaming, rooted to the spot in their fear and fascination. In seconds the sound of an adult voice could be heard shouting,

"What's all this commotion? If you boys have been fighting I'll....Oh my God! Jack! What have you done?"

Miss Plummer almost fainted on the spot, but, to her credit, she maintained her equilibrium enough to send two of the other children running for help. How she did it I can't remember, but she made me open my mouth long enough for her to retrieve the bitten remains of Andrew Denning's ear, which she quickly wrapped in a handkerchief she pulled from a pocket in the side of her skirt. The others were quickly dismissed and Miss Plummer stayed with me and Andrew, who continued to scream until another teacher arrived and escorted him away. Soon afterwards a car disappeared through the school gates carrying the injured boy to the hospital. I learned afterwards that the doctors had sewn what they could of his ear back together, but in truth it would never look right again, and Andrew Denning I'm sure will never forget our encounter. I say that because I only heard these things second-hand. After that incident the headmaster summoned my parents to the school and I was removed from that particular place of education and sent to what is laughingly called a 'special school', where children with 'special needs' are taught. I thought it odd at the time, that no-one really seemed to appreciate what my own peculiar *'special needs'* were.

It wasn't until much later that I would begin to realise just where my life was heading, and what I was destined to fulfil, just after my eighteenth birthday in fact, my 'coming of age' as they call it. That was when things really began to fall into place in my mind, and that is why you and all those who follow you, and Doctor Ruth especially, will never, ever forget me. I'm sorry, I've been remiss. Perhaps I should introduce myself before going any further. My name is Jack, Jack Thomas Reid, and this is the letter that began everything that transpired after that fateful day when I received my legacy from Uncle Robert.

To my dearest nephew, Jack,

This testament, the journal, and all the papers that accompany it are yours upon my death, as they became mine upon my father's death. Your Aunt Sarah and I were never fortunate enough to have children of our own, so it is with a heavy heart that I write this note to accompany these pages. Had I any alternative, I would spare you the curse of our family's deepest secret, or perhaps I should say, secrets! Having read what you are about to read, I had neither the courage to destroy it, nor to reveal the secrets contained within these pages. I beg you, as my father begged me, to read the journal and the notes that go with it, and be guided by your conscience and your intelligence in deciding what course of action to take when you have done so. Whatever you decide to do, dear nephew, I beg you, do not judge those who have gone before you too harshly, for the curse of the journal you are about to read is as real as these words I now write to you.

Be safe, Jack, but be warned.
Your loving uncle,
Robert

As for the rest, I suggest you go and talk to Doctor Ruth. She's the *expert* after all.

Chapter I
A Career Move

Does violent death have a name? Can evil truly be born into the world, evil so deep that it is bred into the genetic make-up of an individual? Until I came to this place, and met the man who made me begin to suspect that such an evil could exist, I'd have been as dismissive as most of my profession at the prospect of such a possibility.

My name is Ruth Truman, and this, I suppose is my confession, my testament to the failure of all I've tried to do, of all I've stood for since the day I took the Hippocratic oath on becoming a physician, a healer, one who makes people better when they're ill, who cures disease and puts a healthy smile back on the face of those who are beset by illness.

My career was always a fast track to the specialisation I'd chosen while at Medical School in London, and so, today, I'm a psychiatrist, and as such am charged with administering treatment to patients who suffer from some of the most dreadful and least understood diseases that afflict us as human beings, diseases of the mind. My career, until recently, has been one of unqualified success, as I rose through the ranks of my profession with almost indecent haste, becoming a senior consultant psychiatrist in one of our country's largest teaching hospitals at the age of just forty one. My work with the most difficult of patients, and with those suffering from some of the lesser known but perhaps most interesting of psychiatric illnesses, in particular bipolar disease, more commonly known as manic depression and some of the more obscure dissociative disorders, led eventually to me being offered the post of Senior Consultant at one of the largest secure psychiatric hospital facilities in the United Kingdom. In this enlightened age of course, we now refer to such places as 'Special Hospitals' rather than the old institutional type of description which would once have been applied to such a facility.

No, in our politically-correct, pre-packaged, health and safety orientated nation of today, the word 'asylum' no longer has a place, and perhaps rightly so. Those who are incarcerated, or should I say treated in the hospital are no longer referred to as 'inmates' but are now simply 'patients'. These patients, of course, by nature of the acts they committed that led to their confinement at Ravenswood, are some of the most dangerous individuals our society can produce. As such they must be treated with the utmost respect in terms of ensuring the safety of those who have to work in close proximity to the assorted rapists, murderers, arsonists and serial criminals of every variety whom the courts have chosen to label as being of unsound mind. Quite often, those patients can, of course, be a danger not only to those who must care for them, but also to their fellow inmates, er, sorry, patients, and occasionally to themselves. The number of incidences of attempted self-harm in a hospital such as Ravenswood are far higher than might be supposed by those on the outside. With the greatest of care and supervision that we can provide, a determined individual will always find a way to inflict grievous harm upon themselves, occasionally with fatal consequences. Such events are, thankfully, a rarity, as most patients are found and treated before they are able to complete the act of suicide.

This then, is the powder keg environment into which are cast a selection of the most damaged members of our society, mentally speaking. As doctors and nurses, the staff must be constantly vigilant and on their guard when dealing with such individuals, and while some achieve their goal of an eventual release from their incarceration in the hospital, others, not so lucky, may find themselves living out the long years of their natural lives within the confines of Ravenswood and other facilities of its kind. We have a number of other staff, not medically qualified, but who in any other similar environment might just be referred to as guards. These men and women are members of the prison service and assigned to take care of the additional security necessary for the calm and efficient running of such a high risk establishment. Without their presence, the 'patients' might just end up inflicting terrible harm on both staff and fellow inmates of the hospital, and pandemonium would reign.

***

The man whose tale I wish to relate, the man who has driven me to doubt the profession and the ethics that I have given my life to, shows no outward sign of being the proverbial monster, the thing of evil, the beast that I henceforth profess him to be. In truth, Jack Reid is one of the most handsome young men I have ever met. He has the good looks of youth, a cheerful and, at times, most charming disposition, and his fair hair and blue eyes, combined with his warm and gentle smile are such that the man is capable of 'charming the birds from the trees' to quote a much used colloquialism. At a little under six feet tall, he has the advantage of height over me, being a mere five feet two, but I have to admit that the towering young man has never used his size to try to intimidate me in any of our meetings. Jack Reid is politeness itself.

When I first arrived here, Jack had been a patient within these walls for just over a month. Not one of the three doctors who'd attempted to 'connect' with the sad and unhappy young man he was at that time had managed even a modicum of success. Jack Reid had been found guilty by reason of insanity of a series of three murders of innocent young women in and around the Brighton area. His barrister had successfully pleaded at the trial that, as Jack had no recollection of having committed the murders, which had been borne out by intensive pre-trail psychiatric examinations by a series of respected psychiatric consultants, then it would be impossible to convict him of 'wilful' murder. It was put forward by the prosecution that Jack had committed the murders whilst on a form of 'fugue state', almost a trance, or while undergoing a personality change wrought by a deep psychotic disorder, a severe schizoid episode. Jack's story, however, was very different and regarded as being so improbable that no-one, least of all the police and the prosecution, gave much credence to it at the time. That story, incredible though it may appear at times, forms the basis of much that I wish to record here.

A 'not guilty by reason of insanity' plea was rejected by the judge, who directed the jury to disregard any such option when arriving at their verdict. Jack Reid, although apparently having no knowledge of his actions at the time he'd committed the slayings, was sufficiently aware of his crimes that he did all he could to cover up the murders after committing each of the killings. He said, and the psychiatrists who examined him believed him sufficiently to accept this, that he'd woken as if from a dream at each of the death scenes, and, knowing that he must be the one responsible for the scenes of mayhem he encountered, and not wanting to be caught and punished he therefore did his best to evade the due process of law. At other times he contradicted this story, saying that he didn't kill the girls, that someone else was responsible, which is where the most elaborate and unbelievable part of his story came in, and which we will focus on quite soon. This illogical and at times pitiful changing from one story to another probably helped the judge to decide there was enough evidence regarding the accused's mental state that a conviction could be made on the grounds stated by the prosecution counsel, and the jury agreed.

How could a man commit such crimes and yet have no knowledge of them, while at the same time take all reasonable steps to avoid apprehension and prosecution? Something about the case of Jack Reid caused sufficient consternation for him to be committed to Ravenswood, the most secure and technologically modern hospital of its kind in the United Kingdom. It was hoped the medical staff here would be able to get to the bottom of this strange and chilling case, and that of course is where I entered the picture.

The Director of Medical Services at Ravenswood, Doctor Andrew Pike, solicited my services with a well-timed approach some weeks before my first meeting with Jack. I'd grown tired of my post at a leading London teaching hospital and was ready for a new challenge. When a friend of mine who'd been privy to one of my long and boring lectures over lunch on the need for a change of career direction met Pike at a psychiatric conference a few days after I'd shot my mouth off, and Pike had told him of the impending retirement of his senior consultant, Paul suggested that Pike speak to me about the vacancy. After a telephone call from the Director, and an interview that was little more than a social meeting between the two of us, Pike offered me the position and I, flattered by the confidence he apparently had in my abilities, graciously accepted my new role. I really felt that I could make a difference, and perhaps bring a new dimension to the treatment of what at one time would have been described as the 'criminally insane' although such phrases are frowned upon in these enlightened times.

It took me only a couple of weeks to make the necessary arrangements for my move to Ravenswood, and to find a beautiful country cottage to rent a mere five miles from the facility. I left my flat in London in the hands of an agent to handle the task of renting it out for me, ensuring that the property would at least be occupied, and the sum of money I received each month would more than cover the rent on my picturesque cottage in the beautiful village of Langley Mead. My employers at the hospital were reluctant to accept my resignation, but there was nothing they could do to prevent me taking up my new post, and thus I found myself within the walls of Ravenswood far sooner than I'd thought possible.

It was April, and the tulips and daffodils were in full bloom in the flower bed positioned just outside the large picture window of my office on the ground floor of Pavlov wing, named in honour of Ivan Pavlov, to whom we owe much by way of our knowledge of modern-day behavioural psychology. A veritable plethora of colours, vibrant reds and yellows, tinged with a few pastel shades of pink and off-white gave the little flower bed the appearance of being awash with far more blooms than were actually planted within it. The illusion created by nature wasn't lost on my logical mind. If the very plants that spring from the earth can cause us to doubt the reality of a situation, then how much cleverer are those whose minds have developed the most warped and misleading codes of ethics, and who would do all in their power to mislead and misdirect those of us who seek to understand them? The irony of the situation was that, although the flowers were free to bend in the breeze and to soak up the life-giving rays of the sun that gave them sustenance, my new patients were, like me, locked securely within the structures that comprise the hospital, away from the sunlight, in safe and secure isolation. Even the window to my office was fitted with bars in the inside, and alarmed to prevent unauthorised opening of the narrow ventilator slits at the top. Even on a hot and stifling day, the window itself didn't open. Those of us incarcerated with our patients within those walls had to count on the air conditioning to maintain a comfortable environment. It is with those strictures in mind that it is, I suppose, possible to be envious of a tulip.

My new secretary Tess Barnes entered my office, smiled a good morning greeting and placed a large pile of patient folders in my in-tray. She paused for a moment before leaving me and as I looked up I could see he was eager to speak.

"Yes, Tess, what is it? If you have something to say please get used to the fact that I'm not an ogre of any sort of description. Feel free to talk to me any time you like."

"I'm sorry, Doctor Truman," she replied. "I wasn't sure how busy you are. It's just that Doctor Roper asked me to ensure that you looked at the file on the top of that pile. He thinks, with respect, that you might want to take personal charge of that particular patient."

"Okay, Tess, that's no problem. I'll look at it straight away if he thinks it so important."

"Thank you, Doctor," she said, and with that she turned on her heel and left my office, closing the door quietly behind her.

Alone once more, I reached out to the in-tray and picked up the file designated as of special interest to me by Doctor Roper, who I remembered meeting a couple of times in the previous two days. He seemed a pleasant and affable man, and gave off an air of confidence and calm reassurance, the perfect demeanour for a psychiatrist. Wondering what he thought was so important about the file that he'd asked my secretary to specifically direct me to it, I placed the beige folder on my desk and looked at the name on the cover of the patient file before me. There, in a neat and ordered handwriting were written just three words.

The file was that of Jack Thomas Reid!

Chapter 2
In the Beginning

Reading the file that had been left so invitingly upon my desk, I soon found myself drawn into the life of the young man whose future treatment, and to some extent, his life from now on had effectively been placed in my hands

Jack Reid had been born to doting parents in the year nineteen ninety six. Tom and Jennifer Reid were what could perhaps be termed an 'average' middle-class couple, with the husband being a respected if a little eccentrically minded computer engineer. Tom Reid worked for a company that specialised in the production of state-of-the-art military hardware for the British Armed Forces.

Young Jack had lived a relatively happy and conventional childhood, though by the age of ten he had developed a marked and quite disturbing preoccupation with the sight of blood. His parents, understandably disturbed by their son's rather macabre interest, took him to a number of different child psychologists and psychiatrists. Tom's own cousin Robert, the boy's official second-cousin, but always referred to as 'uncle', had been a psychiatrist until his death from the effects of a brain tumour in nineteen ninety eight, and though Jack had been too young to know his uncle at the time of his death, Tom had always held hopes that his son might follow either in the footsteps of himself or his late brother. The manifestations of his young son's mind seemed to preclude the second possibility however, as Tom realised that something far from normal was taking place within the cognitive sections of his son's brain. Far from ever becoming a psychiatrist, it looked as if Jack could well find himself permanently under the care of one.

That being said, both Tom and Jennifer Reid loved their son dearly and no expense was spared in their choice of the physicians they selected to try and elicit the best care and potential cure for Jack's odd predilections. Though initially they'd relied on the resources of their own G.P. and the local NHS hospital to care for their son, it soon became clear to them that the overstretched resources of the National Health Service would never provide either short or long term relief for their son's condition, nor would the ministrations of a general practitioner with limited knowledge of psychiatric disorders. They made the expensive decision to seek private care for Jack.

Thankfully, Tom's job with Beaumont Industries provided them with a more than adequate income, and though the family's finances were at times stretched to breaking point, Jack was soon under the care of both a child psychologist, a Doctor Simon Guest, and a psychiatrist, Doctor Faye Roebuck. Between them the two noble members of my profession did their best for the young boy. Both concluded that Jack suffered from a personality disorder, but one which, with treatment, could be controlled and eventually eradicated. Their methods differed, of course, as befitted their different fields of medicine. As a psychiatrist, Doctor Roebuck had tried to work her way into the mind of young Jack, and attempted to control his urges by placing him a regime of medications that she hoped would temper his unusual desires and feelings. Doctor Guest, on the other hand, tried simply to identify anything in the boy's background or home life and upbringing that might have led him to his unusual fixations. He spent hours talking to Jack and his parents and despite finding little to suggest that anything in his environment had caused Jack's aberrant behaviour, tried to instil a new and regimented system of life upon the young man in the hope that continuity and stability in his daily life could be used as a tool to regulate and control Jack's feelings, to clarify things in his young mind, and slowly bring about a change in his mental attitudes resulting in a healthier and more rational outlook by the boy.

Years of treatment followed, and appeared to have been successful when at the age of fourteen Jack was considered well enough to leave the special school to which he'd been allocated after the incident at his junior school, once more to enter the world of regular education, this time at the local Comprehensive school where he settled in nicely and with no further incidents of violence. Jack seemed happy and well-adjusted, and his doctors, and more especially his parents, breathed a sigh of relief.

The teenaged Jack was a popular boy, and his circle of friends thought highly of him. He was academically bright and excelled on the sports field, being a capable footballer and an excellent wicket-keeper and batsman on the cricket pitch. Indeed, so adept was he at the game of cricket that he was selected for the local county schools association team, playing in competitions with other county associations. Jack eventually left school with a clutch of GCSE examination passes to his name, and moved onto the local college, where he began a course in graphic design, hoping to qualify and become a book illustrator. Halfway through his first year at college however his focus changed and without warning he gave up his studies and found himself a job as a trainee nurse at his local hospital.

His parents were at first horrified at the thought that his close proximity to the sick and infirm, and more especially to his being exposed to almost daily exposure to those suffering from open, bleeding wounds, might bring about a recurrence of his earlier problems. Jack was able to mollify them, however, when he explained that one of his friends from college, a young woman no less, had also begun the self-same nursing course. As Jack put it to his parents, he had already received enough treatment from the health services and, as a qualified nurse, he would be able to give something back to the system that had helped cure him of his earlier childhood affliction.

His mother was quite delighted to think that her son had become so responsible and mature in his outlook on life, but his father proved a little more sceptical about the whole affair and decided to reserve judgement on his son's sudden change of career path. Hindsight would apparently prove his reservations to be well-founded.

Initially, though, all appeared well and Jack was a diligent student, attentive to his teachers and scrupulous in his studies. All of his written work was handed in on time and his 'hands-on' practical work under supervision on the wards was reported as being exemplary. In his first six months, Jack Reid earned a reputation as a model student, and his nurse tutors reported in writing that he would, in time, become an excellent and valued member of the nursing profession.

As his eighteenth birthday approached Jack presented himself for his first official assessment of his training. After receiving a glowing report from all of his tutors he returned home that evening to inform his parents that he was considered to be one of the top two students on his course. His mother and father were elated at the news and agreed that at last they could feel a real sense of pride in their son's achievements. Even his previously sceptical father felt sufficiently pleased to crack open a bottle of his very best Chablis, which the small family of three consumed with delight over dinner that evening.

Over dinner his mother tried to draw him to speak on the subject of the girl who'd enticed him to join her in the nursing fraternity. Jennifer thought that if perhaps a relationship was developing between Jack and the girl, she might consider inviting her son's new friend, his first girlfriend as she put it, to dinner one evening. Jack, however, had totally rebuffed any questions from his mother on the subject. Apart from telling his parents that the girl's name was Anna, that she was nowhere near as clever as he was and not worth investing any more of his time in her, she became a closed subject. Jennifer Reid was disappointed, believing that if her son could achieve some sort of normal relationship with a member of the opposite sex, it would be another step towards his total rehabilitation from his earlier, juvenile problems. Perhaps, in the light of events that were soon to follow, Jack's failure to cement any sort of relationship with Anna, who would later testify at his trial, was a blessing in disguise.

Two weeks after that first assessment Jack reached his eighteenth birthday. His parents had asked if he would like to invite any of his friends or fellow students to a celebratory dinner at a local restaurant, but Jack declined the offer. A meal with his parents would be enough, so he informed them. Sadly, his parents, tutors, and fellow students had failed to recognise the gradually expanding bubble of isolation in which Jack was cocooning himself. Something had occurred within his mind that saw him withdraw more and more into himself, and though his studies hadn't become affected, the once gregarious and popular student began to shut himself off from those around him.

Later, statements from his parents would confirm that the evening of Jack's eighteenth birthday was perhaps the last really happy occasion they enjoyed together as a family. Though not particularly talkative, Jack had been in a fairly bright and happy frame of mind and grateful to his parents for the gold watch they'd bought for him to celebrate his birthday. The back of the watch had been engraved with the words, *To Jack T Reid with much love on your eighteenth birthday, Mum and Dad.* Jack loved it, and the evening of his birthday meal passed off amicably and with much good humour in the Reid household. No-one could have foreseen what lay ahead, just beyond time's immediate horizon.

For now though all was well, at least on the surface, and it wasn't until the Reids received notification through Tom's late cousin's solicitor that a package was being held in trust for their son, to be given to him after he'd reached his eighteenth birthday, that events escalated towards the calamity that awaited the family.

From the day the family visited the solicitor and the package was placed in the hands of their son, no-one's lives would ever be the same again. A seed had been planted that was about to bear fruit, and for Jack Thomas Reid, the ripening of that seed would prove to be the harbinger of his own downfall, and the precursor to murder. The storm was about to be unleashed!

Chapter 3
A Link to the Past?

I should perhaps point out at this juncture of my tale that Jack's parents were not with him when their son read the contents of the package bequeathed to him by his late uncle. Whatever was contained within the file of papers handed over to him remained in his possession. His father testified at Jack's trial that he had no idea what his brother had left in trust for Jack, denying any knowledge of what Jack claimed in his defence it contained, therefore having no reason to give that could have caused such a sudden change in his demeanour and behaviour.

Tom Reid went on to describe how, on the night he received his legacy, Jack retired to his room at about nine p.m. and Tom and Jennifer weren't to see him again until he arrived in the kitchen for breakfast at about nine the following morning. He was scheduled to work on one of the hospital wards from two p.m. that day, but told his parents he was feeling unwell, and phoned in sick. His 'sickness' continued for another two days, after which the Reids noticed a dramatic change in their son's character. Almost overnight, Jack had become a morose and sorrowful character, and he appeared as though he was carrying the weight of the world, or at least some great burden on his shoulders. When pressed by his parents to talk about the reasons for his melancholic state of mind he refused to discuss the matter. Presuming it may have some connection to the papers left to Jack by his Uncle Robert, Tom and Jennifer did their best to find out from their son what had been contained in the package he'd received. All that Jack Reid said in reply to their inquiries was "It was something and nothing."

Tom Reid even went so far as to telephone Sarah Cavendish, Robert's widow, to try to ascertain what had been contained in the bundle of papers. Sarah told Tom that she knew of the package and its existence, but Robert had kept it securely locked in his safe and she'd never seen the contents. She did say that she suspected it contained something which had disturbed and upset him at one time, but thought that whatever it was could hardly be a contributing factor in young Jack's current morose and sullen mood. She went on to say that shortly before his death Robert had lodged the package with his solicitor and that was about all she knew. She hadn't even known that he'd left it to young Jack, and reiterated her belief that a few pages of paper couldn't possibly be the cause of such a change in the young man. Tom and Jennifer thought otherwise, but failed to press home their doubts to Sarah. As later events overtook the family, even Robert Cavendish's solicitor would be forced to admit that he had no idea of the contents of the package.

Within days of the receipt of his legacy, Jack's whole demeanour and personality appeared to his parents to have undergone a radical transformation. The happy young man they'd watched develop with such pleasure after the childhood psychological problems seemed to be slipping away from them. He returned to his studies at the teaching hospital but there was no longer a smile on his face either at the beginning or the end of the day. His conversation grew stilted, almost monosyllabic. His mother in particular worried that perhaps his close proximity to the original source of his childhood fixations, blood, teamed with whatever disturbing news he may have read in the papers bequeathed to him by his uncle had in some way brought about this alteration in her son's personality. His father, though he didn't mention it to Jennifer, went so far as to call on Jack's senior tutor at the hospital who was reluctant at first to divulge much in the way of information about one of his students, but who was persuaded to open up to the father in the end. The one-time golden boy of the course had let his standards slip. Jack's work on the wards, once regarded as exemplary, had become shoddy and constantly in need of correction. His written work and other aspects of his study course had fallen below par and Tom was warned that such a rapid deterioration in standards could only lead to eventual failure if not corrected sooner rather than later.

Despite being taken to task by his father on his alleged shortcomings in relation to his studies, over a period of weeks Jack Reid's demeanour and attention to his work underwent an almost total transformation for the worse. In short, the life of the young man, who up until recently had appeared to have a glittering career in the nursing profession ahead of him, simply imploded. Tom and Jennifer pleaded with their son to go and see his own doctor, to talk about the things happening to him, but as far as Jack was concerned everything was as it should be. He saw no need to consult a doctor over what he deemed "his personal business".

Finally, unable to withstand the constant barrage of criticism and questions from his disbelieving and apparently disapproving parents, Jack left home. There was no discussion on the matter with his parents and no forewarning of his intentions. One morning, he quite arbitrarily walked out of the door with a suitcase in his hand and never returned to his parents' home again. Attempts to contact Jack on his mobile phone over the following days proved useless; the phone either being switched off or diverted to voicemail. His father found himself having to comfort his wife, Jack's mother, more and more as the sense of loss cut deeply into her heart and mind. Forced to choose between searching for Jack and looking after the psychological well-being of the woman he loved, Tom Reid chose the latter course of action. He would use whatever time he could afford to try to locate Jack's whereabouts, but his first priority would be his wife, the woman he loved and adored above all others.

Tom was faced with the unenviable task of convincing Jennifer that their son had in all probability regressed to his former mental state. As a loving, doting mother Jennifer was hard to convince, but eventually agreed with her husband that such an event was the only possible explanation for the sudden change in Jack's personality, though both she and Tom possessed a firm conviction that the legacy he'd received on his coming of age from his late uncle Robert had in some way contributed to his sudden regression.

"It had to be that package, or at least something in it. He was fine until he received it," Jennifer stated, without any doubt in her mind one evening as she and Tom tried yet again to rationalise all that had happened in recent weeks.

"You're right, of course, Jen," he'd replied. "And somehow we have to find out what was in it. What on earth can have been so shattering that it changed him so suddenly and dramatically?"

"You know, Tom? I know that Sarah said she'd no idea what the package contained, but you have to admit that Robert seemed a changed man shortly before he died. Could he have been affected by the contents of those papers in the same way that Jack has been?"

"Jen, my darling, Robert died from a brain tumour, you know that."

"Yes, but what about before that? Don't you remember how he lay in a coma after the crash that killed his father, your uncle?"

"Of course I do, but what's that got to do with Jack?"

"Tom, try harder. Sarah said that when he came round he was babbling on about having some sort of nightmares, that he thought Jack the Ripper was out to get him or something like that?"

"Oh, come on, Jen, get real. That was just the ramblings of his mind while he was in a comatose state, probably induced by the amount of drugs he was on for the pain."

"But what if it wasn't just the ramblings of his mind? What if something really happened to Robert that we don't know about?"

"If it had I'm sure Sarah would have said something, or Robert himself, come to that."

"But would they have told us? You must admit that Robert seemed a different person after the accident, and we hardly saw him and Sarah much after that time, right up until his death. Since then we've rarely seen or heard from Sarah, and she used to be so bubbly and full of fun before. Now, she's like a recluse, banging about in that big old house by herself, hardly ever going out or socialising anymore. Tom, I want you to go and see her, please. If you have to, press her on the subject of Robert's mental state after the accident. Try and find out if there was anything that happened to Robert that might have been a trigger for what's happened to Jack."

Jennifer wasn't to be talked out of her plan of action and eventually Tom agreed to visit his late cousin's wife on the following weekend. In the meantime, he engaged Philip Swan of Swan Private Investigations, with instructions to locate his son. He provided the investigator with the names of the few friends of Jack's he was aware of, including Anna. Swan said he'd do what he could, though it might not be much. Tom told the man he could ask for no more from him. Swan never found hide nor hair of Jack, and Tom Reid eventually paid the investigator's bill with some regret at having employed him on the fruitless task.

The weekend arrived, and Tom Reid left his worried wife at home alone as he set off in the family car for the home of his late cousin's wife. He'd purposely not given Sarah Cavendish any advance warning of his arrival. He thought that any such warning could put her on her guard, if indeed there was something she'd held back from them since the death of Robert. He though it preposterous of course, but his wife's pleadings and belief that something in the past tied Robert and Jack's behaviour together made him just the slightest bit reticent in his approach to Sarah.

As he pulled into the sun-drenched, leafy tree-lined avenue where he and Jennifer had shared so many happy evenings with Robert and Sarah in the dim and distant past the dark shadows of his son's mental state seemed to recede from his mind. Here in the heart of English suburbia, all appeared normal and peaceful. One of Sarah's neighbours was outside mowing the pristine lawn in front of his mock-Georgian home. Another was trimming the overhanging branches of an expansive lavender bush threatening to encroach over his fence onto his neighbour's property.

Only as Tom pulled onto the driveway of Sarah's home was he brought back to the reality of the reason for his visit. He pulled up behind Sarah's red Toyota, pleased that its presence probably indicated she was at home. As he stepped from his gleaming black BMW, Tom couldn't help but notice that though clean, Sarah's car appeared to be coated in a thin layer of dust, including the windscreen, giving him the hint that she hadn't been out in the vehicle for a few days at the very least. Jennifer's observation that Sarah had become something of a recluse came into his mind and for the first time, as he stood and pressed the doorbell to announce his arrival and despite the warmth of the day, Tom felt a cold shiver of foreboding at what he might discover in the home of his late cousin. Receiving no reply to his first press of the bell he tried again and again, and after what appeared an age to the increasingly impatient Tom, he heard footsteps from within. Sarah was coming!

Chapter 4
Sarah's Confession

The face that greeted Tom Reid as the door opened was one he knew only too well, and yet something in Sarah's smile rang false in his mind. This was not the happy and carefree woman who'd laughed and swapped jokes and stories with him and Jennifer in the good old days when Robert had been alive. It had been over a year since he'd seen his cousin's widow and she seemed to have aged considerably in that time.

Following Robert's tragic death, Tom and Jennifer had for a time maintained close ties with Sarah, but as often happens in families, the visits to one another's homes grew less frequent until they'd diminished to maybe once a year, until even those occasional visits stopped and the telephone became the chief means of maintaining communication. After all, they were struggling with the problems posed by the adolescent Jack and Sarah had been attempting to rebuild her own life after the death of her husband. Somehow, the two opposing threads had gradually driven an insurmountable wedge between them.

"Well, this is a surprise. Come in, Tom. To what do I owe the honour?" asked Sarah, doing her best to appear welcoming, though Tom felt as though he were intruding upon her privacy and in truth he felt less than welcome as he stepped over the threshold in to the once familiar home of his cousin.

"Hello, Sarah. Sorry to drop in unannounced, but there's something I need to talk to you about and it couldn't wait. It's urgent, and it concerns Jack."

"Jack? Why? What's happened?" she asked with a look of bewilderment on her face. "I'd have thought I'd be the last person to be able to help you with a problem that concerns you and your own son."

"Look, Sarah," said Tom as she led him into the familiar sitting room where he'd often held long and enjoyable discussions on all manner of subjects with Robert in happier times. "I know you said when I phoned you a while ago that you'd no idea what was in the package Robert bequeathed to Jack, but Jen and I are convinced it has something to do with his disappearance."

"His disappearance? Tom, what on earth's been going on? I've no idea why Jack should disappear. When did this happen?"

As Sarah sat with a worried look on her face in the armchair opposite the sofa, Tom related the tale of Jack's apparent descent into psychological trauma following his birthday and the receipt of his 'legacy' from Robert. She didn't interrupt his lengthy discourse on the events that had led to his arrival on her doorstep. Instead, she listened carefully, the frown on her face growing deeper as Tom arrived at the end of his tale.

"So there you have it, Sarah. From the day Jack received that package his life gradually fell apart. All I'm asking you to do is to please tell me if you have any idea whatsoever why that may have been so. Surely Robert must have given you some hint over the years as to what he proposed to leave to Jack?"

"I've told you, Tom, and Jen too, that Robert never mentioned a thing about it to me. I knew he had something he considered important for Jack but he never, ever told me what it was."

"I'm sorry, Sarah. I don't mean to sound disbelieving and I don't want you to think for a minute that I'm harassing you, but you and Robert were so close it's almost inconceivable that he'd keep something like that from you."

"But he did, Tom, and that's the truth."

"OK, Sarah. Let's suppose that to be the case. Can we look at this from another angle?"

"What 'angle' would that be, Tom? I just don't see what all of this has to do with Jack running off. Where is all this leading?"

Tom took a deep breath. He'd no desire to rake up old and painful memories in Sarah's mind, but concern for his son's mental well-being over-rode such considerations as he continued.

"Well, you remember when Robert first came out of his coma? He talked of being hounded or haunted by Jack the Ripper?"

"Oh Tom, really!" Sarah snapped. "Poor Robert had been in a coma, and those were just the fevered dreams and nightmares that he experienced while he was in that terrible state. How on earth can that have anything to do with Jack?"

"Look, I know this is painful for you, and I don't mean it to be, but, well, just suppose that Robert's nightmares were in fact slightly more than that."

"What the hell d'you mean by that? How can they have been more than that? They were nightmares, bad dreams, the hallucinations created by his mind while he was in the coma. How could they have been anything else?"

"I don't know, Sarah. I suppose I'm clutching at straws here, trying to find some logical reason to explain the sudden change in Jack's personality and behaviour."

"I can understand and sympathise with that, but blaming something that may or may not have sprung from Robert's hallucinations while he was in a coma isn't exactly logical, is it?"

"I know, but there has to be something, somewhere that'll give me a clue as to what's brought all this about so suddenly."

Sarah didn't answer immediately, and Tom suspected that she wanted to say something but couldn't find the words to express whatever it may be. He waited, the few seconds pause in their conversation seeming like hours as silence descended on the room and the chill he'd felt on his arrival returned to cause the hairs on the back of his neck to stand up. Sarah finally broke the silence.

"I think we need a cup of tea, Tom. What do you say?"

"Eh? Oh, yes, tea would be nice, Sarah, thanks."

She rose from her chair and without a word left Tom sitting on the sofa as she made her way to the kitchen. Tom thought better of asking if she needed any help. Sarah was far too independent to accept any such offer. He knew her well enough to make that assumption and in the few minutes she was employed in the making of the hot steaming brew he wondered what, if anything, could be the reasons for her sudden silence and reticence immediately prior to the offer of tea. He felt sure that Sarah knew something, or that at least she *thought* she knew something. Would she reveal all on her return? Tom didn't have long to wait, as Sarah soon returned with tea for two, served on a solid silver tray, the tea cups and saucers of the finest Royal Worcester bone china, and sugar provided in the old fashioned way, in lumps served from a bowl complete with silver-plated serving tongs.

"Still take sugar, Tom?" she asked as she poured the tea from a pot that matched the cups and saucers.

"One, same as always," he replied.

"Of course. I thought maybe you'd given it up, the sugar I mean," Sarah smiled at him, though the smile carried a certain falseness about it that Tom found unnerving.

Sarah passed him his tea and Tom went through the motions of stirring it with his teaspoon, and taking a small sip from the cup before speaking again.

"Sarah…" he began, but she forestalled his words by raising her hand.

"Tom, be quiet, please," she said, and she smiled that false smile once again. This wasn't the Sarah he'd known across the years. The woman who sat opposite him now bore the hallmarks of a woman with deep and intense problems of her own. He wondered why he hadn't noticed it before. Even her hair had begun to succumb to grey at the edges, and her once long locks were now cut in a less than fashionable style barely reaching her neck. Tom Reid suddenly realised that his cousin's widow could be harbouring some deep and terrible secret, something that she was afraid to discuss, even with him. He decided not to push the issue but to wait and see if she would eventually reveal what he suspected she may be hiding.

"I'm sorry, I…"

"Tom, please, *be quiet.* I have something to tell you. I don't know if it's relevant to what's happened to Jack and it may be just the ramblings of a lonely widow, but there *was* something odd about the things that happened to Robert, after he came out of the hospital you understand, not directly to do with the coma, at least, I don't think so."

"What do you mean, odd?"

"Well, when he came home it took a few days for him to open up fully and tell me all about the dreams or hallucinations or whatever they were. When he did, he related them to me with a sense of great fear and foreboding. I'm sure he didn't tell me everything, but Robert had been convinced that the spirit, the soul, call it what you will, of Jack the Ripper, had invaded his mind while he was in his comatose state. I pooh-poohed the idea of course, but he was unshakeable in his belief, and in the end I went along with what I thought were his delusions in order to pacify him, as he'd often become quite agitated when relating his stories of the 'Ripper's life' to me. A few weeks after he came home he received a package from his father's solicitor, which he told me contained personal papers and letters, but I know he was greatly affected by something in that package, and he'd often spend long hours in his study, usually late at night, reading through whatever it contained. Later, when he was diagnosed with the brain tumour, I presumed that his rather odd notion about the Ripper might have been caused by whatever was happening to his brain. I never for one moment, of course, believed any of it, but it is possible that the package he received from the solicitor may have been the one that he left to young Jack, though what it contained I've no idea."

"Sarah, what you're saying makes sense and at the same time it doesn't. It seems to me that you're trying to say that the package may have had something to do with his Jack the Ripper delusions, but if they were just that, delusions I mean, then why on earth would his father's solicitor have had them in his possession and why would he hide them away for years and then leave them to my son?"

"That's just it, Tom. I have no idea at all. I don't even know if I should be telling you all this. It doesn't mean a thing really, does it? Like you, I can't see what connection any of Robert's dreams or delusions or fears may have with Jack's current mental state."

"You say Robert had 'fears'. What exactly do you mean by that? He never mentioned any fears to me in the time between his coma and his eventual death."

"Listen, Tom, Robert told me that his greatest fear was that he would end up being cast into a purgatory type of existence, such as that he believed the Ripper's victims had been consigned to. He said that they visited him in his worst nightmares and that he could never shake their names or their faces from his mind. He spoke as if he knew them personally, Tom; Mary Kelly, Martha Tabram, Annie Chapman, Catharine Eddowes, Liz Stride and Mary Ann Nicholls. You see, I even know all their names. His later life became haunted by them, and when he lay dying, his last words, which I've never told to any living soul were, and *"They're here."* He was convinced that they'd come for him Tom, I'm sure of it. He couldn't find any peace at all, not even in his last moments."

Tom looked at Sarah, and he realised all of a sudden that this woman, his cousin's widow, had carried this great burden within her for so long that the weight of her own husband's tortured mind had preyed on her until she was close to cracking. She was so obviously riddled with guilt that she'd been unable to offer him the peace and solace he'd sought so desperately in his last days, even if it hadn't been her fault. Robert's mind had created his own demons, but Sarah had been forced to live with those demons every day since his death. Tears streamed down Sarah's face and

Tom Reid rose from his place on the sofa and moved across to the armchair. Sitting on the arm of the chair he placed his arm comfortingly around her shoulder, and said quietly,

"Thank you, Sarah. I don't know if it helps me with Jack, but I know it's been hard for you to tell me these things. Why on earth you never confided in me before I don't know, but I'm sure you had your reasons."

"Robert begged me never to tell anyone," she sniffed, "But after what you just told me I thought it only fair to tell you. Jack is family after all."

"Look, Sarah, I think that now you've got it out in the open, you should maybe come and stay with me and Jen for a while, just like you did in the old days. What do you say to coming for an extended visit?"

"Thanks, Tom, I appreciate your offer, but I can't, really. I don't get out much these days and I feel much more comfortable here in my own home, where I have my memories of Robert, than I do anywhere else."

"Are you sure, Sarah? It might do you good you know. We'd be more than happy to have you over. You know that."

"I know. I'm sorry. I don't mean to be ungrateful, but please understand what I mean when I say I feel closer to Robert here. I loved him very much you know, and I still do, even though he's gone forever. I'm closer to him here."

"I won't press you, Sarah," said Tom, resignedly. "But please remember that the invitation stands for as long as it needs to. You can come and visit and stay with us anytime you want, for as long as need to. Jen would love to have you with us."

"Thank you, Tom. I appreciate it, really," said Sarah as she wiped the tears away with a tissue from a box she kept beside her chair. Tom suspected that she probably cried a lot of tears in her lonely life in Robert's old house, alone with nothing but her memories of the husband she'd loved and lost to the reaper of death and the ghosts of his nightmares of long ago.

Five minutes later, after saying a difficult and tender goodbye and reiterating once again his invitation to Sarah to come stay with him and Jennifer, Tom Reid eased his car out of the driveway of her home, and as he looked in his rear view mirror, he swore he saw a dark heavy shadow hanging over the house he'd just left, despite the brightness of the sunshine that bathed the rest of the street and the cloudless blue sky above. Could it have been his imagination? Maybe the passage of time and the events that followed provided the answer to Tom's question. For that answer, I shall relate those events as they happened, and leave aside for a moment the trials and tribulations of Tom and Jennifer Reid, and the troubled mind of Sarah Cavendish.

Chapter 5
Laura Kane

In the early hours of the morning on 7th August 1888, the body of prostitute Martha Tabram, sometimes known as Martha or Emma Turner, was discovered in a pool of blood on a first floor landing at an address given as George Yard Building, Whitechapel, in the East End of London. The previous day had been a bank holiday and Martha, in tandem with a friend, Mary Ann Connolly, aka *Pearly Poll,* had spent the evening plying her trade around the pubs on the mean streets of Whitechapel. Pearly Poll later reported that the last time she'd seen Martha had been when her friend had gone with a soldier into George Yard for the purpose of a sexual liaison. Martha was never seen alive again.

When later examined by Doctor Timothy Killeen, her body was revealed as having received 39 stab wounds variously to the lungs, the heart, the liver, the spleen and the stomach. The apparently frenzied attack had concentrated on her breasts, belly and genital area.

In the light of what followed during the reign of terror in the coming weeks, it may seem odd that after the killings in the East End progressed many commentators at the time, and indeed well into the twentieth century, dismissed the murder of Martha Tabram as being unconnected with those of the subsequent victims. Today however, it is accepted by many of those who have studied the crimes committed during the time known as The Autumn of Terror that Martha Tabram was indeed the first victim of the man who came to be known in the coming weeks and months as *Jack the Ripper!*

It may be significant that Inspector Frederick Abberline, one of the officers charged with the hunt for the Ripper was almost certainly convinced that Martha was a victim of the hideous and unknown perpetrator of the heinous crimes that wrought terror in the hearts and minds of the people of the East End in particular, and London and the whole of England in general during that terrifying autumn.

***

Could it therefore have been mere coincidence therefore, that on the night of 6th/7th August in the year that now concerns us, a woman by the name of Laura Kane was viciously murdered and her body left to be found, in a pool of blood on the first floor landing of a block of flats on the outskirts of Brighton, the seaside resort on the South Coast so favoured by many Londoners.

The murdered woman's body was discovered by a milk delivery roundsman, Dave Fowler, at approximately four a.m. as he made his deliveries to the flats. He immediately used his mobile phone to summon the police and emergency services, but Laura, though still warm to the touch, was beyond any medical help that the paramedics who attended the scene could possibly provide. The coroner later concluded that Laura has probably been dead for less than half an hour when Fowler came upon her body, a fact which shocked and dismayed the milk man who realised that the killer could still have been close by when he found Laura's remains, and that he himself may have had a lucky escape.

The Regent Estate where the block of flats was located was a remnant of the town planning nightmares that marred so many English towns during the Nineteen-sixties and the whole area had recently been earmarked for demotion and redevelopment by the town council. At the time of Laura's murder the estate remained a haven for drug dealers, prostitutes and petty criminals, who found the rabbit-warren like system of streets and alleyways the perfect location for their nefarious goings-on. Laura Kane was herself a prostitute and it was thought that her killer was in all likelihood a 'client' with a predilection for the macabre, and that her killing was a one-off, though on what evidence such a theory was based little is known. Later events would prove it to be a nonsense, of course, but at the time it fitted with the police's scant clues and lack of forensic evidence at the scene and with the Council's desire to underplay the whole episode so as not to deter visitors from coming to the seaside resort, which depended so much on both long-term and day tripper tourism. The largest manhunt that Brighton had witnessed in many a year was thus launched by the police, though at first they maintained a low profile approach so as not to detract from the pleasures of Brighton's less gruesome attractions. Perhaps the fact that Laura was a prostitute led to there being less than is usual in terms of press and media publicity.

That being said, Detective Inspector Mike Holland applied himself tirelessly to the case, aided by his assistant Detective Sergeant Carl Wright, and neither man could be faulted for their efforts in attempting to track down the vicious killer. Forty-eight year old Holland, was tall, lean and athletically built. Divorced for ten years he'd served many years on the force, while Wright was five years younger, had never married, and was no less athletic and who possessed a shock of blond hair that always seemed to be in need of a good comb. They made a good team, but found their current case one of increasing frustration and blind alleys.

The forensic officers had been baffled by the lack of trace evidence at the scene of the murder. There was no sign of defensive wounds on the girl's hands or arms and no valuable residue of the killer's DNA could be extracted from beneath her finger nails. There simply wasn't anything there to extract. She hadn't been sexually assaulted and the murder weapon had been carried away by her assailant, and either disposed of or kept on his or her person. At that early stage the police refused to discount the possibility that the killer was female, though they were fairly sure that such a frenzied and protracted assault could only have been carried out by a male. For the time being Holland and Wright maintained open minds in the light of lack of evidence either way.

Checks on twenty-eight year old Laura's background proved singularly unhelpful. Orphaned at the age of three, she'd been brought up in an orphanage in the town of Lyme Regis in Dorset, another coastal town which might have helped explain why she decided to make her life in Brighton when she was old enough to leave the home. Perhaps she'd developed a love of the sea and wished to remain close to it. With no family to question, Holland tried to find Laura's friends but again found a distinct lack of persons to question. It appeared that the young woman had kept herself very much to herself and had formed no friendships either within or without the local community of 'working girls'. Local hostility towards the police on the estate also made extracting information from local residents difficult and Holland and Wright felt as though they were hitting their heads against the proverbial brick wall in their search for Laura's killer. Despite their best efforts no-one confessed to having seen or heard anything on the night of Laura's death and, equally frustrating to the police, no-one was either able or willing to provide them with any background information about the life of the murdered woman. Had Laura Kane been the only victim of the crazed killer who'd struck that night the case may well have been added to the 'unsolved' list that haunts those charged with hunting down those who kill their fellow human beings. Holland and Wright weren't to know at the time, of course, but Laura was to be only the first in a series of murders that would baffle and confound the police force. Thought they didn't know it, they were about to be plunged into a nightmare of blood, gore and terror hitherto unknown in the beautiful seaside town.

There were clues present, but those clues were so vague and so linked with the past that neither Holland or Wright or anyone connected to the investigation could possibly have been expected to make any connection to the murder of a Whitechapel prostitute over a century earlier. If they had, they might have found it chillingly coincidental that Laura Kane's murderer had inflicted exactly 39 stab wounds upon her body, concentrating the attack on her breasts, belly and genital area.

Chapter 6
The Photograph

By the twentieth of August, it was becoming painfully clear to both Holland and Wright that the investigation into the death of Laura Kane was going nowhere fast. Apart from the medical examiner having established the cause of death as being from severe blood loss as a result of multiple stab wounds, one of which had lacerated the girl's throat almost entirely from left to right, they were really no further forward than from the day her body had been discovered. The M.E. had pointed out that he considered the throat wound to have been administered from behind, and that it would have been sufficient to immobilise the girl through shock and would also have prevented her from crying out. He guessed that she would perhaps have been alive when the remaining stab wounds began to be inflicted, a prospect that appalled Holland and Wright and all of those connected with the case.

Unfortunately, the lack of co-operation from local residents, either through fear or apathy or downright opposition to the police combined with the lack of forensic evidence, meant that the investigators had almost nothing to go on, no leads, no clues and no ideas. They had conducted a house-to-house in the locality of the murder, with no success.

As he and Wright sat in his office trying their best to think of a way to move the case forward, Holland reflected on the sad state of the world in which he lived.

"Here we are, in the supposedly enlightened twenty-first bloody century, sergeant and a girl can be brutally murdered, cut to shreds on the landing of a tower block without anyone hearing or seeing a damn thing. It almost beggars belief that no-one on that bloody estate saw or heard anything, or that they don't know who might be involved. Surely, some-one, somewhere must know something!"

"Maybe we have to assume that the killer is from outside the estate sir, or even from out of town. Maybe he's a visitor, someone who was just here for a short time and took the opportunity to carry out a grisly little murder to leave us cops something to do."

"I bloody well hope not, sergeant. If the bastard is from out of town we may never catch him. He could have run off to a bolt hole anywhere in the country and without anything to tie him to Brighton or the Regent Estate, we won't have a snowflake in hell's chance of ever identifying him."

"Unless he does it again somewhere else."

"That's a good point, Carl. Not only that, but maybe this isn't his first kill. We should take a look and see if there've been any similar reports of unsolved murders matching this one *prior* to ours, anywhere in the country."

Wright eagerly seized upon Holland's idea. The sergeant had been particularly appalled by the horrific sight that had presented itself to him when he'd first viewed Laura Kane's body and he as much as his Inspector was committed to bringing the killer to justice and the frustration of recent days was getting to him.

"I'm on it, sir," he said, and immediately left Holland's office to return to his own desk where he painstakingly e-mailed every force in the United Kingdom with a request for information relating to any murders exhibiting similar characteristics as that of Laura Kane.

Half an hour later, as Carl Wright looked up from his computer screen, he saw Holland striding towards him across the office. Within minutes the two men were heading for the Regent Estate once again. Despite the previous thorough forensic examination of the murder scene and of Laura Kane's home in an almost identical tower block to the one in which she was murdered, Holland wanted to go over the girl's home one more time. It was always possible that the forensics team had missed something. Improbable, he knew, but possible.

Number 44, Marchland Towers presented a sad and sorry sight to the two detectives. Located on the second storey of the tower block, the doorway retained the blue and white police tape across the door. The murdered girl's home was still sealed as part of an ongoing murder inquiry and as yet no-one but the police and forensic teams had set foot inside the place since the discovery of Laura Kane's body. After breaking though the tape and using a key to gain entry to the flat, Holland and Wright were met by the dismal vista of the deceased's home. Laura Kane hadn't possessed much in the way of furniture. A battered dark blue sofa stood in the middle of the living room, in front of a well used, probably second-hand TV table on which stood a small television, also second-hand by its careworn appearance, with what looked to be nothing larger than a fourteen inch screen. A rather out of place standard lamp stood in one corner, it's shade a bright yellow, the only slash of colour in the room. A cheap pine effect dining table with matching chairs completed the furnishings in the living area. The carpets throughout the flat were threadbare and had seen better days long before Laura would have obtained them.

Laura's bedroom presented an even grimmer picture to the two men. The bed stood centre stage, and Holland wondered if the girl had ever brought clients back to this room in order to earn a few pounds. If she had, he mused, the clients would have been mad if they'd ever returned a second time. The bed itself lay unmade as she'd left it, a plain blue duvet cover loosely thrown back to reveal a crumpled miss-matched blue sheet of a totally different hue beneath. At least, he noticed, the pillow case on her pillow teamed up with the sheet.

An old wind-up alarm clock, long since stopped, stood on the small bedside cabinet on the window side of the room. Opposite the bed a chest of drawers stood forlornly, its drawers left open and the contents, various items of underwear and a couple of sweaters, three blouses and an equal number of cheap and very short skirts lay neatly where they'd been left by the forensic crew. Holland suspected the forensic people may have been tidier than the victim in their treatment of her clothing.

The bathroom revealed an even more Spartan décor. The bare walls were unadorned with any fixtures or fittings and a small make-up mirror was the only 'luxury' item present in the room, standing forlornly on the window ledge. A pink towel lay draped over the side of the bath, a smaller hand towel in the same material hung limply over the solitary white plastic stick-on hook that hung behind the door. A floral make-up bag with Laura's lipsticks, mascara and other personal items lay discarded on the floor under the wash-hand basin.

"Not one for much in the way of creature comforts, eh?" said Wright as he took in the sad and pathetic sights of the murdered woman's home.

"I can't argue with that hypothesis," Holland replied. "I suppose you noticed that not one of these rooms has any wallpaper on the walls?"

"Couldn't help but notice, sir. Bloody hospital green paint on every wall in the place. It's enough to give you the creeps. How could she live like this?"

"It strikes me that Laura Kane never had much of a life, sergeant. She may have been 'on the game' but what she made from the clients she managed to pick up wasn't enough to keep her in any sort of luxury, that's for sure."

"Maybe she thought she'd one day make it big and have enough to get away from here, what d'you think?" asked Wright, trying to inject some belated optimism into the scenario surrounding the victim's dismal end.

"Maybe, Carl," Holland replied. "We'll never know, will we? I'll bet almost every penny she earned went on fuelling her drug habit. The coroner said she showed signs of prolonged drug abuse. Now, let's start nosing around and see if we can find anything that the forensic boys might have missed."

Twenty minutes later, Carl Wright called to Holland, who was searching and rummaging under the small kitchen sink in the living area. Holland quickly made his way to the bathroom, where he found Wright on his hands and knees in one corner of the room.

"Found something?" Holland asked.

"Just this, sir," said Wright, triumphantly holding up a small passport sized photograph.

"Where was it?"

"When I lifted the carpet, I thought I could make out a bit of white between two of the floorboards. I went back to the bathroom and took the tweezers out of the girl's toilet bag and came back, got down here, and hey, presto!"

He held the photo out towards Holland's outstretched hand and the inspector took a hold of it and studied it carefully. The black and white photo showed the murdered girl together with a young man, apparently clean and well shaven, with longish hair, probably some years younger than herself. It was a typical photo-booth shot, the two of them smiling and leaning their heads in towards each other happily.

"Well, well," said Holland thoughtfully. Maybe we just got our first clue, eh Sergeant?"

"How on earth did forensics miss it?" asked Wright.

"Remember, this wasn't the murder scene. They'd have gone over that with a fine tooth comb, but this was her home and not directly linked to the mechanics of the crime so they probably wouldn't have been instructed to go as far as lifting carpets and floorboards. They'd have been searching for straightforward evidence that might have linked the girl to her killer, but bearing in mind the desolate picture this place portrays, I doubt they'd have spent too long in going over the place. I'm damn glad you thought to lift the carpet though, sergeant, damn glad indeed."

"Now we need to see if we can identify this young man," Holland went on. "So far we've been working under the assumption that Laura had no friends or close acquaintances. This photo tends to prove the lie to that theory."

"What about everyone we've already questioned about her friends, you know, the neighbours and so on?"

"They'll be as good a place to start as anywhere," Holland agreed. "As we're here, let's go knock on a few doors, and then we can go back to the office, have this blown up and copied, and get the beat boys to check with the crowds in the red-light areas once darkness brings them out."

Unfortunately for Holland and Wright, their inquiries around the flats in Marchland Towers proved as useless as before. Either the residents denied knowing or ever seeing Laura Kane, much less the man in the photograph, or they simply refused to open their doors to the officers. The night shift met with almost identical results when they hit the streets later that night, with no-one showing willingness to identify either of the two people in the photograph. To all intents and purposes, it was as if Laura and her mystery friend had simply never existed.

Carl Wright sent the picture to forces around the country and checked the face against all known police photo-fits and mug shots, with no success. Their mystery man remained just that, a mystery.

In a frustrating conversation with his sergeant two days after the discovery of the photograph, Holland reasoned that it was going to take something quite extraordinary to loosen a few tongues amongst the underclass of predominantly less than wholly law-abiding types who lived in the rabbit-warren like flats and corridors of the Regent Estate. Even those decent law-abiding folks who were forced to endure life in the tower blocks of the estate were either too scared or too far removed from the nefarious goings on around them to be of help to the police.

Unfortunately, within days, as the Laura Kane case dragged on towards what would normally might have proved an unsatisfactory unsolved murder case, Mike Holland's 'quite extraordinary' event proved him tragically correct, and the occurrence that eventually opened one or two of those sealed tongues was every bit as gruesome as the murder of Laura Kane had been.

Chapter 7
A Chance Meeting

As events prepared to escalate and Holland and Wright were about to become embroiled in one of the most baffling and gruesome cases of their respective careers, across the town from their office at police headquarters a young man known only to his associates as Michael was waking from a deep sleep. As his eyes opened fully, he squinted against the glare of the shaft of autumn sunshine that cascaded into the room through the uncurtained window a mere three feet from the end of his bed. The room was small, dirty and unkempt and completely matched the two occupants who shared the meagre accommodation. Michael rubbed his eyes, squinted again and turned his head away from the bright rays that met his waking gaze. Instead, he looked across the room to where a second low framed bed stood. Its occupant still slept soundly and though he didn't present quite as filthy a picture as Michael, the young man who lay snoring in peaceful oblivion in the bed also resembled little more than a bundle of unwashed humanity. The single cheap blanket that served as his cover had slipped to the side revealing socks that had holes where the toes showed through, and the frayed hems of what had once been an expensive pair of jeans.

Michael had met his new flatmate a mere four weeks previously. 'Jacob' had been sleeping rough on one of the benches that lined the Brighton seafront as Michael walked home one night after one of his regular excursions to obtain the drugs that had long-ago become the sole focus of his life. At first, Michael thought the young man might prove an easy target for an opportunist theft. His head rested on a rucksack that Michael considered might contain some items of value that he could possibly sell to one of the many 'fences' who he regularly did business with. A return of less than fifteen percent of the value of his ill-gotten gains wasn't much, and he had to work hard to raise the money to fuel his ever-expanding need for drugs.

Unfortunately for him, as he approached the bench, the sleeping man began to stir so, ever the opportunist, Michael instantly changed tack. He might be a druggie, but he was an intelligent one. His brain, slowly becoming poisoned by the cocaine, still had the ability to think quickly and sum up a situation in a few seconds.

"Hey, man, you can't sleep on the benches round here. The cops will soon pick you up and treat you as a vagrant. At best you'll spend a night in the cells and at worst they'll have you up in front of the magistrate and you could end up with a fine and being run out of town."

The sleepy figure rose slowly to a sitting position as Michael appeared to tower over him.

"And why should you care what happens to me?" he asked of the man who'd disturbed his sleep.

"Look, friend, I don't like to see anyone getting into bother with the cops. That's all. I thought that maybe you're new in town and might need a few pointers. What's wrong with being friendly, eh?"

"What gives you the idea I'm new in town?"

"Hmm…maybe the rucksack is a bit of a giveaway, or the fact that you look like you need a place to stay. When did you last have a shave, man?"

"Look who's talking," the man on the bench replied. "You're not exactly Mister Clean yourself by the looks of you."

"Ah, but my appearance is all a part of my persona," Michael replied. "I look this way because I want to. You look like that because you've got nowhere to stay, am I right?"

"Yes, okay, I need a place. I haven't been here in Brighton for long, just a few days."

"And before that?"

"That's got nothing to do with you. I've admitted I need a roof, and that's all you need to know."

"Hey, calm down a bit. Like I said I'm just being friendly. Look, my name's Michael, what's yours?"

There was a slight hesitation from the young man on the bench before he replied.

"You can call me Jacob," he said.

"That's as good as anything I suppose," Michael replied, sceptically.

"It's my name!" said Jacob, defiantly.

"Yeah, sure it is. Like I say, it doesn't matter a fig to me, man, long as I've got something to call you. Now listen, how would like to have a warm bed for the night and a place to stay while you figure out what it is you want to do here in town?"

Jacob appeared suspicious.

"Look, you're not some sort of weirdo are you? Or gay? I'm not into that side of things, or anything like that."

"Listen, it's just a friendly offer of a roof over your head, nothing more, nothing less," Michael lied. He had a plan and Jacob would be just the man he needed to help him put it into effect, if he could convince the young man to throw in his lot with him.

Jacob rose from the bench, pulling himself up to his full height. Michael looked surprised when Jacob appeared to be at least three inches taller than himself. From his position curled up on the bench, the young man had looked smaller somehow. No matter, Michael wasn't intending anything violent. He thought that Jacob might just be the man he needed to help him in a coming venture. For now however, it was necessary to get Jacob back to his home, and try to engender a sense of gratitude in his new friend.

Jacob stretched, looked up and around at the multi-coloured seafront lights suspended between the resort's lamp-posts, and at the dark starlit autumn sky. A breeze was being driven in towards the promenade from the English Channel, and the salt air held the tang of a cool night as it whipped around his face. Wherever Michael lived, it would probably be a more pleasant option than spending another night in the open, and risking arrest for vagrancy by some bored copper with nothing better to do than pick on homeless young people. His mind made up, he agreed to go with Michael and the two young men walked together towards the less salubrious end of town, where Michael's home lay. It was, he explained to Jacob, only temporary. He'd be finding something better soon.

Twenty minutes later, arriving at Michaels flat, Jacob had cause to pause and think that perhaps he might have been better taking his chances on the seafront bench. Michael's flat was squalid to say the least, though Jacob could have added a whole host of less than complimentary terms to that one simple word to describe the place he found himself in. The whole flat smelled of something unclean, though Jacob couldn't put a name to the scent that assaulted his olfactory nerves. Perhaps it was just the fact that he'd spent days living in the fresh air of the seafront, but he almost retched as he was swept into the living area by Michael, who proceeded to flop on the sofa in the middle of the room, gesturing to Jacob to take seat in one of the two tattered armchairs that made up the other components of the three-piece suite that had seen many better days, that was for sure.

"Bet you could do with a hot drink, eh, Jacob?" asked Michael, after allowing his guest the luxury of five minutes relaxation on the sofa.

"Wouldn't mind," Jacob replied, and Michael gestured to follow him into the kitchen.

The kitchen reminded Jacob of something out of a war zone. Pots and pans lay strewn on top of the grease encrusted cooker, the centrepiece of which was a heavily burned and well-used frying pan, that, like everything in Michael's flat appeared to have seen better days. The sink was piled high with used plates and bowls giving the whole area the appearance of a piece of grotesque modern sculpture. The worktops were equally laden with plates that bore the remains of a few take-out meals, well past their sell-by dates by the look of them, and Jacob estimated that anything he ate or drank in this place would probably be guaranteed to give him a dose of salmonella at the very least. He was surprised therefore when Michael opened a cupboard and extracted a couple of clean mugs and a clean spoon produced from a cutlery drawer positioned strategically next to the sink.

"I hate washing up," said Michael, by way of explanation for the culinary and hygienic mayhem that lay before them. "I get around to it about once a week," he went on, though Jacob estimated that once a month might be nearer the mark.

"Is Bovril all right? I ran out of tea and coffee days ago and haven't had chance to do any shopping since then."

Jacob nodded, and Michael quickly had his kettle on the boil.

"You go and clear the coffee table, eh?" he said to Jacob, who dutifully returned to the living room and swept the assorted magazines and old newspapers from the surface of the dirty glass-topped coffee table in the centre of the room. As he did so, Michael took the opportunity to drop two tranquilisers into the hot steaming mug of Bovril that he was about to present to his guest. The hot beef extract drink would easily mask any taste of the tiny tablets, once dissolved, that would give Michael the opportunity to carry out the first part of his plan.

When, twenty minutes later, Jacob at last fell into a deep sleep on the sofa, where Michael had insisted he sit and put his feet up, (after all he needed the rest), Michael at last had his chance. He rummaged through the contents of the rucksack, where he soon found out as much as he needed to know. As he'd thought, 'Jacob' was not really Jacob at all, and it didn't take long for Michael to decide that with a bit of tutoring, his new houseguest could be just the man he was looking for. Before he finally placed the rucksack down and crept off to his own bed for the night, he did, however, find one more item of interest tucked away at the very bottom of the bag, under a small pile of underwear of socks. What he found there quite appalled and intrigued him, and he wondered just how he could put what he'd learned to good use.

It hadn't taken him long to formulate a revised plan. His original idea to use Jacob as a runner and a messenger for some of his less than legal activities were rapidly revised into one where Jacob would provide him with something far more important. He knew someone who just might find Jacob a useful pawn in a little game he was playing.

Now, as he watched the sleeping figure snoring peacefully in the bed opposite his own, Michael smiled to himself. Yes indeed, his chance meeting with Jacob had been a sign from the gods, a message to Michael that things were about to start going his way. All his past cares and troubles were about to evaporate, thanks to Jacob. So what if it wasn't his real name? If the poor sod wanted to be known as Jacob, that would do for Michael. After all, Michael wasn't his real name either.

Any minute now, Jacob would be awake. Michael had plans to make, but for now, he'd play the genial host as ever, and have a good breakfast ready for Jacob when he woke.

Chapter 8
Escalation

Allow me to now trek back in time once more, back to the dark and murky, crime-infested streets of the East End of London, in the year 1888. Such a time slip is necessary in order for me to illustrate the odd connections that began to come together in the beautiful seaside town of Brighton in our own time. Of course, as events began to unfold no-one made any connection between the events in London so long ago and what was taking place in Brighton. At least, not in the beginning.

In the early hours of the morning of 31st August 1888, the body of forty three year old prostitute Mary Ann Nichols, known locally as 'Polly', was discovered by two men, Charles Cross and Robert Paul in a doorway on Buck's Row, Whitechapel. Three police constables were on the scene within five minutes, and one of them, Police Constable Neil, was able to ascertain immediately, with the aid of the light from his lantern, that the woman's throat had been cut. Her skirt had been pulled up, though it wasn't evident at that time that the victim had been subjected to a series of mutilations. The police surgeon, a Doctor Llewellyn, was summoned. He pronounced the victim dead and ordered the body to be taken to the mortuary shed at Old Montague Street Workhouse Infirmary. It was during the stripping of the body at the mortuary that the mutilations to Polly Nichols's body were discovered and Doctor Llewellyn was subsequently summoned to carry out a further examination of the remains.

Though not identified immediately her identity was later confirmed by Mary Ann Monk form the Lambeth Workhouse, where Polly had spent time in the recent past. Mary Ann Nicholls had been married to William Nichols, a printer, and had borne him five children. Following frequent and often violent quarrels, mostly caused by Mary's propensity for drink the couple separated and, as was so often the case amongst the poor of Victorian London, she took to prostitution in an attempt to keep body and soul together. It was an old story and one repeated all too often amongst the decay and squalor that the poorest inhabitants were forced to endure on a daily basis. There were no welfare benefits, no handouts and no pity to be spared for those who made up the sad underclass without whom the vast engine of the British Empire would in all probability have ground to a halt. These were the souls whose sweat and hard labour fuelled the vast factories that had spring up during the industrial revolution, who worked long and hard hours on the docks, in the markets and on the streets of London in order to eke out the barest of livings. The hours were long and the work mostly soul destroying and back-breaking in its physical intensity.

Their homes were for the most part dark and dirty hovels, with often more then one family sharing not a whole house, but a pitiful room, perhaps without furniture, beds, or decent food. Windows were often bare of glass and were stuffed with old newspapers or sacking, anything to keep out the cold of night. Degradation and squalor were the order of the day and nowhere was perhaps as severely affected as the Whitechapel district, where crime, disease and apathy of soul became bywords for those who eventually sought to attempt to improve the lot of those who were forced to endure the privations of life on the fringes of so-called civilised society.

Such was the way of life endured by Polly Nichols and those like her, the poor 'unfortunates' who plied their pitiful trade selling their bodies for a few pence at a time in a pitiful attempt to raise enough money to find a bed for the night in one of the many 'doss' houses that sprang up around the East end to cater for those with no home to call their own. Of course, the handmaiden of the prostitutes of Whitechapel was so often the gin that flowed in the many ale houses and pubs that lined the district's streets, and the temptation was always there to spend whatever meagre earnings they'd obtained in attaining the oblivion of drunkenness in preference to finding that bed for the night. It was certainly the case for Polly Nichols. A woman by the name of Ellen Holland had been the last person to see her alive, reporting her as having been 'drunk and staggering' when she saw her on the corner of Osborn Street and Whitechapel High Street at around two thirty a.m. Perhaps we may hope that her state of drunkenness protected her from the full horrors of what was about to befall her.

Mary Ann 'Polly' Nichols had received such a wound to her throat that the incision completely severed the tissues down to the vertebrae. The lower part of her abdomen had been subjected to a number of wounds, deep and violent in their execution. In addition, bruising was apparent on her face and jaw, as though caused by a blow or blows, and possibly by pressure from fingers on the side of her face. Though not as grotesque as some of the wounds inflicted on later victims in the killing spree that had begun in Whitechapel, they were sufficient to raise the spectre of horror and fear that was soon to engulf the whole of London, and capture the attention of the nation as a whole. The infamy of the killer's reputation would soon spread abroad, far and wide, though as yet, the killer was unknown, nameless and little more than a shadowy figure in the night, unseen and unheard as he went about his grisly work.

With no progress made in the hunt for killer, Mary Ann Nichols was buried in the cemetery at Little Ilford on 6th September 1888.

***

Returning to the present, it is worth noting that Marla Hayes was in no way similar in looks or background to Polly Nichols. She was twenty four years old, not forty-three, and she came from a reasonably well-to do family in Hastings. Her father was a doctor, her mother a librarian and money had never been a source of trouble for the Hayes family. The one thing the two women shared, despite the passage of time between their time on Earth, was the fact that both worked as prostitutes. Marla had fallen in with a bad crowd after leaving school and attending her local college where she initially began a course in animal care and welfare, hoping to one day realise her ambition of working in the veterinary industry.

Soon, she had descended, as do so many others in modern society into the world of the drug addict. Her habit grew worse until she was caught stealing from a local shop in order to fuel her growing habit. A period of probation followed and her father did his best to wean his daughter from the drugs he was only too aware might bring about a sad and sorry death for her one day. Sadly, his efforts were in vain and Marla became more and more embroiled in the world of drugs and drug addicts. It soon became plain to the bright and pretty young girl that there was an easy way of funding her habit. She began to sell herself for sex at the age of nineteen, and a series of arrests for soliciting followed. Her parents were at a loss as to how to deal with their wayward daughter and it probably came as no surprise to them when, soon after Christmas following her twentieth birthday, Marla disappeared from their lives.

She simply left home one evening and never returned.

Mara's crumpled body was found by boat-builder Andrew Mitchell as he walked along Catherine Steer on his way to work at five thirty a.m on the morning of 31ˢᵗ August. It lay in a doorway about halfway along the street, and at first he'd thought the body to be a drunk, sleeping off a heavy night on the front step of her own, or someone else's home. The river of blood that had poured from the girl's gaping neck wounds as he drew closer soon dispelled any such thoughts, and Mitchell stepped back in horror as he realised the full horror of his discovery. Her black mini skirt had been pulled up around her waist and the man had no difficulty in seeing that a series of terrible mutilations had been carried out upon the poor girl. Pulling his mobile phone from his pocket Mitchell quickly summoned the emergency services and waited for the arrival of the police and ambulance teams.

The squad car that arrived on the scene within twenty minutes of the call contained two uniformed constables and, upon seeing the extent of the murdered girl's injuries and realising the similarities between this and the murder of Laura Kane, P.C. Donald Stone quickly placed a call in to headquarters. It wasn't long before the telephone in Mike Holland's bedroom woke him from a deep sleep and within half an hour of waking, the Detective Inspector was on the scene, quickly followed by his sergeant, Carl Wright.

As Wright so aptly understated as he and Holland looked down at the pitiful remains of the once beautiful young girl who lay cold and lifeless on the ground before them, "Bloody Hell, sir, this is getting serious."

Chapter 9
Catherine Street

Doctor Charles Murdoch, known to those who worked closely with him simply as 'Chas' surveyed the scene of death that greeted him upon his arrival at the Catherine Street murder scene. There was little doubt in anyone's minds that this was indeed the site of the actual murder. The amount of blood present at the scene was sufficient to testify that the girl had met her end right there, on the doorstep of a stranger's house sometime during the night. Chas Murdoch was forty two, and had been a medical examiner for over fifteen years. Tall, and slim, brown-eyed, with a shock of light brown hair that never seemed keen on responding to any sort of combing or styling, in the style of Carl Wright, he resembled an archetypal mad professor though his colleagues and members of the police force knew him to be professional, exact and never prone to making snap judgements, thus avoiding the pitfalls of having to change his mind at a later date. Though it could be frustrating sometimes for a detective who was pressing for quick answers, Murdoch never guessed and always ascertained the facts before revealing even the hint of a suspicion about any case he was called to assist with.

Now, as he knelt by the body of the deceased girl he worked slowly and methodically, making sure that nothing pertinent to the actual death scene escaped his gaze or his examination.

"She didn't live here, then?" he asked, looking up at Holland.

"No, we don't know who she is yet, but the people who live in the house were shocked as hell to find us all on their doorstep a little while ago. They've no idea who she is either so it's likely she wasn't from around here. Why do you ask, Chas? Is it important that she didn't live here?"

"Not really. I just wondered whether she might have been killed on the way in or out of the house, that's all. If she had been we'd have needed to carry out a thorough forensic examination of the property."

"We may still have to do that," Holland replied. "We only have Mr and Mrs Harland's word for the fact that they didn't know her."

"You think they may be lying?"

"No, but we might have to make sure."

"Where are the householders, by the way?"

"We've already evacuated them to the church hall, along with the people who live either side of the house. We don't want the locals treading all over potential forensic evidence, now do we?"

"I'm surprised they agreed to leave their homes at this time of the morning," said Murdoch.

"I don't think any of them really fancied the idea of staring out at a corpse and a whole herd of police and forensic officers while they ate their breakfasts or tried to get ready for work. They soon went quietly when we told them what had happened."

Murdoch changed the direction of the conversation.

"Have your men searched for anything that might identify her?"

"They haven't touched the body, if that's what you mean. They've looked around the street and there's no sign of a purse or anything that might have been hers. For now, she's a victim without a name."

"Poor kid," said Murdoch. "She wasn't very old, that's for sure. What a way to end up."

He said no more, and simply returned to his examination of the body. After five minutes, he stood and faced Holland, standing waiting patiently a few yards away, speaking quietly to Wright while the doctor carried out his initial examination.

"Well?" asked the detective inspector.

"Cause of death is almost certainly the deep incisive wound to the neck," Murdoch stated, matter-of-factly. "The other wounds were all in-flicted post-mortem as far as I can tell. I'll be able to fully confirm that at autopsy. At least she was dead before the killer began his butchery."

"Any idea of the time she was killed, doc?" asked Wright.

"Judging by the state of rigor, and the lividity of the skin tissue, I'd say she was killed soon after midnight, maybe between then and two a.m."

"And no-one saw her until the boat-builder came along?"

"It's a quiet street in a quiet area, sergeant," Holland chimed in. "I'd imagine all the residents were tucked up in their beds by the time our killer brought the girl along here to carry out the murder."

"But surely she would have screamed, or struggled, made some sound or done something to alert the folks in the houses," an exasperated Wright went on.

"Not necessarily." This was Murdoch once again joining the conversation. "If the killer got her to turn around so her back was facing him, he could have grabbed her around the face, effectively gagging her, and cut her throat so fast she'd have had no chance to scream. A wound as deep as he inflicted on her would have made damn sure she had no way of crying out for help. All that would be coming out of her mouth would have been blood and gurgles as she gasped her life out."

"Oh, great, thanks, doc," said Wright. "You certainly know how to paint a pretty picture for us, don't you?"

"Sorry, sergeant," Murdoch grinned sheepishly, "but I thought you'd like to know just how he could have done it so silently."

"Yeah, but, there's something I don't get about that theory," said a quizzical Wright.

"And that is?"

"Why would she turn her back on him? The only reason I can think of for her doing that in a dark street in the middle of the night would be if she was about…"

"To have sex with him! If she was a prostitute, like Laura Kane, she would possibly have turned around, hitched up her skirt for him to do it from behind, and that's when he struck." Holland finished Wright's theory for him.

"Exactly, boss. Which means that we might have a serial killer on the loose, one who's targeting prostitutes."

"If that's the case, then this could possibly be just the start, sergeant. He's killed twice already. Why should he stop now? We're going to have to work hard to catch this bastard before he does it again. Chas, can you get those autopsy results to us as soon as you can, please?"

"No problem," said Murdoch. "Now that I've confirmed death and made my preliminary examination, the body can be removed. We'll leave the Scenes of Crime team to search for trace evidence at the scene and I'll get straight on with the autopsy as soon as I get her back to the lab."

"Let me know if you find anything to suggest she was working the streets will you?"

"Apart from her clothes you mean?" Murdoch gestured towards the body, now lying on a black plastic sheet, ready to be lifted into the equally black body bag that was being removed from the back of the waiting ambulance.

"She does look a bit obvious, doesn't she?" said Wright, looking at the girl's short black min-skirt, black patent high heels, and the almost see- through white nylon blouse that left very little to the imagination. The skimpy red thong she'd been wearing had been cut or torn from her body by the killer and had been found beside her body. Her lips were also painted in a vivid shade of red lip gloss that gave her mouth even in death, a lascivious and provocative appearance.

At that moment, a uniformed constable approached the scene, carrying what appeared to be a woman's purse. He'd sensibly picked it up using the end of his notebook pencil, thereby not eliminating any fingerprints or other trace evidence.

"Sir, look what I found in one of the litter bins at the end of the street," he almost shouted in his excitement at making his discovery.

He held it out towards Holland, who stood back without touching the bag, until he'd removed a pair of plastic gloves from his pocket.

"Is it hers, sir?" said Wright as Holland tentatively opened the small black clutch bag with his gloved fingers.

Holland was silent for a few seconds as he examined the interior of the potentially crucial piece of evidence. There were six unused condoms, confirmation perhaps of the girl's line of work. Any money and credit cards she may have possessed were gone, and the purse appeared other wise empty. He looked again, probing the interior with his well trained eyes. In a small plastic window section at the side of the purse's interior, he saw something that caught his eye. Borrowing a pair of tweezers from one of the nearby forensic technicians he carefully removed the small photograph contained within the window.

"It's hers all right," he said solemnly as he held the photo out for Wright to see.

The smiling face that peered out from the photo was that of the dead girl, and on either side of the teenager were the faces of what most probably were her parents. The happy smiles belied the stark appearance of the dead girl now lying before them, lifeless and unfeeling. Holland felt a pang of sadness as he gazed at the happy family scene in the photo. What, he wondered, had happened to turn this young girl away from the bosom of her family, to end up selling her body on the streets of Brighton in the dead of night?

"He must have emptied it as he ran, taking her cash with him," said Wright. "And in the dark he probably didn't see the photo at the side."

"Either that or he didn't care whether we found out who she is," Holland replied. "Her identity was probably of no importance to him. The poor girl was just the target for his perverted lust, I'd think."

"Is there any sign that she'd indulged in sexual activity just before she was killed?" asked Wright, turning to Murdoch again.

"Let me get her back to the lab and get on with the autopsy. I'll be able to tell you more then," he replied.

"Right then," said Holland. "We need to get this photo copied and into the papers and media as soon as we can. Someone out there may have lost a daughter, and we need to find them and identify the girl as fast as we can."

Now that the prospect of a serial killer being on the loose in the town had been raised, and would probably be confirmed by the autopsy, Holland wanted to move fast. Whoever was responsible for the deaths of two women in the space of three weeks might just be ready to kill again, and soon.

"You'll check the wounds, right, Chas? If they were made by the same knife that killed Laura Kane…"

"Say no more. I'm on it." said the doctor. "You go find that poor girl's parents. They must be wondering where their daughter is by now, I would think."

"Let's hope they'll be the last grieving parents I have to confront in this damned case," said Holland, his wishful thinking betraying his own revulsion at the thoughts of the vicious and callous murderer who appeared to be stalking the streets of Brighton, *his* Brighton, *his* home town.

He and Carl Wright left the scene soon afterwards, his uniformed team of sergeants and constables left to carry out house to house inquiries and the forensic team of scenes of crime officers going about their task of attempting to glean information and trace evidence from the murder scene. Holland knew there was little more he could do on Catherine Street for the time being. His own net would have to be cast wider, his first priority being to identify the latest victim. As soon as the photograph had been copied and blown up to a larger size back at headquarters Carl Wright and two constables departed for the red-light district in an attempt to find someone who could identify the dead girl. It may be daylight, but there would always be people around in that area. And if they struck out in their day time attempts, they could always return at night when the victim's fellow prostitutes would be out in force. The weather was warm, and night not yet quite drawing in as autumn approached, and business would be brisk for those who plied their trade on the mean streets by night.

Calls to the local newspapers and television networks would lead to a high degree of co-operation from the media as each agreed to carry the photograph of the dead girl and her parents, as Holland believed them to be, in their late editions and news bulletins.

In the only piece of good luck he'd received so far in the case of the two dead girls, Mike Holland wouldn't have long to wait for the identity of the latest victim to be confirmed.

Chapter 10
The Parents

The sky, as seen from Holland's office window, revealed a patina of blue and white, thin clouds resembling the wave crests that rolled in atop the waves that broke upon the seashore of Brighton's famous beach. The detective inspector stared upwards, lost in thought as he awaited the arrival of the parents of the murdered girl. The television appeal had produced the desired result, in that within twenty minutes of the news broadcast being aired, a phone call to the police had given the police a name to apply to the second victim of the apparently frenzied murderer who now appeared to be stalking the dark night streets of the town.

Holland considered the possibility that he was getting too old for this sort of thing. Aged forty-eight and long divorced from Susan, who couldn't cope with the long hours of loneliness that accompany the role of policeman's wife, he'd had to cope with this type of situation too many times since he'd first joined the force at the tender age of twenty-one. His once luxuriant brown hair had thinned and now revealed traces of grey at the sides and back. His brown eyes had definitely lost some of the sparkle that had once made him attractive to the opposite sex, and he felt tired, tired of chasing the bad guys week in week out only to see many of those he arrested released through lack of evidence or sentenced to short derisory sentences by liberal minded, politically correct magistrates and judges who seemed to care more for the rights of the criminal than those of the victims.

Murderers, of course, gave no thought to their victims. Why therefore should they give any consideration to the families of those they killed? How could they be expected to have a second's thought for the tears, the grief and the lifetime of emptiness that a husband, wife, parent or child might feel over the loss of their loved one, or to the nightmares that would so often accompany the revelation that their nearest and dearest had been the victim of violent and cruel death, inflicted on so many occasions by a total stranger with no apparent motive other than to cause pain in order to satisfy their own illogical or insane blood lust?

Never mind the poor bloody policemen who had to cope with the traumatised families of murder victims, and at the same time remain detached enough to seek every clue in the words and body language of the relatives, to search for every nuance in body language that might identify that relative as a potential suspect. Terrible though it may appear to some, men like Holland and Wright were all too often faced with cases where the killer could be found close to home, from within the family itself. Mike Holland didn't expect such a result in this case. He was reasonably certain that the autopsy on Marla Hayes would show her killer to be the same perpetrator as the murderer of Laura Kane.

Diverted from his reverie by the sudden sound of firm knocking on his door, Holland turned and shouted "Come in".

Carl Wright entered the office followed by the parents of Marla Hayes. Doctor Rowan Hayes looked around sixty, his wife Mary a little younger, maybe in her early fifties. The doctor was obviously trying to maintain his composure, though his wife looked red-eyed and tearful, perfectly understandable in Holland's eyes.

"Doctor and Mrs. Hayes," Wright spoke by way of introduction. "This is Detective Inspector Holland."

"Hello, Inspector," said the doctor in a calm, quiet voice that belied his obvious inner turmoil. He didn't want to be here, didn't want to believe what he already knew. What man after all would want to admit to himself that his daughter had turned to prostitution and ended up dead on the street of a strange town? Mrs Hayes simply sniffed and nodded in Holland's direction.

"Doctor and Mrs Hayes, I'm sorry we have to meet under such circumstances, but I want to thank you for coming in to see me."

"We had little choice really, Inspector, did we?" asked Rowan Hayes.

"No. I know. I'm sorry."

"Are you quite sure it's Marla you've found?" asked the mother. "I know we phoned the police as soon as we saw the news bulletin, but isn't it at all possible that someone might have found that photograph, or taken it from Marla's bag, and..."

"Mrs Hayes," said Holland as soothingly as he could. "The girl we found is the girl in the photograph. There's no doubt about that. I know it's a terrible thing to have to come to terms with but..."

"How do I do that?" she suddenly snapped. "How do I come to terms with the fact that my daughter is dead? Can you tell me that, Inspector Holland?"

Holland took a deep breath and allowed himself to pause for a second or two before he replied.

"No, I can't tell you that, Mrs Hayes. I can imagine nothing worse for a mother to have to try and deal with, I really can't."

"I'm sorry, Inspector," Rowan Hayes said in that quiet, doctoral voice of his. "You see, we married a little later than most couples and we had Marla when I was already in my forties. She was our pride and joy and this has hit my wife, hit us both, terribly hard. My wife is highly distraught as I'm sure you can see. Please tell me what we can do to help you find her killer."

Holland wasn't sure if he should mention Marla's descent into prostitution at this point. The news bulletin had simply mentioned the discovery of the body of a young woman. The police had specifically not mentioned that Marla had been employed on the streets. For now, he'd decided to hold that piece of information back. It could serve no useful purpose and would cause Mrs Hayes in particular even more grief. She'd have to know very soon of course, but there was something else he needed from the parents first.

Little did he know that the girl's parents were already aware of their daughter's chosen profession. So far, there had seemed no need for either side to mention it. If it had anything to do with her death, and Holland was beginning to believe it did, the Hayes's were as yet blissfully unaware of it. That Marla had led a chequered life since her teens was another fact that Holland was as yet to learn. So far his only priority had been in identifying the dead girl, and now, to comfort her parents in their time of need. In time, as he learned the facts surrounding Marla's past, that would change and would have a direct bearing on the way Holland would direct the future of his case.

"Thank you, Dr. Hayes. The first thing we need from you or your wife is for one of you to perform the official identification of Marla's...er."

"Yes, quite! Of course, I understand. I think I'd better do that, don't you, dear?" he said, turning to his wife and placing a reassuring arm around her shoulder.

"I want to see her too, Rowan, please," his wife implored. "If it's the last thing I do I want to see her one more time, just to say goodbye, if that's all right, Inspector?"

"Of course it's all right," Holland replied. "Please go with Sergeant Wright. He'll take you to the mortuary and bring you back when you're done there. Please don't feel rushed. Take as much time as you want."

"Thank you," said Hayes, as he took his wife by the hand and led her from the room, following Carl Wright, who would provide them with all the support he could during the trial of facing the remains of their daughter.

The door closed behind them and Mike Holland slumped back into his leather- faced office chair. He closed his eyes for a few seconds, then opened them once more, spun the chair around to face the window and sat staring for a minute or two at the sky once again. He tried to imagine how he'd feel if he were in the shoes of the Hayes's at that moment, and decided he was glad that he and Susan had never had any children.

God! There are times when I hate this bloody job.

When the tearful parents returned with Wright some time later, the identification of their daughter confirmed, it was obvious to Holland that the mother was in no fit state to answer questions, and he directed his words to the father for the next few minutes. Holland promised to keep them informed on the progress of the case. As the distraught parents left his office escorted from the station by Sergeant Wright, Holland felt relieved that he didn't have to undertake such tasks every day. He'd rather face a gang of knife-wielding thugs than have to confront the grieving parents of yet another young girl or boy whose life had been tragically and abruptly brought to an end by violent crime.

Carl Wright returned after seeing Doctor and Mrs Hayes safely to their car. Holland, seated in his office chair, looked up at his sergeant as he entered the office and said, quite simply though with great conviction,

"Carl, old friend, we *are* going to catch this bastard."

Chapter II
Cousin Mark

Tom Reid was at a total loss. All his efforts to find young Jack had proved fruitless. The private detective he'd hired had gone through the motions, but Tom felt that the man had never held out much hope of finding Jack. Consequently, Tom had paid out a rather exorbitant sum of money to cover the man's expenses, for absolutely no reward.

"But he can't just have disappeared into thin air, Tom," Jennifer Reid said as she sat imploring her husband to do something, anything, in terms of a greater effort in finding their son.

"I've told you, Jen, the best thing we can do for Jack now is to report him as a missing person to the police. They're the best equipped to deal with something like this."

"No way, Tom! No police and that's final. If we tell them that Jack has a history of psychiatric illness, they're likely to list him as dangerous or mentally ill or something, and who knows how they'd treat him if they found him."

"Rubbish, Jennifer!" Tom snapped, without meaning to. "He's committed no crime. Why would they do that?"

"I don't know, Tom. I just don't want the police involved. He's gone because something in Robert's infernal legacy upset or disturbed him. If we could find out what that was then we might have an idea where to look for him."

"But how on Earth do we find out what was in those papers? Even Sarah didn't know, and she was married to Robert for a long time. He didn't even confide in her as to what he was leaving in trust for Jack."

"I know, but what was that rubbish she told you about when you went to see her? Jack the Ripper wasn't it? Robert had become delusional about something to do with the Jack the Ripper case hadn't he?"

"Jen, please. Robert was ill, a very sick man. Don't forget, he never fully recovered from the car crash and no-one knew he'd developed the brain tumour until it was too late. He must have had a hard time concentrating on the realities of life sometimes. The pressure of the tumour must have made all sorts of things short circuit in his brain and I'm not surprised if he became a bit delusional."

"But Sarah said he was reading something in his study late at night, while she was in bed. She thought it was something to do with the Ripper, didn't she? What if that was the thing he'd bequeathed to Jack? What if it contained something so disturbing that Jack's mind couldn't cope with it? Tom, we must find out what was in that package. We simply have to!"

"Like I said, Jen, Sarah said that Robert was convinced the soul of the Ripper had visited him, but that was *because of the effects of the tumour.* Don't you understand that? How could the soul of Jack the bloody Ripper be wandering around the ether for over a century and then plant itself into the mind of Robert in some random possession or whatever?"

"But what if it were true, Tom? What if Robert's rantings were real? And what if it wasn't random? What do you know of your own family's background, back in the nineteenth century? Maybe someone in your family's history had a connection to the case or something. That might explain why the Ripper came back and found a way into Robert's mind."

"For God's sake, Jen, have you heard yourself? You sound like a crazy woman. Since when did you begin to believe in spirits, ghosts or that kind of stuff? How the hell could the spirit of Jack the Ripper survive through the years and then just pop up and inhabit some corner of Robert's mind when it felt like it. There's no such thing as ghosts, Jen, you know that. Jack the Ripper died over a hundred years ago. Whatever Robert may have said was caused by the delusions of a very sick mind, infected as it was by the tumour."

"Look, Tom, something caused our Jack to run away like he did. You have to admit that it's too much of a coincidence that his whole personality changed after he received that package. Humour me, please. There must be a way to find out more about your family history, surely."

Tom Reid sighed. He knew that his wife wasn't about to let him off the hook. She'd decided that the time had come to go searching for skeletons in the family cupboard, and there was no way she was about to back down until he agreed to delve into the past in search of a clue to Jack's disappearance. He knew when he was beaten.

"Ok Jen, listen. There is one family avenue we haven't explored yet, I suppose."

"Which is?" she asked, her hopes rising in the belief that Tom had thought of something important.

"Mark," was Tom's one word answer. "Good old cousin Mark."

"Mark Cavendish? Robert's brother? Didn't he go abroad after Robert's death? No-one seems to have heard from him for years."

Mark Cavendish was the younger bother of the late Robert Cavendish. When their father died the old man had left the psychiatric practice he'd shared with his son to Robert, with the remainder of his estate going to Mark, thus ensuring an equal share of his assets between his two sons. Robert had continued in practice until the day of the car crash that had killed his father and seriously injured him. Although he returned to work after recovering from his injuries and the coma in to which he'd fallen at the time of the accident, his heart never seemed to be in it any longer. He eventually sold the practice, and was diagnosed soon afterwards with the incurable brain tumour that was the eventual cause of his death. Mark was last seen by the family at Robert's funeral. At the wake that followed the interment of Robert's body in the family plot in St Jude's cemetery, Mark had announced his intention to sell his own computer games production business and seek his fortune on the continent. When asked exactly where he planned to settle he'd told Sarah, his sister-in-law that he quite fancied the idea of the Italian Riviera, or at least, somewhere where there was a coastline and he could be near the sea, which he loved. Sarah wanted to know how she could keep in touch with him, but Mark, always something of a loner, told her that he intended to make a new life for himself and needed no ties to the past. He meant no disrespect to her or to Robert's memory, but with his father and brother both gone, and his mother long dead, there was nothing to keep him in the old country any longer. If he needed to get in touch with the family he'd do so through the family solicitors.

"Our Mark was always a bit odd," Tom now replied to Jen's question about his cousin. "Robert was always the calm and level-headed one, but Mark was something of a dreamer. He wanted to be an artist when he was a kid, but never quite developed the skill to make a go of it. I think that's why he went into computers in the end. He actually created some damn good computer games you know. He sold them to some of the big games manufacturers, before realising he could make even more money if he set up his own company, which of course is what he did. I suppose his games became his own special art form, and he really was good at it, like I said."

"But how do we find him if he doesn't want to be found?" Jennifer asked her husband.

"Why, through the solicitors of course. As far as I know he still maintains a controlling interest in Global Programming, the company he started when he branched out on his own. He said he'd keep in touch with the solicitors in order to keep track of things back home. I'm sure they'll have an address for him somewhere in their records."

"And why would they give it to us Tom? It's not as if we were close to Mark is it?"

"But this is a family matter isn't it? I'm sure that the family solicitor at Knight, Morris and Campbell, whoever it is who's handling the family business these days can be convinced to at least get in touch with Mark on our behalf and see if he'll contact us."

"And do you really think that Mark might know something that could help us?"

Tom was silent for a few seconds, and then he sighed and sat back wearily as he answered his wife.

"To be honest Jen, I think we're clutching at straws. Jack could be in any town in this country, and Mark Cavendish might or might not know anything about the family's history in the Victorian era. Robert and he might have talked about stuff we know nothing about, but then again they might not have. All I can say is that if you want us to be doing something that doesn't include walking the streets of every city and town in England looking for Jack, then this seems the most logical path to follow for the time being."

Jen looked at her husband, noticing for the first time how tired and weary he looked. She knew he'd done everything he could to find their son in the preceding weeks, and had slept little along the way. She loved Tom very much and she was grateful that she had him by her side through all of this. Rising from her chair, she moved across the room to where her husband sat in his favourite armchair and gently sat down on his lap, draping her arms around his neck as she did so.

"So, my big handsome husband, "she whispered in his ear." What do we do next then?"

"Well," Tom replied. "First thing in the morning I phone the solicitors and make an appointment. Then we take it from there. As for right now, it's getting late and I think it's time you and I turned in for the night my tired little lady."

"Is that an invitation?" asked Jennifer almost coquettishly.

"I suppose you could say that," smiled Tom. Five minutes later, the house locked up for the night Tom and Jennifer mounted the stairs, and within two minutes of falling into bed together the pair were both deeply asleep, arms locked around each other in a loving embrace. The emotional turmoil of the past few weeks was catching up with them. They were no nearer to finding their son, but the morning would bring fresh hope, and for the first time in a long while, the couple were both undisturbed by dreams as they slumbered.

Chapter 12
Breakfast at Michael's

Jacob lay sleeping on the sofa in Michael's seedy, foul smelling flat. Michael sat opposite his new found houseguest, watching the sleeping form. Jacob slept a lot lately, and was constantly complaining to Michael that he could never seem to clear his head. Michael knew the answer to Jacob's problem of course, though he'd no intention of revealing that information to the sleeping man. The constant infusion of sedatives and other narcotics that Michael added to Jacob's tea, coffee and occasionally to the take-away Chinese meals they enjoyed from time to time ensured that Jacob had become highly susceptible to Michael's will, and also to some extent dependant upon his so-called benefactor.

In fact, Jacob had become everything that Michael had wanted him to be when he'd first seen him on the bench on the sea front. Armed with a street map, Jacob didn't seem to mind being put to work carrying messages from Michael to various contacts throughout the town. Occasionally there were small packages to be delivered too, which Jacob had no trouble in discerning contained drugs of some description. As far as Jacob was concerned, it mattered little to him. Michael had provided him with a home of sorts and in return for his efforts on Michael's behalf, Jacob effectively received a few pounds a week, free food, board and lodgings. Michael had long sought an accomplice who would be a convenient and cheap runner for his less than legal activities.

By ensuring Jacob's dependence on his goodwill, he'd ensured a degree of safety and immunity for himself from some of his competitors and from the police. Jacob after all was clean cut, well-spoken and best of all, unknown in town. That made him a valuable commodity to Michael, who had experienced one too many run-ins with the law and with some of the more violent small-time drug dealers of the area. Michael provided a service and for the most part, violence played no part in that service. There were times of course when a little strong-arm work was needed, but that was rare, and he avoided any such actions unless it was absolutely necessary. When he did deem it essential he could be as brutal as the next man, but like all such specimens of the human race, the thought of someone actually committing an act of violence against him was abhorrent and terrifying to Michael. He hated physical pain and Jacob was one way of ensuring that he didn't have to place himself in the front line quite so often.

The sleeping man had another use of course, one that Michael was already making very good use of. He'd need to be careful and vigilant in the way he handled Jacob in this respect however, and Michael even considered introducing Jacob to the world of the addict by slowly introducing something more addictive to his food and drink. That would be a last resort however, as Jacob would serve Michael's purpose far better if he remained 'clean' of such contamination. For now, everything was going well, and as long as things continued along their current path, there'd be no need to change the regime.

Michael knew that very soon, Jacob would wake and he'd soon be on his way out of the flat. Jacob had a daily routine that Michael knew very little about. He seemed to spend most of his days on the streets, searching for something or someone. Michael knew of course exactly what Jacob was searching for. His search of the young man's rucksack on their first night together at the flat had told him that.

Michael had put all he'd learned from his illicit search of Jacob's rucksack to good use since that night and now all he had to do was ensure that Jacob failed in his attempt to discover what he was looking for. That was going to be relatively easy to achieve, as Michael had already discovered. He'd barely believed it when he'd found the source of Jacob's goal, the reason for his arrival in Brighton tucked away amongst his personal belonging s in the rucksack, but, when he'd done so, and realised the significance of what he'd learned, the rest had come easily to Michael.

Now, everything was going well and would continue to do so as long as he could keep Jacob under his control until the plan was complete. Michael had help of course, of the best kind imaginable and he was confident that nothing could go wrong, and if it did, then what the hell, they had the perfect patsy ready and waiting, sleeping right here on the sofa, in front of him.

Jacob began to stir. Michael had no wish to be around as his guest rose, stretched and made his way to the kitchen for his regular daily intake of corn flakes and milk. God! The man's routine was interminable.

As Jacob finally opened his bleary eyes and rubbed his temples against the throbbing of the headache that never seemed to leave him nowadays,

Michael quietly closed the door as he left the flat and made his own way into town. He had errands of his own to run that morning, and he needed to see someone urgently. There were plans to be made, and Michael knew his friend was eager to move on to the next stage of the game.

Jacob finally snapped wide awake and was immediately struck by the air of silence that pervaded the flat. Even without looking around he knew Michael was out. That was strange to him, as it was rare for the man to leave the flat during the morning. He rubbed his temples once more and slowly rose from the sofa. The pain in his head seemed worse when he was up and about, and he quickly made his way to the kitchen, fixed his breakfast and just as quickly returned to the sofa, where he set the bowl in his lap before devouring the corn flakes hungrily. Whatever was wrong with his head certainly hadn't done anything to diminish his appetite.

As he ate he tried to recall the previous evening. For some reason, he appeared to be experiencing a mental blank. He hoped that the thing that had happened to him once before hadn't happened again. Michael had helped him that time, would he have done so again, Jacob wondered? Then again, how could he have done? He wouldn't have known where Jacob was going, so would have been unable to assist him a second time.

Jacob paused in his eating to look at his hands. They were shaking, like the last time. He searched for tell-tale signs, but there were none. He was clean, absolutely clean. He sighed in relief. It couldn't have occurred again. He was sure of it.

Breakfast finally over and his mind clear of dark thoughts and the fear that had temporarily gripped him earlier Jacob washed, shaved and made his way out of the flat, remembering to lock the door with the spare key entrusted to him by Michael. Jacob wasn't sure he trusted Michael, but at least for now he had a roof over his head, and Michael's 'business' though not strictly or in fact in any way legal, at least provided Jacob with the means to go about his own task during the days.

He felt sure that the answers he sought were to be found here on the South Coast. He just wished to hell he knew how to go about finding them.

Chapter 13
The House on Abbotsford Road

Abbotsford Road stands atop a hill that runs almost parallel with Brighton's coastline. Situated about a mile inland, its height affords those who reside in the homes that line one side of the road commanding views of the town, the Royal Pavilion and the English Channel. Those who live on the opposite side of the road are not of course so lucky, though some of their upper storey rooms do afford a lesser view of the sea and perhaps a small fraction of the town, as seen through the gaps between the houses on the town side.

The houses on Abbotsford Road were at one time the height of elegance and refinement, being built during the height of the Regency period and affordable only to the rich and wealthy who took advantage of the town's royal connections to ensconce themselves in the vicinity of the wealth and opulence that those connections brought to the town.

In keeping with the original owners' desires to secure uninterrupted views, no trees were allowed to be planted along the road, unusually for the time, and today the treeless tradition continues, and though not enshrined in any local by-laws or council minutes, it would be unthinkable for anyone to consider planting a tree anywhere along the length of the road.

Most of the houses along the road retain their original names, having been grandly given such appellations as "Sussex House" or "De Savory Manor" and even a rather cheekily named "Regent's Folly". Some have had their names changed over the years of course, but the house that perhaps possesses the most fame, or perhaps infamy is the only one on the street that bears no name at all, just a number. It was here, at number 14, that 'Bertie' the Prince Of Wales, and later King Edward the Seventh, would enjoy a number of dalliances with one of his lesser known mistresses in the years prior to his assuming the throne of England. This was the home of Mrs Amelia Lassiter, widow of Colonel Henry Lassiter of the Royal Horse Artillery, who'd succumbed to fever during a posting to the Indian sub-continent. Introduced to the prince by one of his military friends,

Amelia soon became close to Bertie, and his visits to her home continued for a period of over three years until he became bored with her increasing years and moved on to other, younger women who took his fancy.

Much of the elegance of those days has now departed from the houses on Abbotsford Road, and number 14 is no exception. Still possessing its impressive wrought iron gates, solid oak front doors and high ceilings with wood-panelled walls, it does however exude an air of rather faded elegance, and the current batch of residents on the road are a far cry from the opulence and wealth of the original residents of Abbotsford Road. That's not to say that the houses here are cheap of course. They are in fact among the highest priced in the town, though perhaps the views that the homes on the ocean side of the road have something to do with that. Perhaps it's just that today's residents are less class conscious and maybe just that bit less able, in the current financial climate, to lavish thousands and thousands of pounds on maintaining the exteriors of their homes in the manner of their forerunners.

The late summer sun was at its Zenith as Michael reached the door to number fourteen. The day had grown warmer and warmer as he'd walked the two miles from his flat. He wasn't one to waste money on taxis when the weather was fine, though he did wish he'd taken one by the time he reached the top of the hill and walked those last few yards to the house. Sweat dripped from his brow and his shirt felt as though it was plastered to his back. Even his hair felt as wet as if he'd just stepped from a shower.

Michael reached into the pocket of his denim jacket, (wearing that had been a mistake in this weather too), and extracted a bunch of keys. Selecting the correct one, he inserted it into the lock of the heavy oak front door to the house, turned it and entered number fourteen as confidently as if he owned the place. He closed the door behind him as he entered, and walked slowly but confidently across the marble floored hall until he reached the door to what at one time would have been designated 'the drawing room', or perhaps, 'the sitting room'. He paused for a second, listening at the door, and then knocked quietly and waited until he heard the single word, "Come" quietly spoken from within.

"Welcome, dear boy," said the man who sat reposing in an old fashioned floral cloth upholstered armchair that was positioned beside the currently unused fireplace at the far side of the room from where Michael entered through the heavy brass handled door. "Do come and sit down."

Michael walked across the room and seated himself opposite the man in an identical chair to that occupied by his host.

"How are you?" asked the man, who Michael thought to be at least sixty years old but who was in fact just past his fiftieth birthday. His hair was greying at the temples, and his moustache had also lost much of its natural brown colour. About five feet ten tall when standing, he reminded Michael of a Victorian gentleman, sitting there in his plush red carpet slippers, a brown paisley patterned silk smoking jacket and black trousers that sported knife-edge creases down the front. The room in which the two men sat mirrored the look of fading elegance that the exterior of the property exuded. The oak panelled walls gave the place a dreary, overpowering air, and the three paintings that hung in heavy wooden frames all depicted historic sailing ships, one an un-named tea clipper in full rig, another the famed 'Cutty Sark', and the third an eighteenth century fully armed Royal Navy fifty gun ship of the line, its battle ensigns billowing from the rigging as it sailed to war against some unseen enemy.

Books of ancient origins lined the bookshelf that took up the wall adjacent to Michael's chair, and a heavy solid oak table stood at centre stage of the room, it surface covered with maps, an antique sailing compass and a host of very old seafarers navigation instruments.

To the casual visitor, though there were none at number fourteen, it would have appeared that they were in the home of some decrepit ancient mariner. They would have been wrong.

Everything in that room gave Michael the creeps. Something about the man and his house seemed steeped in the past. An almost ghostly air pervaded every wall, every inch of the slightly threadbare Axminster carpets. It was as if the house itself had been frozen in time, and that time was long, long ago. Michael knew it was stupid, it couldn't possibly be, but nevertheless the thought that the man he sat facing at that moment belonged to another time and place always leaped into his mind whenever he was called upon to make one of his visits to number fourteen.

"I'm ok," said Michael in reply to his host's question. He doubted that the man cared either way about his health, it was simply an introduction to whatever he'd been called here for.

"You appear a little grumpy this morning."

"I'm not grumpy, just tired and bloody hot. It's a long walk to get up here and it's a scorching day out there."

"Ha! The young of today. Scorching day? It's barely sixty five degrees out there young man, and look at you, all sweat and panting as though you'd run a marathon. Next time I send for you, get a taxi!"

"Taxis cost money, old man. You gonna pay for it are you?"

"Don't I pay you enough already? And don't you ever call me 'old man' again, or I'll see to it that something very nasty happens to you. You can count on it."

The man's voice rose to a crescendo that forced Michael to sit back in his chair. The temper had appeared from nowhere, and the younger man knew better than to answer back. He'd seen the man like this before. His volatile nature frightened Michael. Though the man was much older than he, Michael had no doubt that he could handle himself well if forced to. His looked strong and lithe, his arms muscular and well proportioned despite his age. Michael could be violent as well of course, but his drug abused body probably meant that the two men would be much more equally matched than would normally be the case if it came to a fight, and Michael didn't dare take the risk. He depended too much on his host.

"I'm sorry," said Michael. "No offence intended."

"Hmm, it might help if you stuck to selling those drugs to the poor misbegotten souls out there instead of using them yourself. You might have a bit more wind with which to make your way up the hill if you were fitter. And isn't it time you had a shave and a damn good wash? When did you last have a bath, or a shower?

What my neighbours must think if they see you coming up my drive-way, God only knows."

Michael didn't reply. Instead he waited. He knew the man hadn't called him to the house to discuss his bathing and sanitary arrangements.

"What? Nothing to say to me? You're a bloody coward and a liar, that's what you are. Why I bother with you I just don't know. If you weren't useful to me I'd..."

The man let his last words hang in the air. The inference wasn't lost on Michael. He knew that his host could be violent if he wished to be, and Michael had no wish to be on the receiving end of that violent streak.

"You asked me to come here today." Michael said quietly.

"Yes, I did, didn't I?"

The man leaned forward, took a Davidoff cigarette from a packet that stood on the small side table beside his chair, inserted it into a silver cigarette holder that he extracted from the pocket of his smoking jacket and proceeded to light it using a well used Zippo lighter.

"Well, I presume you have something to say to me about last night?"

"Oh you do? You presume do you? That's rather eloquent of you isn't it? "You presume? Well, well. As a matter of fact, young man, you're quite correct. I do wish to discuss last night with you, and in some detail. This morning too, if you don't mind."

The man leaned back in his chair, took a long drag on his cigarette and with an ease that had always baffled the younger man on previous visits, began to produce a steady stream of smoke rings that billowed forth and rose towards the ceiling before dissipating and forming a cloud that would hang just below the level of the ceiling through out their conversation. Michael hated these 'little talks' as the man referred to them. They always made his flesh creep, and his nerves would be on edge from now until he eventually left the house and returned to the fresh air of the outside world once again.

"Well?" asked the man. "Are you going to tell me about your house guest or not?"

Michael shivered. The air in the room seemed to have grown colder. As he began to relate the information required of him the man closed his eyes and listened intently, hanging on every word of Michael's, absorbing every fact and every detail of the narrative that the younger man laid out before him. It took some time for Michael to convey everything he needed to and the man never once interrupted him or asked a question. He never did. He was content to listen and absorb Michael's words, always sitting as he did now, eyes closed, smoking his cigarettes using that long silver holder that added to the air of Victoriana that Michael felt clung to the man like a thick fog.

When he'd reached the end of his report, Michael himself sat back and allowed himself to relax a little. He waited. At length, the man spoke once again.

"You've done well, young man, very well indeed."

Reaching into the inside pocket of his smoking jacket, the man removed a wad of notes from within and quickly counted out what appeared to Michael to be an inordinately large amount of money. Passing the notes to Michael the man smiled, a smile that Michael felt could chill the soul of any man. There was death in that look, he knew it for sure.

"Here. Take it. You've earned it. I'll let you know when I need you again. In the meantime you keep that house guest of yours sweet, you understand?"

Michael nodded.

"Now go, and don't come back until I send for you again, got it?"

Michael nodded, rose from his chair and walked slowly across the room until he felt the reassuring brass of the doorknob in his hand. Opening the door he turned to speak to say his goodbyes to the man. It never hurt to be courteous to the old bugger, thought Michael. He needn't have bothered. As far as Michael knew there was only one door to the room and he'd just opened it himself, but when he looked at where the man had been sitting there was no-one there, and the room was empty!

A minute later as he walked through the front door and out into the sunshine of the day once more, and moved to walk back down the hill towards the town, Michael at last allowed himself to breathe normally. He realised that he'd been tense and holding on to his breath unnaturally as he'd left the house. He increased his pace as he passed through the gate and he could almost swear that the temperature out on the street was at least ten degrees warmer than it had been in the grounds of number fourteen Abbotsford Road.

He hoped it would be quite some time before he was called back by the man. He wasn't to know it of course, but the next call he received from his less than genial host would plunge Michael into an escalating world of danger and fear from which he'd find it ever harder to escape. But that was for the future. For now he was glad to be in the warmth of the sunshine, the walk down the hill being far more pleasant than the lung-bursting climb he'd had to endure to reach number fourteen. Relieved to be back in the 'real world' Michael actually whistled to himself nearly all the way home.

Chapter 14
Post Mortem

Chas Murdoch stood up straight and stepped back from the autopsy table. Laid out before him were the mortal remains of Marla Hayes. The large 'Y' incision in her torso had been stitched and sealed, Murdoch's work completed. Mike Holland and Carl Wright stood off to one side about six feet from the table. They had seen autopsies before and although not unduly bothered by the sights and sounds that accompanied the procedure, they never actually encroached any closer than their current distance. It was possible to see too much sometimes!

"Well, Chas?" asked Holland. "Can we be reasonably certain that we're looking for the same killer who butchered Laura Kane?"

"In my opinion, the wounds inflicted on Marla Hayes were done so with the self same knife that killed your previous victim. There's little doubt about it. The knife has a particular ridge on one side and it leaves a fairly obvious track in the flesh as it enters the body. The track is present in the remains of both girls. You have a serial killer on your hands, there's no doubt of it."

"And the actual cause of death was the wound to the throat?"

"Oh yes. Just like the first girl, this one had her throat cut with such severity that the spine was almost severed. Whoever did this has strength, possibly accompanied by great rage, I'd hazard a guess."

"What about the other wounds Doc, the ones he inflicted after cutting her throat? They were inflicted post-mortem, I hope?" Carl Wright inquired.

"Yes, sergeant, they were. The girl was dead before the other wounds were inflicted upon her. I think he killed her and then took his time to carry out his mutilations on the poor girl's body."

"Are the wounds indicative of any specialist anatomical or medical knowledge?" Holland asked.

"You mean, could it have been a doctor? Yes, it could have been, but then again it may not have been. The cuts were certainly inflicted with confidence. There are no hesitation marks where he cut into the body and the incisions are all clean and made with confidence I would say."

"Didn't they ask that question at the beginning of the Jack the Ripper inquiry back in 1888?"

The question came from Carl Wright, who made a habit of studying old cases, particularly unsolved ones, and no unsolved case was as well known as that of the infamous Whitechapel murderer.

"Yes, they did, as I recall," Holland replied. "But that was then and this is now. We need to get some degree of focus on the case. If someone is going around targeting the town's prostitutes he or she, though I'd suspect a man in a case like this, must have a motive, a trigger that's set him off on his course of action. We need to get a team of officers into the red light district with specific orders to try and discover if the prossies have noticed any strangers perpetually hanging around lately, or if they know of anyone who may have developed a grudge against them in general."

"You're working on the assumption that the girls may have known their killer?"

"Correct sergeant. We know that in the majority of murder cases the killer is known to the victim, and there's no reason why that might not be the case here. We just have to find the common denominator that links the girls with the killer. Let's not get bogged down with theories of mad doctors or anything like that for the moment. Like Chas says, the killer is just as likely to be a plumber or a waiter or a stockbroker, eh, Chas?"

"Hmm, yes, I believe I said something like that," said Murdoch, "though not in those exact words."

"But that's what you meant. Just because the killer knows how to wield a knife and target certain areas of the body doesn't make him a medical man, correct?"

"Correct."

"Right then, is there anything else we need to know as a result of your examination?"

"Only that whoever did this terrible thing does know where he's aiming for when it comes to the mutilations. Every incision was made in exactly the right place in order for him to ensure he gained access to the girl's inner organs without having to hack around once he'd got in to the body. In that respect there is care and deliberation present in his 'work' if you wish to call it that, but then he also virtually hacked at her genitalia until they were almost unrecognisable, hardly the work of a calm or skilled person, I'd say."

"Which inner organs in particular did he target?" asked Holland.

"The womb, uterus, bowel and intestines. It appears he removed about six inches of the large intestine and I'm afraid in all probability he carried it away with him. It certainly wasn't present at the scene of the crime and it's nowhere to be found in the body."

"A trophy, d'you think, sir?"

"Maybe, sergeant, maybe."

"What else could he have taken it for?"

"I don't know, but it seems odd doesn't it? Just six inches of intestine? Why not something more high profile?"

"Who's to say how a killer's mind works?" Murdoch returned to the conversation. "Maybe he took it simply to taunt or to add confusion to the police's case, you know, make you think and start guessing as to his motives?"

"Just like we're doing now, eh Doc?" said Wright.

"You should have been a detective, Chas," Holland smiled.

"I often think of myself as a detective of sorts you know," said the doctor. "After all, every time I have to cut one of these poor people open I begin an investigation of my own, searching for clues as to what killed them, and of course, my reports to you boys in blue often lead to the arrest of the killer in cases of murder don't they? You tell me what that is if it's not the art of detection?"

"Well, well, that's quite prosaic of you Chas my old friend. You're right of course. You are a detective, perhaps even more of one than we are. We have to catch the bad guys, sure we do, but you often have even less to go on than we do when you start to search for the clues that the dead provide."

"Exactly Mike. You at least have live witnesses to speak to, to interview and give you leads that might help in the solution of the crime. My only witness is the deceased, and they have a completely different way of talking to me. Having said that, the dead can't lie, Mike, and when I find something at autopsy, there can be no denying the truth of it. It may not always fit with the known facts, but the truth is the truth, and that's it. You have to go with what I and my colleagues find and build your case around it because to do otherwise would leave any future prosecution open to question, am I right?"

"Spot on, Chas, as usual. So, anything else you can tell us about Marla before we go in search of the elusive 'Brighton Ripper' as I'm sure Carl here would love to dub our killer?"

"Just that your killer is right handed, as evidenced by the direction of the wounds he inflicted on the girl, and he wore rubber gloves, probably of the surgical variety when he carried out his mutilations."

"Alright Sherlock, the right-handed bit I'll admit was probably easy to establish, but just how did you work the rubber glove bit out?" asked Holland with a quizzical smile on his face.

"A ha, my dear inspector," Murdoch grinned. "That was easy as well. There's no mystery involved. Surgical gloves usually come in sealed packets. You've probably seen me take them out on a hundred occasion or more. They also have a fine dusting of powder on the inside that makes it easy to slip them on to the hand. Some of that powder was present on the girl's body, probably where it fell as he was stretching the gloves in order to put them on. It also explains why there are no fingerprints anywhere on her body or clothing. He was gloved, and that would also prevent her blood staining his hands, making it harder for the police to establish any contact with the dead girl if your boys had picked him up."

"But there'd possibly be traces of the dusting powder on his hands or under his fingernails, right?" asked Carl Wright.

"Maybe," Holland chimed in. "But that in itself wouldn't prove that he'd killed anyone, only that he'd worn a pair of surgical gloves, right Chas?"

"Exactly," replied the doctor. "Many people use that type of glove for all sorts of reasons, maybe while filling their cars, or while gardening, or doing jobs that might cause some staining of the fingers, the list is almost endless."

"So he's a clever bastard as well as a vicious one."

"Correct, Sergeant. Clever, and very careful if you ask me," Murdoch added.

"Well, thanks Chas. You've given us something, not much, but something. I'll wait for your written report which you'll have for me... by?"

"By tomorrow Mike. I know it's urgent and I'll have it typed up this afternoon and on your desk first thing tomorrow. Will that do?"

"Yesterday would be better."

"Tomorrow morning, Inspector Holland. You wouldn't want me to rush and leave something vital out, now would you?"

"Tomorrow morning it is then," said Holland as he and Wright left the autopsy room with sighs of relief. The smell and oppressive atmosphere that always seemed to pervade the room never failed to make Holland and his sergeant a little queasy and to escape from the room into the outer corridor brought a sense of relief that was almost tangible.

They may have had to wait another few hours for the autopsy report, but for now there was much work that had to be done, and Holland and Wright weren't prepared to waste a moment as they returned to police headquarters to continue their investigation. They both knew that they had to move quickly on the case, as it was almost certain that the killer would strike again. When, they didn't know, but the longer it took for them to bring the perpetrator in, the more chance there was that another girl would die horribly at his hands.

Holland soon had a team of uniformed constables heading for the town's red-light district. They had instructions to speak to anyone and everyone in order to find out if anyone had noticed a suspicious character in the area in recent weeks, or if any of the girls had experienced trouble with a new client, perhaps one who wanted them to indulge in something out of the ordinary. Next, he went through the statements provided by Marla's parents. He'd been surprised when they'd told him they knew about their daughter's line of work. They were philosophical about it however, and showed a lot more understanding of their daughter's lifestyle than most parents would have done, in Holland's opinion. He'd asked them to try and recall anything from her life at home, during her first forays into the world of drugs and prostitution that might have led to something like this happening. They couldn't. Apart from trying their best to turn Marla away from the life of degradation she'd apparently fallen into, they knew little about the seedy world into which she'd disappeared. There was nothing in the information they'd provided that would help in locating or identifying her killer.

Carl Wright had meanwhile left Holland's office with the intention of going through the autopsy report on the first victim Laura Kane with a fine tooth comb. Murdoch had not noted any of the dusting powder from the surgical gloves as being present on the first victim's body. Maybe that was an added refinement he'd evolved after getting too bloody during the first murder. Maybe, Wright had thought aloud to his boss, they'd missed something else that might indicate a change in the modus operandi of the killer, something that might be significant.

A full ninety minutes had passed before Wright knocked and entered Holland's office once more, this time with a folder and a number of files under his arm. Mike Holland looked up from the papers he was reading as Wright entered. He couldn't help but notice the worried frown that his sergeant wore as he approached the desk.

"What is it Carl? You look as if you've seen a ghost man. What've you found?"

"Sir, I want you to humour me if you will. I've found something that I think might be highly significant to the case. It was a whim of mine to check the Laura Kane autopsy report against one from an earlier case. Just take a look and don't say anything until you've read both of these, please."

Mike Holland knew his sergeant well enough to know that the man wasn't given to flights of fantasy or 'whims' as Wright had put it, without having some reason for his actions. Holland held out his hand and Wright passed him the files and folder he'd brought into the office. The top folder contained the autopsy report and forensic reports on the scene of crime in relation to Laura Kane. The second folder that Holland looked at contained a recently photocopied document, obviously taken from a book or some other source, and bore no victim's name. Intrigued by his sergeant's request to examine the two reports and not to speak until he'd read them both, he motioned for Wright to sit in the visitors chair, and Mike Holland did as he'd been asked. He began to read!

"You know I've read this one in detail already, Carl," he said to Wright as he began to read the Laura Kane file.

"I know sir, but please, read it again and then go straight on to the other one."

"Ok, I'll say no more until I've finished, but I hope there's some point in this."

"There is, sir. Now please…"

"Okay, okay, I'm reading."

It took Holland no more than five minutes to read through the report on Laura Kane's autopsy. He'd read it so many times in recent days that he almost knew it by heart. He put the file containing the report on one side and opened the other file, the one that held the un-named photocopied document.

Another five minutes passed as he perused the information contained in the document. As he read his face at first took on a quizzical look, then changed to one of mystification as the implications of what he was reading began to dawn upon him. He began to tap the fingers of his left hand on the desk top, a sure sign that something was beginning to bother him. Carl Wright knew the signs. He'd seen it often enough in the past. He knew that his actions in bringing the document to his boss had been justified. Mike Holland was now seeing exactly what Carl Wright had seen, and though he might not like what he was reading and being asked to come to terms with, Wright knew that Holland couldn't just dismiss his findings out of hand.

Chapter 15
A Few Words from Doctor Ruth

I feel it worth a few words at this point in my narrative to pause and place a few things into perspective. Of course, it would be very easy with hindsight for me to make judgements, to say perhaps "Why didn't so and so do this or that?" or, "Why didn't they know about this or that?"

The point is of course that the benefit of hindsight was not available to those involved in the case at the time the events I'm relating took place. This tale is in itself a composite, drawn together from the various interviews I've conducted with the police officers involved, the family and friends of Jack and those closest to him and the sad facts of the case.

At this stage of Jack's story, and it *is* Jack's story despite the fact that he appears absent from most of the proceedings so far, it has to be remembered that the events as they unfolded were known to only small sections of the participants at a time. The actions and movements of Tom Reid, his search for Jack for example, would have been unknown to Mike Holland or the police officers investigating the case in Brighton. Equally, the mere *existence* of Jack Reid was unknown to Holland. If it had been otherwise, would things have been different? Would the police investigation have shifted directly into a search for the missing teenager? I doubt it, for there would have been no evidence to implicate Jack in the crimes that were taking place in the seaside town, or even to place him anywhere within a hundred miles of Brighton, and even less to suppose that he was in any way implicated in the murders of the women in that town.

I suppose the reason for my injecting this short pause for reflection is because it was around this time in the proceedings that I became aware of the Brighton murders. Though not directly involved at that time, as I was still employed in my previous position I, like millions of my fellow citizens was witness to the news stories which began to invade the national television news bulletins. The press and TV media, ever eager and willing to sensationalise a juicy murder story in order to increase sales or viewing figures had jumped on the Brighton murders and, much to Mike Holland's chagrin, had dubbed the killer 'The Brighton Ripper' much as he'd mentioned the name in scorn in his conversation with Murdoch and Wright.

I was probably as horrified as any right-minded citizen when those bulletins first appeared, describing as they did, in some detail, the terrible mutilations that had been inflicted upon the two victims. I suppose that the police had to release certain details to the media in the hope that sufficient disclosure and adequate coverage in the press, on radio and television might lead to someone with knowledge of the crimes getting in touch with information that might lead them to an arrest.

It never happened of course. There were no witnesses to the crimes, and no friends or relatives waiting to come forward to give the perpetrator up to the police.

At that time in the case, I would never have guessed that the time would come when I would become personally involved with the man convicted of the murders in Brighton, or that my own knowledge of the case, and my relationship with a number of those involved in it would lead us all to a shattering conclusion that even today, some people find hard to believe.

That of course, is something for the future. When I eventually reveal that information, it will be up to you, the informed and perhaps sceptical reader, to decide on the facts as I will present them. For now though, the story will be best served by returning to the events that led Jack to his place in the history of crime, and into the care of me and my fellow medicos here at Ravenswood.

Chapter 16
Good News, and Bad News

Sweeping rain hammered against the window of Holland's office. The sudden thunderstorm had taken everyone by surprise. The black clouds had appeared as if from nowhere, suddenly rolling in from the sea carrying the deluge straight towards the resort town. Thunder boomed from above and forks of orange lightning rent the clouds and zigzagged towards the earth, and in the offices of the town's police headquarters officers and clerks alike switched on lights to illuminate their workplaces as the day turned to darkness. Against the backdrop of the storm, Mike Holland looked across his desk at his sergeant. Having read the two reports Wright had placed in front of him the inspector knew that something out of the ordinary was taking place, though for the life of him, for the moment he had no idea what the significance of what he'd read boded for the future.

"Okay, sergeant, you have my full attention. I'm assuming that this other document is not part of the report on the death of Laura Kane." Holland placed the photocopied papers on his desk. He had an idea where his sergeant was coming from now, but he wanted Wright to confirm it himself.

"Correct, sir. Those pages are copied from a book, and constitute all that is known about the findings of the doctor who carried out the post-mortem examination of a woman named Martha Tabram, who died on exactly the same date as Laura Kane, in Whitechapel in 1888. Most contemporaries of the day dismissed her as a victim, but later theorists now seem to accept that the woman was in all probability the first true victim of Jack the Ripper. The original autopsy report was lost years ago it seems, but those are the salient points of the examination carried out by a Doctor Timothy Killeen. As you can see, there are some bloody disturbing similarities present between the two cases."

"Similarities? Bloody hell man, I think you're deliberately understating the facts aren't you, to get me to point out the obvious?"

"Go on sir, please. Tell me what you think," Wright urged his boss.

"What you've shown me here is a comparison between two murder cases over a hundred years apart where it appears that the second killer, *our* killer, has adopted not only the same method of despatching his victims, but has done so on exactly the same date, and using precisely the same number of wounds as the original killer. He's inflicted the wounds, as far as is possible, in exactly the same areas of the body as the original Ripper and left his victim in the street to be found by whoever may have come along and blundered upon the poor woman. You appear to be suggesting we have a copycat killer on the loose, one who appears to be recreating the murders of Jack the Ripper?"

"Exactly sir, and that's not all. The second murder sort of confirms my theory because Marla Hayes was also killed on the anniversary of the Ripper's second murder. Polly Nichols was murdered on the same date and in the same way as Marla."

"Bloody hell, sergeant. Thank God that you're an aficionado of old murder cases. I'm sure that someone would eventually have made the connection between the dates and the Ripper killings, but at least we've caught on to the copycat theory sooner rather than later, thanks to you. Not only that, but I hope you realise just what else your discovery has given us."

"You tell me if you're thinking the same as me, Boss."

"The killer has given himself away hasn't he? Well, almost."

"That's what I thought sir. He's almost telegraphing his intentions to us isn't he?"

"He damn well is sergeant. If he sticks to the Ripper scenario that means he'll strike again on the same date as the Ripper struck when he killed his third victim. We'll be bloody well ready for the bastard this time, sergeant, by God we will."

Wright hesitated for a second before replying to Holland's last comment. Then, taking a deep breathe threw the proverbial spanner into the works.

"Well sir, it's not going to be quite that simple. Just how much do you know about the Jack the Ripper murders, if you don't mind me asking?"

"Not as much as you Carl, that's obvious. I know that he killed a number of prostitutes in the Whitechapel area of London in 1888. He was a bloodthirsty, vicious bastard who was never identified and caught, despite the police flooding the streets with officers, and the biggest manhunt that Britain had ever seen up to that point in history. I also seem to remember reading that he removed parts of some of the women's bodies, a kidney in one case I believe, and that his last murder was of a woman called Mary Kelly, that name I do know, and it was the most horrendous killing of the lot. The poor girl was butchered, from what I've read about it in the past. Now, what's your point here? Why isn't it as simple as I think to predict his next move?"

"Sir, if the killer sticks to the pattern established by the original Ripper, we're going to have a problem. You see, the next victim, Annie Chapman was killed on the eight of September, just two days away, and then, on the 30th September 1888, Jack the Ripper struck again, but this time it was what was called 'the double event'. You see sir, he killed twice that night. Both Elizabeth Stride and Catherine Eddowes were killed within an hour of one another. Stride was killed in the Metropolitan Police's manor, and Eddowes was just over the boundary in what was the territory of the City of London Police, which led to some confusion in the following days, with different forces involved for the first time in the series of killings. Our problem will be that the killer is going to be trying to kill twice on that night."

"Shit, sergeant. How the bloody hell are we going to get enough men to cover the whole of the red-light district? In the first place, we have a potential murder about to take place in two days time, followed by two more on one night less than three weeks hence. We'd need men on every street corner and even then we don't know what the bastard looks like or how he lures the girls to their deaths. So far no-one's seen or heard a damn thing. Our men could easily walk straight past the bastard and not realise who he is and if he has a way of getting the girls to go with him without a struggle he could just as easily take them off the street to kill them and we still wouldn't be any the wiser until the bodies turn up."

"It's not just that sir. If he sees loads of uniforms on the street he'll know we're on to his game and he might just go to ground."

"Ah, now that's where I think you're wrong my friend. He won't go to ground, not this one. He's got a timetable to adhere to. If he doesn't stick to the original Ripper's dates and times the plan gets screwed up doesn't it? No, he'll do it, or try to, and he's so bloody confident that he can carry out his plan he obviously doesn't care if we know he's copying the original Ripper killings. He obviously thinks he can kill with impunity, carry off his own 'double event' and get away with it. He must know we'll work out what he's up to, and yet he's going to go ahead with it, you mark my words. He's a confident, cocksure bastard, and he must have worked out a way to do it and still keep out of our hands."

"That's a bloody scary scenario, Boss. To be that confident, he must think we're absolutely incapable of catching him."

"Or just too stupid to do so, when he's virtually telling us when he's going to strike again. The bloody question we have to answer sergeant and we have to do it in the next two days, is *where* is he going to strike, and then, in a couple of weeks time, how is he going to get from one murder scene to the other without being covered in blood and being seen by someone on the streets?"

"There's no guarantee he'll stick to the red-light district is there sir? He could strike anywhere if he knows we're likely to be patrolling the area."

"You're right of course, sergeant. That's how he's going to try and throw us off the scent. He's probably counting on the fact that we'll work out his copycat scenario, and that we'll flood the red-light district with uniforms to try to get our hands on him, and while we're doing that the murderous sod is going to strike somewhere else in the town."

The two men looked at one another. What had at first appeared like a breakthrough had turned into a nightmare of epic proportions. There was no way that the police could patrol or keep watch on every street in the town. By counting on the fact that the police would work out his Ripper strategy, the killer was playing a very clever game with the forces of law enforcement. Mike Holland knew he had some hard choices to make. Should he use the men at his disposal to cover the red-light district, even though his instincts told him that the killer was second-guessing his intentions? Should he try and blanket the rest of the town with as many men as he could muster? Even then it would be an inadequate number of uniforms for the size of a town like Brighton, even if they cancelled all leave and for that, he'd need help from above. It was time to call his own boss, Detective Chief Superintendent Andy Wallace. He wouldn't like what Holland had to report, but what the hell? If anyone could give him the manpower he needed to try and catch the bastard who even now was probably planning his next killings, it was the Chief.

Ordering Carl Wright to pick up the reports that lay on his desk, Mike Holland rose from his chair and turned to his sergeant.

"Better bring those with you. We're going to see the Chief Super. It's time we stepped this inquiry up a gear. I will not let that bastard get the better of me sergeant. I'll be damned if I do."

As he followed the inspector out of his office and up the two flights of stairs that led to the floor where Chief Superintendent Wallace's office was located, Carl Wright thought to himself that the original detectives who led the hunt for Jack the Ripper probably said precisely the self-same things as they hunted for the Whitechapel Murderer, and he couldn't help but think of the futility of that particular inquiry. He hoped that he and Holland might be blessed with better luck, but somehow, he couldn't bring himself to be too optimistic.

Chapter 17
The Office of Giles Morris

The offices of Knight, Morris and Campbell, solicitors and attorneys at law are situated on a narrow street, reminiscent of a Victorian Terrace, not far from the law courts in Guildford. Although Victorian in appearance, the whole street is a fairly modern appendage to the town, having been created soon after the second world war in a post-war building boom that had seen Guildford grow into a much larger town than it had been prior to the outbreak of hostilities. The planners had decided to their credit to give the new building project a feeling of permanence and history and in so doing had added to the charm and overall feeling of wealth that pervaded that particular part of town. It was no surprise therefore, that over the years most of the houses that lay along the narrow streets were gradually acquired by various solicitors, doctors and stock brokers, anxious to impress their clients with a show of architectural refinement.

The Cavendish family solicitors had been in situ on Cambridge Terrace since nineteen fifty eight and were one of the longest established businesses on the street. The original partners were long gone and only one of the current heads of the firm bore the name of any of its founders. Giles Morris was sixty eight, and retained a mind as sharp as many men half his age and it was into his office that Tom Reid was shown by an attractive blond secretary as he continued his search for the truth surrounding young Jack's legacy. At first it was hard for Tom to make out the face of the man who sat behind the large oak desk that dominated the chambers of the elder statesman of the firm. Bright sunshine streamed through the large window situated behind the sitting man and the rays were sufficiently strong to cause Tom to squint against the glare, and for a few seconds, Morris appeared as little more than an apparition, framed by a bright sun-driven aura of light. As his eyes adjusted to the light, Tom was eventually able to discern the features of the man who may or may not be able to hep him in his search for information.

Despite his age, Giles Morris had a full head of hair, dark brown with barely a hint of grey evident in his rather opulent sideburns and at the temples. His brown eyes appeared as alert as a thirty year old, and his hands bore no trace of the mottling or liver spots often associated with the aging process. In short, Morris was a man whose physical appearance appeared to defy the years and that in itself gave Tom Reid cause for optimism. If anyone at the firm could help him, he felt certain that Giles Morris would be the man.

"Mr. Reid, do please come in and sit down," Morris said in a deep gravel-like voice, and gestured Tom towards a luxurious and very expensive leather armchair as he walked slowly across the room, his footsteps silent as he trod the rich, deep-pile carpet that adorned office floor. The chair creaked with reassurance as Tom sat.

"Thanks for seeing me at short notice, Mr. Morris."

"Oh, please, let's not be too formal eh? Please call me Giles. I'm too old for all that old-fashioned stuff and nonsense, and it's Tom isn't it? Is it alright if I call you Tom?"

"Well, yes of course, er... Giles. I must say I was surprised to find out that you were personally handling the family affairs. I thought David Chandler was in charge of the Cavendish family portfolio."

"Ah, yes, you won't have heard I suppose as your branch of the family hasn't had any need of our services for a number of years, but David left the firm a couple of years ago. Gave it all up to go and live on a sun-drenched island somewhere in the Indian Ocean. Never married of course, just made loads of money and now has the chance to live it up a bit. Lucky beggar I say! Anyway, when he went I sort of took over most of the lesser used briefs he'd held for a number of years, the ones that, like your family affairs, were to all intents and purposes, dormant files."

"By dormant, I suppose you mean those with not much active work to be done on behalf of the clients."

"Well, yes of course, but in the case of the Cavendish family, it quickly became a case of no work at all to do."

"But how could that be, Giles? Surely the business interests of Mark Cavendish would still have required some occasional work?"

"I'm sorry Tom, but I would have thought you'd know?"

"Know? Know what Giles? I don't understand what you're getting at."

Oh dear, this is rather embarrassing. I shouldn't be the one to have to tell you this really. You're his cousin after all. I'd have thought he'd have told you himself."

"Told me what himself? I've not heard from him since soon after Robert's funeral. Please come out with it, Giles. You're leading me around in circles without telling me anything at the moment."

"Well, you're obviously completely unaware that Mark Cavendish sold all of his interests in Global Programming two years ago and severed all ties with his business associates before leaving the country. The last contact we, as his solicitors had from him, informed us that he was relocating to a villa on the island of Malta."

"Malta?"

"Yes, somewhere overlooking the harbour at Valetta I believe."

"Did he give you a forwarding address, or perhaps a telephone number he could be reached at?"

"Nothing at all I'm afraid, Tom. Mark Cavendish was very precise in saying that he wanted to completely sever his ties with the United Kingdom. We have no way of contacting him, and no way of knowing if he's still in Malta. For all we know, he could have moved on by now, and be living anywhere in the world."

"But surely, if he's in Malta, there must be way of tracking him down."

"There most probably would be, if someone really wanted to find him. Of course, we were just his solicitors and we acted solely on his instructions. If a client decides to leave the country and not leave a forwarding address then there's nothing we can do about that, and it certainly isn't within our remit to go chasing after them or tracing their whereabouts unless it's necessary for legal reasons."

"Yes, of course. I wasn't suggesting that you should. I was just thinking aloud."

Giles Morris could see that Tom was quite disturbed by his cousin's disappearing act and thought long and hard before divulging his next piece of information. In the end, loyalty to the family as a whole overcame any reluctance Morris might have felt when he said,

"The odd thing is, Tom, that you're not the first person who's come here seeking information about Mark in recent weeks."

"What?"

Tom Reid was flabbergasted by the solicitor's statement. It was surely too much of a coincidence that another person might be searching for Mark as well as Tom unless that person had something to do with the family, and that logically led him to think of his son.

"Before you say anything Tom, I can assure you it wasn't your son. In fact it wasn't a man at all. The young woman who came in search of Mark was, so she said, acting on behalf of a client who was owed money by Mark, from his days at Global Programming. Apparently he'd promised her client a large royalty in payment for a game design that Mark eventually patented and released under his company's name. He never paid up, so she said."

"So this woman was a…"

"A private detective, yes," said Morris. "At least, that was what she told me when she sat right there in the same chair you're sitting in now."

"You sound as if you had reason to doubt her veracity."

"Well, let's just say that I thought her a little too young to be conducting such an investigation. Her credentials as she presented them to me appeared impeccable and I gave her nothing more than the information that Mark had left the country and was last heard of in Malta. It was only after she'd gone that I began to have a few doubts about her, and I picked up the business card she'd left me and telephoned the number on it."

"Are you telling me the company didn't exist?"

"Oh, it existed alright and the name on the card was quite genuine, but the real Helen Symes, which was the name she used, is in fact fifty years of age and one of the company's best detectives. At the time that the impostor visited me the real Symes was pursuing an inquiry into a small scale company fraud in the Midlands and was nowhere near Guildford. So you see, the young faker took me in completely. I suppose they're right when they say there's no fool like an old fool. She was young, pretty and appeared wholly credible when she sat in that chair. Great legs, I recall. I should have checked into her credentials sooner rather than later."

"I'm sure it wasn't your fault Giles. After all, why would you have suspected that there was anything odd about someone trying to trace Mark? And the story she gave you was completely plausible, after all."

"Well, yes, you're correct, and I wasn't to know you'd be coming here today asking the same sort of questions, was I?"

"Precisely. Please, don't you worry about it, Giles. I'm sure the woman was, as you say, interested in getting money from Mark, perhaps on her own account, or maybe for someone else, but I doubt it had anything to do with Jack, or his disappearance."

Tom Reid was disappointed with the outcome of his visit to the firm of Knight, Morris and Campbell, and left the office of Giles Morris no wiser as to the whereabouts of his son, or to the contents of whatever documents Robert had bequeathed to Jack. The chance that Mark Cavendish may have had some inkling to the workings of his brother's mind had been a small one at best, but the fact that Robert's brother, and Tom's cousin had disappeared from the country without leaving any means of contacting him had pretty much closed that avenue of investigation.

As he drove home to report the failure of his mission to Jennifer, Tom reflected on the incident of the mystery woman who'd visited Giles Morris in search of information about Mark. As he'd said to the solicitor, it would be highly unlikely that she'd had any connection to Jack and his disappearance, for after all, what could Jack have wanted from his Uncle Mark?

Then again, as much as he tried to shake the thought, Tom couldn't escape the niggling feeling that he'd missed something significant. As he drove onto the gravel driveway of his home, he saw Jennifer waving to him from the bay window that overlooked the front garden of their home and the thought of having to tell her of the negative aspects of his visit to Giles Morris drove all other thoughts from his mind.

Chapter 18
Jacob's Awakening

Jacob felt as though his eyes had been glued together. He'd slept for longer than usual and was finding it increasingly difficult, almost every day, to wake up with any degree of clarity. He was no fool, in fact he was far from it, and the realisation that he was perhaps being drugged had already entered his mind. The question was, why? He'd done all he'd been asked to do by Michael, and in return had received the benefit of a place to stay where he could develop and put into effect his own plans, and in so doing he'd never once disturbed the routine of his host. Now, as he finally managed to open his eyes and the sunlight that penetrated through the window temporarily caused him to feel as though he'd been blinded, he decided that he had little choice but to confront his host. He'd had the feeling for over week that something was happening to him, something not right, and that Michael was the one responsible for whatever it might be, and Jacob thought he knew just what that something was. The strange, 'out of body' feelings he'd been experiencing, the headaches, the inability to wake up with a clear head, they all pointed to only one thing in Jacob's mind.

He could hear Michael clattering around in the kitchen, probably making some of the terrible tea that Jacob had become used to, made with the cheapest and probably the most tasteless tea bags in the world.

Jacob swung his legs out from under the duvet and slipped his feet into the pair of battered leather slippers that waited by the side of the bed. Wearing just his boxer shorts and t-shirt, he padded across the floor and quietly peered around the door to see Michael at work, as he suspected, creating a pot of the hideous brew he so often inflicted on them both. *At least,* Jacob thought, *he enjoys it because he makes it the way he likes it. How the hell can he imagine anyone else relishing the stuff? Maybe his taste buds died a long time ago and he can't really taste the abject apology for a cup of tea he produces.* He saw that Michael was in the process of preparing two cups, obviously intending to wake him and share a brew and a cuppa together. How domestic!

"Morning Michael," he said as cheerfully as he could as he strode through the door and sat down at one of the rickety chairs that lay around the Formica-topped table that really belonged in another era, long before the twenty-first century.

"Bloody hell! Look at you. You look bloody awful," Michael grinned at him. "Couldn't you have got dressed? You could scare someone walking into a room looking like that."

"I'm not feeling too good this morning," Jacob replied truthfully.

"Why? What's wrong? Can I do anything to help?"

For a second Jacob could have believed that his host was actually sincere in his concern for him, but only for a second, and the thought quickly died a natural death.

"No, I'll be okay, but it feels like I've got a hangover, and I didn't even have a bloody drink last night. My head is thumping and my eyes didn't want to open just now in the bedroom."

"My, my, you are in a bad way aren't you? Here, get this down you. It'll make you feel better."

Michael placed a chipped white mug with a picture of a bulldog across the table. The steaming hot liquid smelled almost as bad as Jacob knew it was going to taste, but he forced himself to smile, say thanks, and he gingerly sipped at the foul witches brew.

As soon as Michael sat down opposite Jacob, the younger man decided to seize the moment and make his move. Better not to waste any time, just get on with it.

"Michael?"

"Hmm?"

"What have you been giving me?"

"Eh? It's tea, same as always, you dummy."

"I don't mean the tea. I mean, what drugs have you putting in the tea, or in my food or whatever?"

"Drugs? What fucking drugs, man? I haven't been giving you any drugs. How the hell could you even think that?"

"Listen to me Michael. I'm no dummy, and I'm no fool. I know a hell of a lot more than you could even begin to imagine, especially about drugs. I've known from the moment I met you that you're a user as well as being a small-time pusher, but that didn't matter to me. You gave me a roof to sleep under and I thought you were an okay sort of guy, despite the drug thing, and I didn't even mind running your illegal little errands in return for the pittance you've been paying me, but all the time you were fucking drugging me with something. Don't deny it, you creepy little shit. I know it. It's the only explanation for the way I've been feeling. At first I thought it was just the shitty way I've been forced to live since I moved in with you, the lousy food and that awful stuff you have the gall to call tea, but it wasn't that at all, was it?"

"Look, Jacob, "Michael protested. "I don't know where you've got these crazy ideas from, but I promise you…"

"Don't fucking well lie to me, you bastard," Jacob shouted as he leapt up from the chair and ran around to Michael's side of the table. In a flash his hands were around Michael's throat and as if it was the easiest thing in the world to do, he began to exert pressure on the seated man's windpipe.

Michael began to gag as the pressure of Jacob's hands slowly cut off the supply of air to his lungs. He kicked out and his flailing legs knocked the table over, the two cups of tea flying across the surface and the cups sliding off to smash on the floor. Still the pressure increased, until Michael began to believe that Jacob was going to kill him, right there and then, without giving him an opportunity to tell him the truth. His eyes felt as though they were about to pop from his head, his lungs were bursting from lack of air and his mind began to go blank, and then, just as Michael believed he was about to black out for the last time, Jacob released the pressure on his throat and slowly let his hands fall away from the death grip in which he'd held his victim.

Michael fell forward on to his knees, gulping in precious lungfulls of life giving air, coughing and spluttering, gasping with relief. . A trickle of blood ran from his mouth and dribbled down his chin. He realised he'd bitten his tongue during Jacob's onslaught. He dabbed at the blood with the back of his right hand.

"Jesus Christ, man! You almost killed me."

"I still might, Michael," Jacob spoke menacingly. "You'd better tell me the truth, and tell me now."

"Look man, it was just a prank, a silly game, that's all."

"Do you think I'm daft enough to believe that? You don't drug someone to the point that they don't even remember what they're doing just for a prank, Michael. Do you really think I remember nothing at all? I know you took me out on at least two occasions when I was drugged up, and I remember being in a mess at least once when we got back. You cleaned me up because I was covered in something. It was blood, wasn't it? What the fuck have you been doing to me? I want to know, or so help me, I'll finish what I just started."

Michael's mind was racing. He knew that if he told Jacob the truth, he might just be signing his own death warrant. On the other hand, if he said nothing at all things could work out just as bad for him. He had to think of a compromise that would tell Jacob something, though not everything, about the events of the last few weeks. The trouble was, someone else had to be considered, someone who could be just as vicious and possibly a hundred time more deadly then Jacob if he knew that Michael had blabbed. Then again, Jacob was the immediate problem. Michael had been amazed at the strength the young man had displayed as he'd almost throttled the life out of him. Oh yes, Jacob was the here and now, those hands of his quite capable of locking around Michael's throat once again, and with that knowledge, Michael's decision was made. He knew just what to tell Jacob.

"Listen man, I'll tell you all I know," he spluttered, "But I need to make a phone call first, okay?"

"No phone calls, Michael. You tell me what I want to know, and you tell me *now!*" For starters, I want to know why I woke up in such a state on two occasions, and why my clothes smelled funny, as though they'd come straight out of a washing machine and been quickly dried in a tumble-drier. What the hell did you do to me while I was in a state of drugged catharsis, eh?"

Damn! Michael had hoped to call the man, to tell him what had happened and get his advice on how to handle the situation. That option had been denied to him, so he quickly decided on his story and in a hushed, rasping voice, still affected by the terrible pressure that the other man had exerted on his windpipe, Michael began to relate his diluted and highly adulterated version of the truth to Jacob. He hoped it would suffice, and that Jacob would leave him alone when he'd finished.

For the next twenty minutes Michael talked, and Jacob listened. Michael thought it strange that throughout his narration, Jacob never spoke, not a single sound came from his lips, no interruptions, no questions, nothing. He simply sat opposite Michael with a deadly sick grin on his face, and for the first time, Michael realised that there just might be something seriously weird going on in his guest's mind. A shiver of fear ran through his body, but he continued with his story, slowly and as precisely as he could, trying to make every word sound like the gospel truth. He suddenly knew that without a doubt, his life did indeed depend on the other man believing in his tale.

Jacob simply sat and listened, hanging on every word that came from the still bloodied mouth of his so-called friend. Michael looked briefly at his watch, and wondered how long the other man could sit there without saying a word. Meanwhile, he continued talking as though his life depended upon it.

As Michael's highly edited version of the truth spewed forth from his bloodied lips, Jacob sat listening intently to every word. When Michael eventually fell silent, Jacob stared at him for long seconds, which to the other man felt like hours, then Jacob rose, took hold of the frightened Michael by the scruff of his collar, and pushed him into the sitting room, finally throwing his victim onto the sofa, where he landed in a heap.

"What now?" asked a terrified looking Michael.

"Now," Jacob said, threateningly, "you're going to make a phone call, you lying little bastard. Then, we're going to find out just how much of the truth you've been telling me. We're going visiting!"

Chapter 19
The Tale of Jack the Ripper

In contrast to the house on the hill at Abbotsford Road, the suburban home of the man leading the investigation into the Brighton murders was small, neat, and far less ostentatious and opulent in its outward appearance. With clean white net curtains hanging in the windows, and recently painted woodwork adorning the exterior windows and doors, number forty-eight Acacia Road looked every inch the typical English middle class home. He'd rented the place soon after his divorce, his ex-wife having retained the marital home as part of their divorce settlement. Not too far from the centre of town, the house had been built in eighteen ninety, soon after the series of killings in the Whitechapel area of London that now appeared to have had their ghosts resurrected by recent events in the seaside town. Though late at night, any passers-by couldn't fail to notice that of all the homes on the street, this was the only one where all the downstairs lights still burned brightly despite the hour.

D.I. Mike Holland stretched his legs across the full length of the sofa, and placed the book he'd been reading on the coffee tale. Next, he stretched his arms behind his head to their full extent and looked across at the mantelpiece where the cock read eleven thirty five. It was getting late and he'd barely moved from the sofa in the last four hours. A mug of coffee, long ago gone cold, sat beside the book on the table and Holland listened for a minute or two to the sound of the wind as it whistled along the street outside the warm cocoon of his home. The sound reminded him of the power of nature, the ability of something unseen and yet so powerful to disrupt power lines, damage property and even to drive ocean going ships aground at will. Man may have thought he'd harnessed the power of nature, wind farms used to generate electricity, the wind itself used to drive the sails of ships and smaller, private vessels used for sport and recreation, and yet he knew only too well that such beliefs were nothing more than an illusion, a feeble attempt to pacify our own insecurities. Nothing in the realm of man could ever hope to compare with the power of nature, the awesome ability of wind, storm, lightning or flood to decimate cities, end countless lives, and bring man to his knees in fear and terror.

Fear and terror! Those were the two words with which much of Holland's evening had been occupied in studying. The reign of terror that had been produced over a hundred years earlier by a murderer so elusive, so damnably clever that not only had he succeeded in killing with apparent impunity, never to be caught and apprehended, but even after the passage of so many years, his identity was as yet unknown, with the police, the public and the world at large still no nearer to being able to identify the force, not of nature, but of the twisted evil that lay within the mind of the man whom history knows only as *Jack the Ripper.*

The reasons for such thoughts lay on the coffee table before him. The two hard cover books had been provided by Sergeant Carl Wright. Holland's assistant had long been a student of unsolved murder cases and none came with as high a historical profile as that of the Whitechapel Murders of 1888. His study of the Ripper case had long been a source of amusement among some of his colleagues, who thought his time might be better spent trying to ascertain the identity of some of the more recent killers who appeared to have escaped detection. After all, some of them had voiced to him, what use was it after all this time to try and find out who Jack the Ripper really was? What could it mean to the living to reveal the identity of a man long dead, one who admittedly had escaped detection for over a hundred years, but who was after all way beyond the reach of the law. Wright simply explained that thousands of people around the globe still felt a need to try and solve the case, he being only one of them. If someone couldn't understand his motives in attempting to arrive at a solution to the case, that was their hard luck, in his mind. Holland had spent the best part of the evening poring over the books, trying to commit to memory as many facts about the case as he could. In addition to the books, he'd managed to obtain a dossier from the Metropolitan Police, sent by e-mail that afternoon, which also provided him with as many details as he could possible require about the case, this time from the police of the time's point of view. There were case files, interview reporters with various witnesses, before and after the fact, as no-one ever saw the ripper at work.

With too many similarities between the case Holland was currently investigating and that of the Whitechapel Murder of 1888, Mike Holland had decided that it would be folly to ignore the possibility of a link, however tenuous, between the two even if it were no more than the fact that they had a crazed killer on the loose in Brighton who had determined to replicate the murders of the original ripper. The fact that the two killings on Holland's patch had occurred on the same dates as the first two Whitechapel murders and that both victims had been prostitutes was too coincidental to be ignored at this stage of the investigation.

Holland eventually shook himself from the lethargy of tiredness that he felt slowly engulfing him, rose from his sofa and made his way to the kitchen, mug in hand, where he quickly boiled the kettle and replenished his coffee with a freshly made, steaming hot mug of the dark elixir. Returning to the sofa, he began to read through the notes he'd made earlier when correlating the information he'd gleaned from Wright's books and from the old Scotland Yard reports.

Knowing that 'knowledge was power' he'd become determined to learn as much about his current nemesis as possible. If the Brighton killer was using the Jack the Ripper murders as a template for his own crimes it was obvious to Holland that the man must have studied the intricacies of the original murders in order to carry out his macabre re-creations of the murders, and Holland had therefore set out to arm himself with every scrap of knowledge that might give him an 'edge' no matter how slight, in his search for the murderer. Holland needed to know everything there was to know about the Whitechapel murders of 1888, and so, he continued his studious reading of his notes.

***

The crimes of Jack the Ripper had been played out against the backdrop of filth and degradation that pervaded the Whitechapel and Spitalfields areas of Victorian London. In what become known as 'The Autumn of Terror' the world's first officially acknowledged 'serial killer' stalked his prey and carried out his hideous campaign of murder and mutilation amidst the streets and alleyways of the veritable rabbit-warren of streets that reeked of human effluent, mirroring the poverty and deprivation that stared out at the rank thoroughfares from the windows of the squalid, bleak buildings that housed the employed, the unemployed and the unemployable of the city's vast underclass of the poor. Even to be employed proved no guarantee of a healthy or a long life within those mean streets, with the work available to the denizens of Whitechapel usually being that of the manual labourer, back-breaking work with long hours, poor pay and no assurance of job security. Often such work, perhaps in the markets of London or at the vast docks that helped fuel the engine of Empire with the comings and goings of the great ocean going ships that carried goods to and from the capital was of the casual, transient kind, a day here or there if the worker was lucky. Each day huge queues would build up wherever the prospect of earning a few shillings, or maybe just pennies presented itself.

For women the prospects were even gloomier, with little education being available to girls and marriage often the only means of escape from total destitution. Such marriages in themselves often led to the eventual descent of many a woman into the ancient art of prostitution. Sometimes, it would be the only way for a woman to supplement the meagre earnings of a poorly paid husband, or, often tragically, the only way for a widow, (and there many), to keep body and soul together after the loss of a husband's earnings. It is perhaps often forgotten that the majority of the victims of Jack the Ripper were at one time married women, mothers, and with the exception of the final victim, Mary Jane Kelly, all were what today would be termed 'mature' women.

So the streets of Whitechapel teemed with those least able to cry for help in a society that cared little for those whose efforts powered the great city's factories and dockyards, or who worked in the great houses of the rich, and returned home each night to the squalor and deprivation of the East End of London, and those very streets would provide the perfect hunting ground for the killer who would be remembered by history as none other than *Jack the Ripper.*

Somewhat perversely overlooked from almost every angle by the spire of Christ Church, Spitalfields, Jack the Ripper's killing ground covered only a small geographical area and spanned only a few weeks in time, yet his reign of terror would reach out to touch the hearts and minds of almost everyone within the vast metropolis of London and far beyond, as the notoriety of his crimes became known throughout the country and afar. There were those who would later attempt to attribute other, later killings to the Whitechapel murderer, but most scholars are of the opinion that the murders of Jack the ripper ended with that of Mary Kelly on the 9th November 1888.

There was indeed some speculation and disagreement at one time as to who was indeed the Ripper's first victim, with many wishing to blame the killing of Martha Tabram on some other, unknown assailant. It is now generally believed and accepted however, that Tabram was the Ripper's first victim, and so we will take the date of her murder, 31st August 1888 as the beginning of the Ripper's terrible killing spree, ending with the butchery of the unfortunate Mary Kelly on 9th November, a mere ten weeks from start to finish.

As has been illustrated earlier in this narrative, the murders of Martha Tabram and Mary Ann Nicholls took place on the 7th and the 31st of August respectively. Following the death of Nicholls, it would be a mere eight days before the killer struck again, this time with even greater severity. At that time the name 'Jack the Ripper' had not yet been coined for the murderer, the name being applied to the killer only after the receipt of a letter, mailed to the Central News Agency on 27th September, and reproduced in the morning newspaper *The Daily News* on 1st October. Often regarded as a hoax by modern Ripperologists, the 'Dear Boss' letter nonetheless identified the killer by the name with which he will always be remembered, being signed "Yours Truly, Jack the Ripper."

The letter read:

25 Sept 1888

Dear Boss

I keep on hearing the police have caught me but they wont fix me just yet. I have laughed when they look so clever and talk about being on the right track. That joke about Leather Apron gave me real fits. I am down on whores and I shant quit ripping them till I do get buckled. Grand work the last job was. I gave the lady no time to squeal. How can they catch me now. I love my work and want to start again. You will soon here of me with my funny little games. I saved some of the proper red stuff in a ginger beer bottle over the last job to write with but it went thick like glue and I cant use it. Red ink is fit enough I hope haha. The next job I do I shall clip the ladys ears off and send to the police officers just for jolly wouldn't you. Keep this letter back till I do a bit more work, then give it out straight. My knife's nice and sharp I want to get to work right away if I get the chance. Good luck.

Yours truly

Jack the Ripper

With those few words, a terror was born, a name given to the faceless assailant who appeared free to roam and kill at will and the people of London and the world would forever associate the crimes of that autumn with the man who, though never captured, identified and brought to justice would always live in memory as Jack the Ripper.

That terror, the fear of the ordinary citizen and the anger at the police force's seeming inability to apprehend the killer grew to massive proportions when, twenty two days after the murder of Annie Chapman the as yet un-named Whitechapel murderer claimed not one, but *two* victims in one night.

Swedish born Elizabeth Stride, (nee Gustavsdotter), aged forty-five became the third victim of the ripper, her body being discovered in Dutfield's Yard by Louis Diemschutz, a street seller of cheap jewellery as he drove his horse and cart into the yard at around 1 a.m. Her body had not been subjected to the mutilations present in the bodies of Tabram or Chapman, but Diemschutz testified that he believed he may have disturbed the killer before he was able to carry out such mutilations and so perhaps fuelled the killer's need to find another victim upon whom he could satisfy his evil lust that night.

That second victim of the night and Ripper's fourth victim in his reign of terror was forty six year old Catherine Eddowes, a native of the city of Wolverhampton, who had long since descended into a life of prostitution on the streets of the capital. Her savagely mutilated body had been discovered by a police constable, Edward Watkins, at around 1.15 a.m in the southwest corner of Mitre Square. Watkins saw and heard no-one as he entered the square and Eddowes proved to be the most brutally mutilated victim of the killer thus far, perhaps a victim of his savage frenzy at being interrupted in his 'work' upon the body of poor Elizabeth Stride earlier.

The post-mortem examination of her remains was carried out by Dr. Frederick Gordon Brown and his report provided disturbing reading to say the least. Catharine Eddowes throat had been cut, "to the extent of about six or seven inches." The big muscle across the throat had been completely divided on the left side. The large vessels on the left side of the neck were severed. Her larynx had been severed below the vocal chord and all the deep structures of the throat were severed to the bone. The cause of death was haemorrhage from the carotid artery and Brown estimated that death would have been immediate, and that the mutilations were carried out post-mortem.

On examining the abdomen he found that the front walls had been opened from the breast bone to the pubes. The liver had been stabbed and slit through by a sharp object. The intestines had been drawn out and placed over the right shoulder, with one section having been cut away completely and placed beside the poor woman's body. The face had been heavily mutilated, with the nose almost being cut away, one ear virtually severed, mutilating cuts about the face resulting in flaps of skin being formed around much of the face. The womb had been cut through horizontally, and the woman's left kidney had been carefully and precisely removed from the body. These were but some of the injuries listed in Brown's post-mortem report and serve to show the escalation in severity of the Ripper's attacks.

The police investigation continued, hampered slightly by the fact that Eddowes' body had been discovered within the boundaries of the City of London, thus coming under the jurisdiction of the City of London Police Force as opposed to the Metropolitan Police who had been in sole charge of the case up until that time. A public clamour soon broke out, with demands that the police take action and discover and bring to heel the murderer. There were demands for the resignation of the Commissioner of Police, and vigilante committees were formed and took to the streets at night in the hope of catching the killer.

Despite the police flooding the streets with uniformed and plain clothes officers, not one shred of viable evidence was found that might have led to an identification of the man responsible for the terrible crimes that were being perpetrated, seemingly at will upon the citizens of Whitechapel.

Within days however the killer had an almost universally known name, as the 'Dear Boss' letter appeared in the press and the name of *Jack the Ripper* was being shouted from every street corner by the newspaper sellers and the fear that had gripped the East End of London grew with every passing day that brought no results in the police investigation.

Whether by chance or by design, the whole of October passed without another killing on the streets of Whitechapel, and though the public continued to demand action from the police in tracking down the killer, the public outcry that had greeted the first four murders began to calm down. Perhaps, some thought, Jack the Ripper had gone, left the country or simply ceased his evil ways and that the terror had passed. They couldn't have been more wrong. Jack the Ripper's most heinous crime was yet to come, an act of barbarism and butchery so terrible that grown men, hardened police officers used to seeing the most hideous sights that man could inflict upon his fellows, actually broke down and cried when confronted with the scene that met their eyes on the morning of 9th November 1888.

In a room in Millers Court, off Dorset Street in Whitechapel, the body of Mary Jane Kelly was discovered by Thomas Bowyer as he attempted to collect the rent she owed on her room. Aged around twenty five, Mary Kelly proved to be the youngest victim of the Ripper and the mutilations carried out upon her body were so terrible and so vile that little was left of the woman that could be positively identified.

Her breasts had been cut off, the right arm slightly abducted from the body and rested on the mattress. The whole of the surface of the abdomen had been removed and thighs had been removed and the abdominal cavity emptied of the viscera. The tissues of the neck had been severed all the way round, down to the bone. The viscera were discovered in various places around the body. The uterus, kidneys and one breast were found under the head, the other breast was by the right foot. The liver was between the feet, the intestines by the right side and the spleen by the right side of the body. The flaps of skin that had been removed from the abdomen and thighs had been laid on a table. The woman's face was gashed 'in all directions'. The nose, cheeks, eyebrows and ears were all partly removed. The lips had been cut by several incisions down to the chin. The neck was cut through together with the other tissues down to the vertebrae.

In short, Mary Jane Kelly had been murdered, and then systematically butchered by the most heinous killer yet known to the British Police, or to the public at large.

***

Mike Holland laid his notes and the books belonging to Carl Wright aside. He'd read enough. Jack the Ripper had never been identified, never been apprehended. The largest police investigation ever undertaken up to that time in history had failed to produce a single shred of tangible evidence against one credible suspect. Either the man had been cleverer than the combined brains of the entire police force at Scotland Yard, or perhaps, as Wright had told him some suspected, there had been a cover-up of the facts at the time in order to protect an individual or perhaps a number of individuals with connections to the higher echelons of British society. Either way, Mike Holland had been sickened by much of what he'd just read. The post-mortem reports had been concise and exceedingly thorough for their day and the injuries inflicted upon the bodies of the Ripper's victims certainly corresponded with those inflicted on the recent Brighton victims.

Holland yawned. Tiredness had been slowly creeping up on him and it was now all he could do to keep his eyes open. Sleep beckoned. He'd managed to take in a mountain of facts about the Whitechapel murders of 1888. Now all he had to do was try and figure out how they could help him solve his own case, that of a twenty-first century ripper who appeared determined to copy the style and the acts of the original serial killer. There had to be something in the copious notes and in the vast number of books written on the case that would help him find a way to stop the latter day ripper in his tracks, but that would be a task for him to address in the morning. Laying his papers and books on the coffee table, and shivering with tiredness Mike Holland yawned once more, put his feet up on the sofa and laid his head upon the pile of cushions at one end. Not for the first time, his bed remained cold and untouched upstairs as he felt his eyelids growing heavier. He was asleep in seconds.

Chapter 20
The Morning After the Night Before

It had proved to be a long, difficult, sleepless night for Michael. Though he'd felt exhausted after the trauma of Jacob's ferocious attack the previous day he'd been too fired up to allow himself the luxury of a good night's sleep, afraid that Jacob just might decide to repeat his assault. Trying to rest with one eye continually on the door had left Michael feeling cold and low in spirit, precisely the way he didn't want to feel that morning. After Jacob's attack upon him the previous day, Michael had done as the other man had instructed and used his phone to call the man in the house on Abbotsford Road. Unable to speak openly with Jacob listening, he'd told the man that Jacob knew he'd been drugged, wanted to know why and for what purpose and wouldn't be deflected from his desire to find the truth. The man, sensing perhaps that Jacob was listening in on the conversation had told Michael to bring Jacob to the house at precisely eleven a.m the following day, this very morning to be precise. Although Jacob had protested and insisted that he wanted to resolve the situation there and then, the man had instructed Michael to tell Jacob that all would be revealed if he displayed a little patience. The man explained that he had people to see that day and wouldn't be free until the allotted time. Surely, he'd said, Jacob could wait a little longer in order to discover what he needed to know. Despite Jacob's protestations the man would not be swayed and Michael had told Jacob that this was not someone who would take orders or be threatened by anyone, least of all someone like Jacob. He could be dangerous, so he explained and Michael professed to be surprised that the man had agreed to meet with Jacob at all. After all, he was hardly a great friend of Michael's and probably cared little for the fact that Jacob had given him a thoroughly good beating.

The arrangements having been grudgingly agreed there followed the longest day of Michael's life. Jacob refused to let Michael out of his sight and if it hadn't been for the fact that Michael had a supply of his own narcotics in the flat he'd have been going crazy by the time evening arrived. As it was it suited Jacob to allow Michael to get 'high' on the stuff as Michael's drugged state rendered him easy to control and watch over.

Jacob had confiscated his phone, leaving Michael totally cut off from the outside world and only at bedtime did Jacob allow Michael the privacy of the use of his own room to sleep in, though Michael sensed rather than saw the presence of his young nemesis just outside the door through the night, seated in the tattered armchair that the young man had dragged across the floor to a position by the door. Michael felt like a prisoner under close surveillance in his own home, a feeling he hated more and more the longer the night wore on.

Now, with the coming of the dawn, all thoughts of sleep finally evaporated from his mind. A leering Jacob entered the room and Michael could almost smell the aura of latent potential violence that emanated from the other man.

"Sleep well, Michael? Don't bother to get up. Just stay where you are. I can talk to you just as well while you have a lie-in."

"What do you think? With you standing guard outside my door and me not knowing if you were going to murder me in my sleep, just how was I supposed to sleep?"

"Now, why on earth would I want to murder you in your sleep? You're the one who's going to take me to meet whoever's orchestrating whatever's been happening to me, aren't you? You can't do that if you're dead can you, Michael?"

"Look, I told you. Nothing sinister's going on."

"Bullshit! You don't drug someone until they're incapable of remembering what they've been doing without some sort of nefarious motive. You certainly didn't do it for the good of my health. I should have carried on beating the hell out of you yesterday until you'd told me the whole truth and nothing but the truth, as they say, instead of giving you the chance to pass the buck on to this mysterious friend of yours."

"I've told you, he's not exactly a 'friend'. He's someone I met who helps me out from time to time and I do the same for him."

"In other words, he's your supplier and a dealer and you sell the stuff for him as well."

"He's not a drug dealer, Jacob, honestly. Yes, he makes sure I'm well supplied but I don't sell the stuff for him. That's a totally different thing. You know I sell the stuff, yes, but only small time and I don't get my stuff from him. You should know that because you've picked up enough packages of the stuff from Andy in the tavern."

Jacob had to admit that much was true. As part of his 'bed and board' deal with Michael he'd undertaken various excursions to the old Crown Tavern in one of the seedier areas of town where he'd met with the mysterious 'Andy' who was always ready and waiting for his arrival and who'd hand over a brown-paper wrapped parcel in exchange for the envelope of cash that Michael sent in return. Unless Andy was the man to whom Michael had spoken on the phone the previous day, which was unlikely given his deferential tone to the speaker at the other end of the line then it was evident to Jacob that in this matter at least, Michael was being totally honest with him. As though to confirm the point Jacob said,

"So it's not Andy we're going to see today, am I right?"

Michael laughed nervously.

"Andy? You must be joking. You don't think I'd be this nervous if it were just Andy who was involved, do you?"

"Just why are you so afraid of this man? What sort of hold does he have over you?"

"I can't explain it all to you, man. Just take my word for it that this is one dude you don't want to cross. He's never actually been violent towards me, but you can tell just by being with him that there's something weird about him. Something that bubbles just under the surface. You can't put your finger on it, but you just know that he could probably kill you as easily as you or me would swat a fly. It's like he's evil through and through. He sort of smells evil if you know what I mean."

"Now I know you're talking rubbish. How the hell can anyone *smell* evil?"

"I told you I can't explain it. It's sort of like he lives in another world, another time altogether. His house just seems like it's trapped in time, old and gloomy and just, well, different."

"Sounds to me like he's got you well and truly spooked, Michael. If you ask me you've shot one too many veins full of crap before you've been to see this character. He won't bloody well scare me, I'm telling you."

"We'll see about that when you meet him, won't we? I'm telling you he's unlike anyone I've ever met before, almost as though he doesn't really belong in this world at all. I don't even know his name after all this time. There's no name listed under the phone number he gave me and as far as

I know, the house is supposed to be empty. The owner lives abroad some-where, that's all I've ever been able to find out about the place."

"What are you trying to say? He's a ghost?"

"No, of course not, but there's just something not quite right about him, man, that's all. I know I've done things to you on his orders but I never meant you no harm, honest. Just be careful when we get there, ok?"

Jacob considered Michael's words carefully. Despite his obvious fear of Jacob, developed as a result of the beating meted out to him the day before, the young druggie appeared to be even more frightened of the man who was pulling the strings behind whatever was going on. It was plain to Jacob that he'd have to be on the alert for any sign of treachery when Michael took him to the man's house later that morning. It looked like being a *very* interesting morning, if Michael's description of his strange employer was to be believed. For now though he had to make sure he was prepared for the day ahead and that meant breakfast. Keeping his conver-sation with Michael as brief as possible and thus maintaining his air of superiority and threat towards his host he moved toward the door, smiling that slightly leering smile of his once more at the man in the bed.

"You just leave the man to me. I'm fucking amazed you don't even know his name, you prat. How can you work for someone doing the things you do for this weirdo without even knowing his name? You must be more stupid than I thought."

Michael appeared as though about to answer, but Jacob cut him off with a dismissive wave of his hand

"Now, let's have breakfast. We've got a busy morning ahead of us, and this time, Michael, I'm making the fucking tea!"

Chapter 21
A Plan of Action?

"You look bloody awful, if you don't mind me saying so, sir."

Detective Sergeant Carl Wright had walked into his inspector's office just after eight a.m. to find Holland looking as dishevelled a sight as he'd ever seen his boss appear. Shafts of sunlight pouring through the plate glass window of the office served only to highlight the appearance of the inspector who sat bathed in the halo produced by the sunlight that diffused around him from behind his back.

The D.I. looked as though he'd slept in his clothes, which he had of course and his chin showed traces of stubble that suggested a not too close encounter with his razor that morning. His hair, never his best feature due to it's propensity for thinning and making him look older than his years, appeared even more unruly than was usual for the time of day.

"Well, I daresay you're correct, sergeant, but I have to say that you're probably the chief reason for me getting hardly any sleep at all last night and the little I did get was spent curled up on my sofa, hardly the best place for a restful night, wouldn't you agree?"

"Now how on earth could I be the cause of your sleepless night, boss?"

"Those damn books, Wright, that's how. I started reading them and the contemporary reports from Scotland Yard on the Jack the Ripper case and couldn't put the bloody things down. By the time I did it was the early hours of the morning and I just didn't have the energy to climb the stairs, get undressed and get into bed. They made riveting reading I must admit. I'd no idea that Jack the Ripper was quite as gruesome and ghastly in the degree of his mutilations as I discovered last night. Like everyone, I'd heard of him, who hasn't? But to read the details in graphic detail was something else. No wonder you and your fellow 'Ripperologists' as you call them find the case so intriguing."

"I know, sir. It's hard to believe that someone could get away with such blatantly grisly and horrific acts on the streets, be obviously stained with the blood of his victims and not be reliably seen by anyone, even once. It's as though the man were a wraith of the night, appearing from the shadows and simply disappearing back into them again after committing the murders, unheard, unseen and unknown, even to the present day. So if you don't mind me asking, what are your thoughts as to how it connects with our current case?"

Holland took a deep breath. He knew he was about to commit himself to a train of thought that others including his superiors might find incredible, but he needed his sergeant to be one hundred percent behind him as he took the inquiry down the road he intended to follow and absolute honesty between them would be of paramount importance.

"Well, Carl, I think it's bloody obvious, as I think you also suspect that our killer is attempting to recreate the Ripper murders. It can't be a coincidence that his killings have taken place on the anniversaries of the murders of Martha Tabram and Mary Nicholls and that both victims have been prostitutes."

The sergeant nodded, but said nothing as Holland continued.

"The thing is, if he sticks to the original Ripper's timetable we have less than two days to try and work out who he is and a way to stop him. The Chief Super has given us extra manpower, as many men as he can spare and it's up to us to use them the best way we know how. That meeting we had with him went better than I thought it would, but he was a little hesitant to admit to a real-life Jack the Ripper copycat being loose on the streets. He did say he thought the dates might have been coincidental, but you and I know better, don't we?"

Carl Wright nodded again. The Chief Superintendent had indeed granted Holland the extra men, both uniformed and plain clothes that he needed, but had qualified the grant of the extra manpower by demanding that his D.I. produce results and fast. No-one needed to tell Holland or Wright about the requirement for speed in their inquiry. Both men were well aware that the Brighton killer, if he was slavishly following the original Ripper's timetable of events would claim his next victim in just over twenty four hours. Whatever methods they decided to employ to identify the murderer and bring about an arrest would have to be formulated and put into effect almost immediately. Holland and Wright spent the next hour deliberating on the problems they faced. They were both agreed that the killer would strike somewhere in the red-light district of Brighton at sometime during night of the following day. That left them with just over twenty four hours in which to either catch the killer, or at least to do enough to dissuade him from carrying out the next murder in his re-creation of the Ripper murders.

"The Chief Super gave you the extra men you asked for, sir. Why don't we send them all out on the streets tomorrow and even put the plain-clothes guys in uniforms. It might be sufficient of a deterrent to put the bastard off."

"And then again maybe it won't, sergeant. Can you imagine the field day the press and TV people would have if we flooded the streets with police officers and the murderer still managed to carry out the next killing? They'd bloody well want to string us up if that happened."

"I know, sir, but what do you suggest? We can't just sit back and do nothing can we? Some poor woman's life is depending on what you decide to do."

"You think I don't know that? The trouble is, he's a clever bastard and always seems to be one jump ahead of us. We could get the media to announce that we know he's ready to strike again and why, but that might just cause a bigger panic than we need right now. Can you see it? "*Jack the Ripper comes to Brighton*" or some such headline blaring out from the newspapers and the TV screens? The people would go crazy and it would kill off the tourist trade overnight. As for the prossies, some of them might stay off the streets but there'll always be the hard core who are so in need of cash that they'll brave the streets whatever the risk, just to earn enough to pay for their next fix."

"At least, as you say, some of them might stay at home even for one night. It would narrow down the numbers we'd have to try and protect. I can't see how we can avoid telling the press something, boss. They might be our only hope of avoiding the third murder. You never know, he might even target some innocent holidaymaker who strays into the wrong area after dark and at least this might keep that particular section of the population away from the target area."

"You're right of course, sergeant. I'll go and see the Chief Super after we've finished here, get him to liaise with the press and TV people. He'll come up with something diplomatically and politically expedient that won't scare the populace too much, I'm sure."

"I'm sure he will, sir, I'm sure he will."

Both men were only too well aware that the Chief Superintendent was tied to a varied set of rules and regulations and had to be almost as adept as a politician as he was as a police officer in his dealings with the press and the public. If anyone could get the words just right, he was the man to do it.

"We'll get to that in a few minutes, sergeant. For now, you and I need to decide what we're going to do with the manpower we have available tomorrow night."

Over the next thirty minutes Holland and Wright slowly came to the conclusion that the only option they really had was to follow Wright's suggestion and to flood the streets with uniforms in an effort to deflect the killer from his intended purpose. Both men were only too aware of the fact that over one hundred years ago, the police in London had done the very self-same thing in their search for Jack the Ripper and had met with total failure in their attempts to catch him, or even to find a reliable witness to his presence in the killing grounds of Whitechapel, where he appeared to be able to roam and kill at will with absolute impunity. By the time Holland left the office for his meeting with the Chief Superintendent another hour had gone by, an hour that brought the killing of the third victim that much closer to becoming a reality.

Alone in Holland's office Sergeant Carl Wright pored over a street map of the area they would have to patrol in their attempt to foil the killer. As he did so, he couldn't help but feel that although forty men, the number of officers at their disposal, might sound a lot, they would be hard pressed to adequately cover the labyrinthine streets that made up the killer's hunting ground if indeed he intended to stick to the red-light district. Holland and Wright's biggest fear was that the killer, who was clever enough to realise that the police had worked out his strategy, might move beyond the boundaries of the area and commit his next murder in a totally different part of the town. He began to make notes, to draw up a patrol roster that he hoped would give them the best coverage of the area possible given the manpower available. The day had warmed considerably and bright shafts of penetrating sunlight now lanced through the large plate glass window of the office, their rays bouncing off the polished floor and reflecting from the walls. Wright felt little of the warmth, however, as his mind wandered to thoughts not of bright, sun kissed days, but of cold, dark nights, and the spectre of death that hovered over every one of those streets on the map.

Who are you bastard? Where are you? Come on, give us a clue, you bloody fiend. Where the hell are you going to strike next? were the thoughts that ran through his mind as he looked at his watch, the second-hand inexorably ticking off the next minute. Carl Wright knew without needing to be reminded, that time was running out and that the clock was inexorably ticking away towards what could be yet another grisly and very bloody murder. Despite the warmth of the office, the sergeant shivered.

Chapter 22
The Man in the Dark Room

At precisely five minutes before eleven in the morning, the taxi carrying Jacob and Michael drew to a halt on the street outside number fourteen Abbotsford Road. Michael had been pleased when Jacob had insisted they use a taxi for the journey. In truth, after the treatment meted out to him by the other man the previous day Michael had felt in no mood for the long walk up the hill in the rising heat of the morning. His throat was still painful from the pressure exerted upon his windpipe and his whole body felt as though it no longer belonged to him. Michael was running on empty, though Jacob appeared to be on a high, pumped up by an adrenalin rush at the prospect of solving what he saw as the riddle of the reason for Michael and the stranger combining to place him under the influence of drugs. Neither man had spoken on the journey from Michael's flat to Abbotsford Road.

The taxi driver had tried and failed to make polite conversation with the two young men, concluding from their silence that perhaps they were a pair of gay lovers who'd had a row and now refused to speak to each other. He couldn't have been more wrong of course, though his only real concern was whether the pair would be able to pay the fare on their arrival at their destination. He had an inbuilt instinct that the scruffier of the two, the one with the longer hair and facial growth was a junkie. He'd carried enough of that ilk in his cab over the years to know them on sight, and Michael certainly fitted into his conception of the archetypal junkie without a doubt. He was unsure when it came to the other man. He appeared quite clean-cut and well-groomed and didn't give off the usual aura of the drug abuser. It was a relief to the driver when he pulled up at the address the scruffy man had given him. He was ready to chase them if they made a run for it.

The two men alighted from the cab, the heat of the day meeting them as they exited the cool air-conditioned interior of the car. Jacob made no effort to put his hand in his pocket and reluctantly, much to his chagrin and the driver's relief, Michael found himself paying for the ride.

Gravel crunched beneath their feet as the two young men traversed the driveway and approached the front door of number fourteen. Michael was sweating profusely, a mixture of the heat of the day and his nervousness about what may or may not take place. In truth, he'd no idea what the man waiting in the house was likely to do. He'd been backed into a corner by Jacob's demands, or so Michael believed and anything might happen once he and Jacob entered the domain of his strange acquaintance. Following the man's instructions, given to him over the telephone the previous day Michael refrained from knocking on the door. He simply turned the door knob and walked in, closely attended by Jacob who'd felt a sense of exhilaration as he'd looked up at the old house on their approach along the gravel driveway. He whistled through his teeth as he took in the appearance of the house, sensing its former grandeur but also recognising the rather dilapidated state of the place as it now stood before him. Whatever the state of the place he was anxious to meet the strange inhabitant of number fourteen. Jacob knew he was close to finding out what the hell was going on. He was sure of it.

As Michael closed the front door behind them Jacob was at once aware of a change in the atmosphere of the day. While the outside world was warm and bright, suffused with rays of the bright sunshine the house seemed to be pervaded by a chill that reached out and gripped him as he walked across the hallway. There was little light and the tiled floor added to the overall felling of coldness. *Could Michael have been right about the place, about the man?*

Jacob quickly banished the thoughts as he followed Michael to an interior door at the far side of the entrance lobby. Now, at last, he did knock. A voice seemed to come from far away bidding them to enter and Michael led the way once again as they stepped into the room that lay beyond the door.

The room that Jacob entered took him by surprise. It was large, high ceilinged, and dark. Heavy velvet drapes curtained off the windows blocking off the sunlight that warmed the outside world. He could make out the shapes of the furniture, make out the bookcases and the large mahogany table that formed the centrepiece of the room though he couldn't quite make out the objects that festooned its surface. At the far end of the room, in front of the curtained window stood a desk, behind which Jacob could make out a figure sitting, waiting for them. Suddenly a bright light flared from the desk, a high intensity shaft of light catching both he and

Michael in its beam. He shielded his eyes with his hands but couldn't see what lay beyond the light, in other words the man who sat behind the desk.

"Welcome, Jacob. Do come in and sit down," said a voice from behind the desk. "Forgive my precautions but I'm not ready to let you see my face at this point, as welcome as you are."

Jacob tried to place the voice, which had a slightly familiar ring to it, but the man had obviously used some means of disguising his voice, as he had his face, which even in the darkness Jacob could see was shielded by a mask of some kind.

"Welcome? You bloody well welcome me with a blinding light, refuse to show your face and expect me to just sit down and exchange pleasantries with you? I'm not a damned fool you know. Just what the hell is going on here? What have you been doing to me?"

"Now, now, so many questions and such an attitude. Ah well, perhaps that can be forgiven in light of certain circumstances that only we are aware of, eh Jacob, or rather, perhaps you wouldn't mind if we dispense with the charades and call you by your real name? That would be much better for everyone, don't you agree, Jack?"

Jacob, or rather Jack looked stunned. He whirled round to face Michael, ready to accuse him of somehow discovering his secret but the man was gone, slipped out the door while the man had been speaking.

"Don't bother looking for Michael. He had instructions to leave us to talk in private as soon as you were inside the room. He can be quite obedient at times, rather reminiscent of a faithful dog, wouldn't you say?"

"Never mind him. How the hell do you know me, or rather how do you know my real name? And what do you want with me? Why the hell have you been using your faithful lap dog Michael to drug me until I've been incapable of remembering anything I've done?"

"Oh dear, like I said, questions, questions, so many questions. But please don't worry, Jack. You'll get your answers soon, lots of answers, but first please sit down. You'll find the chair on your left quite comfortable, and there's a carafe of fresh water and a glass on the side table beside it that you might find refreshing during our little talk."

Jack grudgingly took a seat in the armchair the man had indicated. He couldn't help himself. There was too much he needed to know.

"Look, just who are you? At least tell me that, and how you know my real name."

"Listen, Jack, as to who I am, that really isn't important, not right now. As to you, well, I'm afraid you can blame Michael for that one. When you first went back to the flat with him you slept for a long time and he was able to go through your belongings as you slept. He found the journal Jack and the letters from your uncle and you're your great uncles and so on. I know *who* you are, Jack Reid, and I know *what* you are. I know *everything*."

"What do you mean, you know who and *what* I am? Just who are you?"

"Ah, Jack, I've been searching for something for so long and I know you've been searching too and now at last I've found what I've been looking for, though you still have some way to go in order to fulfil your own search for your uncle."

"How do you know about my uncle? There's nothing about that in my papers."

"Oh, but there was, Jack. The letter from the girl who you'd sent to the solicitors?"

Damn, thought Jack, he'd forgotten about that.

"Okay, so you know all about me. What has that got to do with whatever it is you say you're searching for. And why have you had me drugged?"

"Patience, Jack, patience, please."

"My patience is running thin. So far, you seem to hold all the aces, but what's to stop me getting up and running across to you and..."

"And attacking me as you did poor Michael yesterday? Poor boy, he's really rather a coward, isn't he? Jack, you may be young and you may be strong, but let me assure you that if you were to even attempt such a move against me, you would most certainly find yourself in a very painful position. I'm far stronger than I may appear. Oh I'm sorry, I don't appear as anything behind this light, do I? You must take my word for it, Jack, that you will not succeed should you attempt any act of violence in my direction. That is a promise and one you would do well to remember."

Something in the man's voice reached deep into Jack's mind. He recalled the things Michael had told him about this man and he felt something of the things Michael had described. There was something strange about this faceless, nameless man who seemed to know everything about Jack, whereas he knew absolutely nothing about the man. Jack also sensed something of Michael's feeling about the man being not quite of this world. Something in his words and the way he spoke them was at odds with the modern world. The man seemed to belong to a bygone age, not the present.

As Jack sat silently pondering the things he'd just been told, the man spoke again.

"Now, Jack Reid, are you ready to listen to what I have to tell you?"

As the chill of the house mingled with the uneasy feeling that the man's voice generated within his mind Jack Reid silently nodded and with that small gesture, the man began to speak, his voice level and firm. Jack didn't interrupt him, not even once, as he spoke for an hour, answering some but not all of Jack's questions. As he spoke, the room grew colder and Jack Reid began to shake not just with the cold of the house on Abbotsford Road but from the fear that the man's words were instilling into his mind and into his very soul.

There was no sun, no warmth, no outside world any longer. Jack found himself wishing he'd never set foot in Brighton, never met Michael or gone to the house on Abbotsford Road. But of course, by then it was too late, not just for Jack but for too many others. As Jack shivered the voice of the man droned on and Jack's mind began to assimilate the horrors contained in the words he heard.

Chapter 23
Questions and Answers

Jack Reid tried hard to see past the glaring beam of the halogen light that continued to glare at him from just behind the man at the desk, but to no avail. The beam was so intense that even shielding his eyes with his hands brought no respite from the unremitting shaft of high intensity light that lanced across the room straight to his position in the armchair. What, he asked himself were the man's motives in concealing his face in such a way? Could it be that it was someone who Jack knew or would recognise? He'd detected something familiar in the man's voice right away, though he felt that even the voice was disguised in some way, making any recognition impossible. Then again, maybe the man was disfigured in some way and wished to remain hidden. That theory was quickly dismissed from Jack's mind for after all surely Michael would have told him if the man had been some hideously deformed freak. Was it simple theatrics, a ploy to add drama to the meeting? No, it had to be that Jack would or might recognise the man if he saw him. At least that was his conclusion as he sat waiting for the man to begin his explanation for the strange set of events that had overtaken him.

Jack had hoped that as his eyes became better adjusted to the glare, maybe he might just be able to make out a little more of the shape that represented the man behind the desk, but no, the beam of the light was far too strong to allow even for that possibility.

"You may as well give it up, Jack," said the man, as though he were able to read Jack's thoughts. "You'll never see past the light. It's specially positioned and is of a precise intensity that means no-one can see through the shaft of its light. Even if you could, you wouldn't know me, not at all. Just in case you entertained any thoughts of rushing me, let me tell you that there's a small calibre pistol trained on you right now as we speak. I'm a very good shot, Jack, and any sign of movement on your part will result in great pain for you, believe me. Nod if you understand."

Jack nodded. The man spoke.

"Good, now let's see. Ah yes, your name is Jack Reid, son of Tom and Jennifer Reid, nephew or should I say second cousin of the late Doctor Robert Cavendish and his brother, Mark. No, don't speak, just listen," said the man as Jack made as if to ask a question. Jack fell silent and the man continued.

"You recently attained your coming of age, and on so doing, you received a legacy from your Uncle Robert, namely a collection of papers and letters and, not to mince words, the journal of the long-departed serial killer, Jack the Ripper. Before you begin to ask how I know all this I must tell you that Michael did a very good job of obtaining the papers etcetera from your holdall and copying everything and bringing them to me. You were employed as a trainee nurse, a most honourable profession young Jack until you received the documents and realised just what kind of a heritage you shared with your forebears. Having made the shocking discovery you began to revert to the state of mind that so disturbed you in your earlier childhood. Oh yes I know all about that, too, Jack. Why do you think that was? Why did you find the dark thoughts of your formative years returning to haunt you, I wonder? Please don't try to answer, as I hope that I'll be able to do that for you before long.

You read and re-read the journal didn't you, Jack? You read every letter and every note placed within its pages. Robert Cavendish's great-grandfather was most informative was he not? The great physician himself, Burton Cleveland Cavendish, that great pillar of the community, the great healer, and of course, the great philanderer himself. Did it not shock you, Jack to discover that Robert and Mark's great-grandfather, your own ancestor had an affair, an affair that led to the birth of a monster? Yes, Jack, I'm sure you were shocked to learn that the bastard spawn of Burton Cavendish grew up to be the man we know as *Jack the Ripper!*

But that wasn't all you discovered was it, Jack? I also read every one of those pages, and I know what you know. His blood, and I mean Burton Cavendish's, flows in your veins, doesn't it, Jack, as it did in the veins of Robert and Mark and their father and grandfather before them? It flows in the veins of every direct blood descendant of Burton Cavendish, which gives a share of the Ripper's genes to your own father, Tom Reid and of course it flows in your veins, too. How does it feel to be cursed with the bloodline of Jack the Ripper, Jack, and by a wonderful quirk of coincidence to carry the name 'Jack' as well? How delightfully symbolic and ironic that your unfortunate parents should give you that name, don't you think?"

"Listen, I…"

"*Silence*, please. You may speak when I've finished. For now, I ask that you give me your full attention."

Jack fell silent once again. His secret, or what he thought had been his secret, was now known to this man and to Michael obviously, and Jack needed to know what the man intended to do with the knowledge as well as finding out why the two men had conspired to drug him and try to make him forget certain parts of the recent past.

"I'll try and keep this short, Jack, don't worry," the man continued. "To put it in simple terms, when you discovered all of this you realised that perhaps you knew why you'd led such a disturbed childhood. Your blood fixations, your bouts of moodiness and occasional violence could suddenly be explained, couldn't they? You're a descendant of The Ripper. That thought, coupled with the knowledge of your previous troubled childhood was more than your feeble mind could cope with. You needed to get away, to seek solace and solitude and so you began a search for the one man who you thought might be able to help you. You knew from hearing your own family speak over the years that your Uncle Robert had led something of a disturbed life in his later years, leading up to this death and you put two and two together and realised that his state of mind had probably been affected by his reading of the journal. After all, it was having the same effect on you, too, wasn't it, as it still is?"

Jack could keep silent no longer, and now he deliberately and forcefully interrupted the man. He would not be silenced.

"Just how the hell do you know so much about my Uncle Robert? He was injured in a car crash, the one that killed his own father. He lay in a coma for weeks and when he came out of it he was never the same man again. I was only young, but I do remember a lot of it. He was eventually diagnosed as having a brain tumour and that's what killed him. What the hell is all this nonsense you're spouting at me?"

"Oh, come now, Jack. Give me a little credit please. I know that while he was in his coma Robert Cavendish suffered from appalling nightmares and visions of Jack the Ripper and his crimes and that even though he was told it had all been a dream, a figment of his tortured brain while in the coma, within weeks of going home he received the awful legacy that he subsequently passed on to you, his nearest thing to a male heir. Even then, he delayed the legacy until you reached the age of eighteen; I suppose in order to shield you, at a tender age from the effects of reading that journal you carry in your holdall."

Jack's mind was working overtime. This man knew so much, he had to have been close to Robert Cavendish at some time. There was also the familiarity in his voice. He gambled on trying to force the man to reveal his connection.

"You knew him, didn't you? What were you, one of the nurses or orderlies in the hospital, even perhaps one of his doctors? Is that how you know so much about what happened to him in the hospital? Or did you work for the solicitors? Did you sneak a peek at the documents years ago and realise what they were? What I don't understand is why you want them now, why you want to do what you've been doing to me."

"Ha," the man laughed. "You'd love to know, wouldn't you, Jack? I could tell you, but at this time I choose not to. I do know that you're here searching for your Uncle Mark, Robert's brother in the hope that he may be able to tell you something of what really happened to your Uncle, something that the brothers may have shared in a moment of intimacy, something that Robert may not have shared even with his wife. Why Brighton, Jack? You must have heard from the pretty little mole you sent to the solicitors that Mark had left the country, sold his assets and gone to live in the sun. Ah, I can see by your face that you did. But you're cleverer than most, aren't you, Jack? You learned somehow that Mark Cavendish retained one small business interest in this country, didn't you, one that his solicitors knew nothing of? You found out about the guesthouse in Brighton, am I right?"

Jack slowly nodded.

"The Arcadia Hotel was jointly owned by Mark and his old friend Simon Davis, but all the paperwork was in Davis's name, and he used a different solicitor to your family so there was no way they could know about it. You came here thinking that Mark may have kept in touch with Davis, didn't you, but you found out that Davis had disappeared six months ago. No-one knows what happened to him, where he went, anything."

"Are you Simon Davis?"

"No, I'm not, Jack. I doubt anyone will see the man again to be honest with you."

With those words, delivered coldly and slowly, Jack somehow knew that Simon Davis was dead, and that the man behind the desk in all probability was the man who'd killed him, or who at the very least had arranged his death.

"Perhaps you should know that Mark Cavendish is also no more. He's gone forever, dead beneath the waves near his home on the beautiful island retreat he'd chosen for himself. He knew something you see, something that scared him and he couldn't live with the knowledge any longer. I was there when he disappeared beneath the sea for ever, Jack. So you see, he can tell you nothing about what your Uncle saw in his mind or the things that came to him when the nights were dark and the figures from the past, described in the letters he left you with the journal came to visit him."

Jack now felt sure he was in the presence of a very dangerous man. In that, at least, Michael hadn't lied to him. Perhaps he was even responsible for the death of Mark Cavendish.

"But why? And what has all this to do with you?"

"I told you, I was searching for something and I found it in you. I needed to know certain things about myself and your arrival here in Brighton and the words of the journal, the letters from your male ancestors, from Burton Cavendish through to Robert himself have given me what I needed."

"But, I still don't understand your involvement at all. Why did you need to know these things and why did you have Michael drug me?"

"Ah yes, the Rohypnol."

Rohypnol, thought Jack. So that was it. The date rape drug that had gained notoriety in recent years. The drug would render the recipient pliable and drowsy, unable to control their movements, or to remember what had happened to them whilst under its influence. *But, why?*

"Before you say anything, let me reiterate that I know who and what you are, Jack Reid. I knew as soon as I read the journal and the accompanying papers that you were the spawn of Jack the Ripper and that you had, or should I say *have*, a destiny to fulfil. Your Uncle Robert was troubled by the journal but his own training as a psychiatrist, his superb mental control meant that he was able to avoid falling victim to the true nature of the journal. You on the other hand have been troubled since birth with, shall we say, the effects of the 'dark side' of your inherited genes? It was only a matter of time before they began to take control of you and once you'd read the journal and the letters, you began to slowly realise what that destiny was. That's why you went in search of your Uncle Mark, isn't it?

You thought he could help prevent you from turning into exactly what you have turned into."

"What do you mean, what I've turned into?"

"D'you mean to tell me that you still haven't caught on? Even after what I've told you? You have the soul of the Ripper within you, Jack. I knew that, which is why I ordered Michael to lace your food and drink with the Rohypnol. I knew that when the time came you'd begin your own version of the Autumn of Terror. It was just luck that brought you here to Brighton and into my sphere of influence, where I could observe and try to control the limits of your excesses. By drugging you I had thought that we could control your movements enough to prevent the deaths of any innocent victims, but I was wrong wasn't I, Jack?"

Jack's face took on a puzzled look. He had no idea what the man meant.

"I don't know what on earth you're talking about," he said. "What have I got to do with the deaths of innocent people?"

"Oh, come now, surely you can't be so naïve. There've been two murders in the town in recent weeks. Who do you think was responsible?"

"You can't seriously expect me to believe that I've killed two people without knowing anything about it. I'm not so gullible as to be taken in by a story like that. Just what the fuck are you trying to do to me?"

"Listen to me, Jack. We drugged you in the hope that we could prevent your mind, which was already teetering on the verge of murderous intent, from going over the edge. I had a feeling that after your experiences with the journal and all that it means you'd be easy fodder for the influence that emanates from its pages."

"What influence? What the hell are you talking about? How could my mind be influenced by reading the journal?"

Even as he spoke the words Jack knew that the man was correct. All the while he'd read the pages of the journal of the long dead Jack the Ripper, he'd felt that something real was contained within the yellowed pages of the ramblings of the murderer. He'd known instinctively that his Uncle Robert Cavendish must have felt the same things and that had been confirmed by Robert's own notes, inserted at various intervals between the pages. He'd suffered from the same terrible dreams that his uncle described, haunted by images of the tortured souls of the Ripper's victims and of the Ripper himself, an amorphous, wraith like entity that swirled around his mind, encroaching upon his innermost thoughts and feelings.

So disturbed had Jack become after reading the journal that he'd soon
realised that he needed to leave home, to be alone as he sought the truth,
as his mind began to feel the extraordinary pull of the ethereal force that
virtually oozed from the aged pages. He had to find a reason for what was
happening to him. He'd quickly recognised the evil that lived within the
journal, as though the soul of the Ripper lived on in his twisted words.

He'd truly believed that Robert's brother Mark may have held the key
to solving the riddle of what had truly happened to his uncle, but with the
knowledge that Mark had died, or rather had taken his own life, that hope
had now been dashed. What if Mark had also fallen victim to the same
aura of evil that Jack felt with certainty lay within the journal? Mark was,
after all, Robert's brother and as such he would also have shared the same
bloodline that now appeared to have laid its curse upon the hapless Jack.
As though from nowhere, he suddenly realised that the man behind the
desk was speaking to him again.

"The reason for the drugs was simple. I wanted to see what would
happen if you were allowed to remain conscious, but in a controlled state.
I thought that you'd be pliable, easily controlled and I gave Michael instructions as to the exact dose to administer to you, after which he was to
observe what you did and report back to me.

"Unfortunately, he failed to stop you from killing the first prostitute.
He foolishly thought that my orders to observe also meant that he shouldn't
interfere in anything you did while under the influence of the drug. In
point of fact, it served to prove that the power of the journal far out-
weighed the power of the drug. Can you believe it, Jack? The words contained in those pages hold a stronger power than the narcotic that flowed
in your bloodstream. Words more powerful than science, just incredible!"

"I don't believe a word of it. You're lying. I didn't kill anyone!"

"Oh, but you did. Do you remember waking one morning to find that
Michael appeared to have undressed you and put you to bed? That was the
night of the first killing. He'd taken you home after watching what you did
to that poor girl, undressed you and washed every trace of blood from
your clothes, placed them in the dryer and then put them on the back of
the chair. He was amazed to learn from you the next morning that you'd no
idea at all what you'd done the previous night. When he told me, I was
surprised and delighted. Although I'd originally intended to try and control your murderous urges I now decided to see just what you'd do if
allowed to continue. As a controlling part of the experiment I made sure

that Michael continued to administer the drug. Sure enough, you did it again, with no recollection at all of the killing and mutilation you'd carried out in the night. You did have some residual thoughts the second time and you reported strange nightmares, remember? You also found some bloodstains on your hands. Michael had of course cleaned and dried your clothes once again, but he told you he'd fallen and cut himself on the way home from the pub late the previous night and that you'd helped clean him up. You accepted his explanation as you were too mind-befuddled to think otherwise. You were already suffering from short term memory lapses and your mind was becoming easy to control, at least some of the time."

Jack still found the man's words impossible to believe. He couldn't possibly believe that, even allowing for the influence of the journal, he could possibly kill two women without retaining a single memory of either event.

"Listen to me," said Jack. "You have Michael bring me here, tell me I'm a murderer possessed by the soul of Jack the Ripper or something like that and yet you won't even show me your face. Tell me who you are, or offer me any proof of these things I'm supposed to have done. You must think I'm stupid."

"Oh no, not stupid, Jack. Disturbed of mind perhaps, but never stupid. You ask for proof? I made sure Michael kept a record of whatever happened while you were under the influence of the Rohypnol. Please feel under your seat and you'll find an envelope. Take it out and examine the contents in the beam of the lamp. I think you'll find it contains all the proof you require."

Jack fumbled around under his chair for a second until he felt the envelope. He quickly grabbed it and opened the flap, finding two photographs within. In the glare of the high intensity lamp, he stared with disbelief at the pictures.

The first showed him on his knees beside the bloodied body of Laura Kane, the second a similar representation of him, knife in hand beside the unfortunate Marla Hayes. His face was clearly visible, peering in the direction of the photographer, who he assumed must have been Michael.

"Little Laura Kane and Marla Hayes were both clients of Michael's. You must have known that, Jack, which made it easy for you to target and murder them. The police announced that they have a photograph of Laura with a man. Was it you, Jack? Did you wine and dine her, romance her first? Or did you just lure her with false promises and then take her to that place where you gutted the little whore?"

Jack Reid slumped in the chair as belief and grief in equal measure washed over him in a tidal wave of fear and confusion, the shaft of light from behind the man burning a path into his soul, and within seconds, his mind and his world crumbled to dust around him.

Chapter 24
More Facts, No Clues

"Come on, Carl," said Holland to his sergeant. "We need to re-create the next Ripper killing on paper. If we can do that we may be able to figure out how our own killer's mind is working. We need an 'edge,' something that can give us an insight into his mind. If he's going to be on the prowl for his next victim tomorrow night, I want to have at least an even money chance of bringing the bastard to heel."

Carl Wright nodded and rose from his chair on the opposite side of Holland's desk. He quickly picked up the chair and carried it around to Holland's side of the desk, where he placed it down on the floor and sat next to the inspector. Together, they began painstakingly going through everything they had on the murder in 1888 of Jack the Ripper's victim, Annie Chapman.

Annie, born Eliza Anne Smith, had been born not too far from the scene of her eventual demise, in Paddington, London, in 1841. She had married a domestic coachman, John Chapman in 1869 and later gave birth to two daughters and a son, the family living at first in Bayswater and later for some time in Windsor where Chapman worked again as a coachman. Surely, of all the victims she had the greatest opportunity to enjoy a normal happy married life? Unfortunately, for reasons we are unaware of Annie abandoned her family and returned to London in 1882, shortly before the death of her daughter Emily. It is easy to assume that she'd acquired a drinking habit and that this unfortunate circumstance led to the breakdown of her marriage to the man who to all intents and purposes appeared to be as respectable a choice of husband as she could have made. Allegations of her infidelity have also been put forward as reasons for the marriage split, but no true evidence of this has been produced to date.

Certainly, it is known that John Chapman continued to support his wife until his own death from cirrhosis of the liver and dropsy in 1886, after which she appeared to have scraped a living by selling her own crochet work, selling matches or flowers and eventually, when unable to obtain money from a number of men friends who occasionally provided for her, Annie descended into prostituting herself on the streets of Whitechapel.

Her lifeless, mutilated corpse was discovered at around six a.m. on the morning of September 8th in the back yard of number twenty nine Hanbury Street, Whitechapel. Her dress had been pulled up around her waist and as could be clearly seen by John Davis, the man who made the grisly find, her intestines had been draped across her left shoulder. Police surgeon Dr. George Bagster Phillips who carried out the post-mortem examination of her remains reported that the woman had been "terribly mutilated." As in the previous killings, the throat had been cut and in this case a number of the abdominal organs had been removed. The uterus, the upper portion of the vagina and part of the bladder were missing and no trace of these organs was ever found. This was, to date, by far the worst example of the Ripper's mutilations and it would have been little comfort to the relatives of the deceased to be told that she probably had little time left to live in any case due to the presence of lung disease and lesions on the brain.

Unusually in the case of a Ripper murder it was ascertained that Annie Chapman had been relieved of two brass rings which she'd been known to be wearing on the evening prior to her death. Jack the Ripper had taken trophies, so it was assumed. The rings, like her murderer were never traced. She was buried in the cemetery at Manor Park in London on Friday 14th September, her funeral being attended by members of her family.

Unfortunately, as far as Holland and Wright were concerned, the facts of the case ended there. Apart from an in-depth post-mortem report and details of the police force's failed attempts to secure the apprehension of the killer, a few witness reports which detailed the known movements of Annie Chapman in the hours leading up to her death, no further helpful information was available to the latter day detectives. Holland and Wright simultaneously leaned back in their seats, stretched almost in unison and looked at each other.

"It doesn't help us a lot, does it?" Holland volunteered to his sergeant.

"Not really, sir, no. It's typical of the whole scenario surrounding Jack the Ripper. Apart from the names of the victims and the people who were involved with them prior to their deaths and those who found the bodies, it's the same in every case. No-one saw anything, heard anything or remembered anything that might have given the police a real clue to the killer's identity. Jack the Ripper was like a phantom, a wraith who appeared out of nowhere in the dead of night and returned whence he came without leaving an evidence of his presence."

"But we know that he wasn't a bloody phantom, was he? He was a man, a blood and guts evil son of a bitch who was simply too clever for the forces of law and order as they existed at the time. I'll lay odds on the fact that someone back then did know who he was and either kept quiet out of fear or because they actually wanted to protect the bastard."

"Who the hell would have wanted to protect someone like that?"

"Who, indeed? A wife, a lover, a doting indulgent father? Who knows? But someone would have known him, Wright. They had to have done. As the police conjectured at the time, he must have been covered in blood after carrying out his mutilations. If he had a family one of his relatives must have seen the state of him after the murders, surely."

"But if he was single, sir?"

"Even then, he must have had friends, parents or siblings perhaps. There had to have been one person at least in 1888 that had a bloody good idea who the Ripper was and who, for their own reasons, kept silent about it. Either way, it doesn't help us much at all in tracking down the evil sod that's ready to go out and kill again tomorrow night, presumably in honour of the original Ripper."

"You think that's what this all about, sir? Some sort of twisted hero worship?"

"I don't really know what to think," Holland replied. "So far, our killer is proving as elusive as the original Whitechapel version. The fact that he's trying to recreate the crimes down to the exact dates is a bit of a giveaway though, don't you think, sergeant?"

"Maybe, sir, though there could be something in his motives that we haven't caught on to yet."

"You're right of course, but we have so little to go on. I suppose we're clutching at straws and they're all damn well slipping through our fingers before we can get a grip. We've got one day left before we expect him to strike again and we have no idea what he looks like, why he's really doing it, or who he's likely to target apart from the reasonable certainty that it will be another prostitute."

"You know, sir, it's often been assumed that Jack the Ripper had an in-built hatred of prostitutes, perhaps because he'd caught a venereal disease from one of them at some time. Do you think it's possible that our current Ripper is also infected with something he's picked up from one of the local girls and is carrying out some sort of revenge attacks using Jack the Ripper as his model?"

"By God, sergeant, you just might have something there. If we're dealing with some prat who's picked up a dose of V.D. from a local prossie then we might just have a chance of nailing the bastard."

"But how, sir? The clinics at the local hospitals treat everyone confidentially. They won't tell us a bloody thing about the patients they've treated and even if they did there'd probably be too many for us to check out in the space of twenty four hours."

Holland, who a moment ago had actually believed his sergeant had hit on a possible theory to explain the reasons behind the killings had to agree with Wright. Even if it were true that the Brighton Ripper was killing prostitutes out of a perceived need for revenge against women of the street in general, there was no way he could force the medical profession to divulge confidential patient records to him on the basis of a hunch or a theory.

"You're right of course," said Holland to his sergeant. "But I do think you may have hit on a potential motive for our killer. I want you to speak to the boys in vice. Try and see if they have a list of all known users of the local girls, those who've maybe been picked up for kerb-crawling in the last year, say. If they've picked up one or more men on a number of occasions and we can compile a list of regular frequenters of the red-light district we just might find our man lurking somewhere on it. It's along shot I know and we don't have much time, but we have to try something."

Carl Wright wasted no time in leaving Holland's office and making his way to the office of the vice Squad where he was soon involved in deep conversation with Sergeant Mary Kelleher, a seasoned detective who'd spent the last two years working in vice and who knew the local scene as well as anyone in the local force. Irish by birth, Kelleher wore her hair long, the fiery red, wavy locks speaking of her ancestry as if her soft lilting brogue wasn't enough of a giveaway.

"So, there you have it," she said as her computer printer spewed out a two page list of known users of the local red-light district. "Page one is a list of the men who've not only been caught picking up girls, but who've actually been prosecuted and fined or bound over by the magistrates. The second page lists those who've been let off with a police warning. In all cases on the second page they were first offenders. I doubt you'll find your man there."

"Hey, come on, Mary. You know as well as I do that it only takes once with an infected girl in order to pick up a case of something nasty."

"That's true," Kelleher replied, "but I'm thinking that the man you're looking for is more likely to be a seasoned user of these girls. From what I've heard about your case he seems to be a man on a mission and there haven't been any signs of trauma on the bodies to indicate that he physically forced them to go with him to wherever he killed them, am I right?"

"Yes, but I fail to see the significance of that."

"Listen, Carl, trust me," said the pretty vice cop. "A beginner, someone with little knowledge of the scene down there would probably be nervous. He'd in all probability approach the girls from his car, drive to a secluded spot where he'd think they couldn't be seen and then screw the girl in the front or back seat before dropping her off back on the streets. I think the man you're looking for is more confident than that. He probably picks the girls up on foot, walks with them for a while, talks to them, leads them on a bit and before the poor girl knows what's happening he directs them to wherever he wants to do the deed and then kills them in his own time. No, if your man is a user of prostitutes then I'd stake my life on the fact that he's a serial user. Concentrate on page one if you want to stand a hope of finding him, assuming you and your boss have hit on a workable theory."

A short while later, after saying his thanks and offering to meet with Mary Kelleher for a drink one evening after work in order to keep her up to date on the case Carl Wright made his way back to Holland's office. Knocking and entering, he was surprised to see that the D.I. had a visitor, one who bore a face that Wright knew very well indeed.

Chapter 25
Prisoner

A pall of oppression weighed heavily on Jack Reid's shoulders. The stygian gloom of the room in which he sat combined with the awful and terrifying evidence he held in his hands served to add to the terrible sense of guilt that now gripped the young man's heart. The camera never lies, so they say and Jack couldn't fail to be convinced by the sight of his own image captured as it was at the scenes of the two murders, the blood of the young victims on his hands, the knife clearly held by no-one else but he. The beam of light from the floodlight positioned behind his tormentor served only to accentuate the darkness around him and despite its highly intense beam it failed to add illumination to the feeling of terror that held him glued to his seat. Jack couldn't have moved if he'd wanted to.

"I see you've changed your attitude considerably, Jack. Not quite so arrogant now, are you?"

The voice of the man behind the desk broke into Jack's thoughts, pushing aside the mind-numbing reality of the photographs as his words struck home.

"You mean that I…"

"The proof is there, in your own hands. Not only have you killed twice, but left unchecked, you will most certainly kill again, and soon."

"What d'you mean by soon?"

"By soon, Jack, I refer to the date of the killing of the next historical Ripper victim and that date is tomorrow."

"No!" Jack cried out in anger and frustration. "I won't kill again. I won't. You can't make me and if I stay indoors, locked in a room perhaps, you could do that couldn't you, then there's no way I could leave and go out and do it again? You have to stop me. Please."

"Now, now Jack, calm yourself, dear boy. You're rambling. Pull yourself together and listen to me. I've already told you that in the first instance, my knowledge caused me to want to see if I could hold back the urges that the journal had kindled in your mind. When I realised that wasn't to be, I instead decided to monitor and document your actions whilst under the influence of whatever power the pages have instilled within your mind. I have no intention of stopping you, Jack. You have a legacy to fulfil, and it will be my mission to note and to photograph every aspect of your transition into the being that lies within your soul."

Jack could hardly believe what he was hearing. This man who appeared to know everything there was to know about him was cold-bloodedly prepared to allow him to carry on what appeared to be his own re-enactment of the crimes of Jack the Ripper for whatever perverted reasons might lurk within his own, obviously twisted mind. Jack knew that he must have murdered the first two girls, but every fibre of his being screamed to him that he must do all he could to break the cycle of terror, to prevent himself from killing for a third time. Whatever the man behind the desk might say, Jack felt he had to find a way to stop his own murderous urges from getting the better of him. He had to try everything at his disposal, even it meant turning himself in to the police. Before Jack could speak again and appearing to be capable of reading the young man's thoughts, the man spoke, his deep voice resonating through the darkness of the room.

"And don't even think of going to the police, Jack. Do you think they'd believe your story? I think not. You'd go along to them with this preposterous idea that you're a descendant of Jack the Ripper, that a man in the house on the hill paid a drop-out small-time drug peddler to drug you and then took photos of you carrying out the murders. Let's see what they'd do, shall we? They'd ask you to produce the journal. I've made sure that Michael has removed the journal from your possessions, Jack. It's now in a safe place where only I can access it. By the time the police arrived here, I'd be long gone, I can assure you of that and so would Michael. There'd be no trace of us and no trace of the incriminating photographs, which I have no intention of allowing to leave this room. In fact, I think it would be highly advisable if you stayed right here until tomorrow. I don't think it would be safe for you to be allowed to wander the streets with all of that terrible knowledge in your head, do you?"

"Safe for whom? You or me?" asked Jack, his voice breaking as tears welled in his eyes.

"Let's say, safer for both of us," said the man.

"So you're going to keep me a prisoner here, is that it?"

"Not a prisoner, let's say more of a guest."

"A guest? Hm, that's rich. What sort of guest isn't allowed to leave a room, or a house? And how do you intend to keep me here against my will?"

The man fell silent, making no attempt to respond to Jack's last remark.

Suddenly, Jack sensed rather than heard a movement behind him. So intent had he been on the terror of his situation and the words of the older man that he'd failed to notice the almost silent re-entry into the room of Michael, who now hovered above him, a syringe strategically held in his right hand.

So stunned was Jack by the appearance of the other man that he had little or no time to react as Michael's hand moved quickly towards him and he felt the sudden stinging prick as the point of the hypodermic needle penetrated the skin of his neck.

As a warm blackness began to engulf his conscience mind, Jack saw only the gradually dwindling beam of light from the floodlight as darkness overwhelmed him and all sense of who he was, where he was and what was happening to him receded in time with the dimming of the light. All sense and memory of reality diminished entirely and then there was nothing but blackness.

"I think the cellar will do nicely," said the man as Michael slowly hoisted the inert body of the unconscious young man over his shoulder and turned to leave the room.

"And make sure the padlock's secure."

Chapter 26
Alice Geraldine Nickels

"Alice!" exclaimed Carl Wright as he entered Holland's office. "Good to see you, but what on earth brings you all the way down to Brighton?"

The thirty-something year old woman who sat in the visitor's chair smiled back at Wright and rose to greet him, wrapping her arms around him in an affectionate, old-friend style hug. She was dressed in a smart black business skirt suit, with a white blouse, and a black and white polka dotted neck scarf tied at her neck. Her dark brown hair was neat, shoulder length, obviously expensively styled. Her attire was such as would identify her to most professional people as a solicitor, or perhaps a doctor. Stepping back from the sergeant she replied to his question, still smiling.

"Your case, Carl, is what brings me to Brighton. I had a feeling that your boss here might be in need of some help and he's been gracious enough to see me and to hear me out. You see, I've been watching the news about these killings and I have a theory."

Carl Wright was amazed to see Alice Nickels in his inspector's office. She was in point of fact a highly respected member of the legal profession, a solicitor with the firm of Macklin, Bennet and Cross in the city of London. Outside of her work however, Alice led a senior position within an organisation known as *The Whitechapel Society 1888*, an organisation set up to study not only the murders committed by Jack the Ripper but also life in Victorian and Edwardian London in general. Wright had met her on at least five occasions when he'd made trips to London to attend meetings of the society at their headquarters in Whitechapel itself. He knew only too well that the lady now standing warmly holding his hand in friendship was one of the leading authorities on the Whitechapel murders of 1888. There was little she was ignorant of, either in terms of the facts and the myths that surround the case of Jack the Ripper. For her to have taken the time to ditch her usually busy schedule to come in person to speak with Holland must mean that she had a good idea that she could be of assistance, a fact confirmed in Holland's words as he spoke.

"Miss Nickels has been most informative, sergeant," he said, as Wright released his grip on the hand of their visitor. "According to her, it appears that you and I have been almost spot-on in most of our deductions so far, few though they are, but we appear to have missed one point that may be of vital importance in laying our hands on the murderer."

Alice Nickels sat down once again as Wright seated himself in the only other chair in the office, a typist's chair that stood before the computer to the side of Holland's desk.

"It must be a very important point for you to have come in person, Alice," said Wright. "A phone call would normally have sufficed."

"Ah, Carl, my dear boy, a phone call would have been next to useless. You see, in order to show you and the inspector what I believe to be happening here, I really do need to be here in person so that I can physically *show* you what I think is happening. If I'm correct in my reasoning I believe I can show you pretty much exactly where your killer will strike again if you haven't apprehended him by tomorrow night."

"But, how?"

"Ah, sergeant," sighed Holland. "You and I have been a little narrow in our thinking, according to Miss Nickels."

"Please, Inspector, call me Alice."

"Very well, Alice it is." Turning back to the sergeant, Holland went on. "So, as I was saying, according to Alice, we have been correct in our assumption that our killer is a copycat, someone who is re-creating and copying the murders of Jack the Ripper in as great a detail as he can. The one thing we haven't taken into consideration in our case though is the *locations* of the killings."

A small chink of light began to burn in Wright's brain at those words. He had an idea where the conversation was about to lead, and he was soon proved to be correct as Holland beckoned him over to his desk, Alice Nickels stood at Wright's side and for the first time he saw the documents that lay spread out across the top of Holland's desk.

"Perhaps you'd like to explain, Alice," said Holland. "It's your theory after all."

Alice leaned forward and gestured towards the maps that Wright had seen as he approached the desk. She'd obviously been busy, or at least she'd had her secretary hard at work in preparing the papers that lay before the three of them. Carl Wright caught a hint of expensive perfume as he moved closer to Nickels in order to get a better view of the desk top.

"As you can see," she began, "there are actually two maps here. The first one is a map of Brighton as it is today, with the murder sites of both Laura Kane and Marla Hayes marked clearly by the red crosses I've placed there. The second map is of Whitechapel as it was in 1888, with all the sites of the Ripper's verified killings and some of the possibles later attributed to him also marked. The definites are marked with black crosses, the others in green. I've had the Whitechapel map transposed onto this transparency so that we can overlay it and still view the Brighton map underneath. Now, watch what happens when I place the Whitechapel map on top of the Brighton one."

Very methodically, she placed the transparency on top of the Brighton map and began to line them up slowly and accurately until she was satisfied with the positioning of the two documents. As the labyrinth of Victorian streets began to superimpose themselves on those of contemporary Brighton, Wright and Holland at last began to see the reasoning behind the woman's theory. The red cross that marked the site where Laura Kane's body had been discovered on the Regent Estate was covered exactly by the black cross that marked the site where Martha Tabram's body had been found in the George Yard Buildings. Perhaps even more telling was the realisation that the cross that showed the location of Marla Hayes's body was equally obliterated by the black cross depicting the location on Bucks Row, where Mary Ann Nicholls had been found back in 1888.

"Bloody hell!" said Wright.

"Exactly," Holland added.

"You see," said Alice Nickels. "He's not only re-creating the murders, but he's also committing them, or at least leaving the bodies, in places that match the locations of the discoveries of the bodies of the original Ripper's victims. You'll see that the cross that marks the location of Annie Chapman's body, found on 8th September in Hanbury Street lies directly over a place here called Hastings Close, and that gentlemen is where I firmly believe your killer will strike, or at least deposit the body of his next victim, tomorrow night."

"It's so bloody simple, it's actually brilliant, Alice," Holland exclaimed excitedly. "Why the hell didn't we think of it?"

"My fault, sir," said Wright dejectedly. "I'm supposed to be the one with the inside track on the Ripper crimes, and I should have thought of it."

"No, sergeant. I won't have you taking responsibility for missing something that I would never have thought of. Let's face it, you were the one who latched on to the Jack the Ripper connection in the first place. If you hadn't been so fast in doing that, I might still be totally in the dark about our oddball killer and his motives."

"He's right, Carl," said Alice Nickels, reinforcing the inspector's view.

"I only thought of it when I decided to try and think outside the box a little. It was plain to me that you were dealing with a copycat of some description and I wondered just how far he'd gone to create a total re-enactment of the original crimes. It was only then that I got a hold of a map of Brighton and checked my idea, and I was fortunate to see that my theory did in fact bear close scrutiny. Now, we also know that poor Annie Chapman was found just prior to six in the morning, having been supposedly witnessed talking to a man at around five-thirty outside a house in Hanbury Street. If your killer sticks to the original Ripper's timetable and the witness sighting from 1888 was correct then you can assume that, if he's a stickler for detail your next victim will meet her end at some time between five-thirty and six a.m. in the morning."

"Which means we've got a little more time than I thought," said Holland. "When everyone was talking about tomorrow night I assumed we were talking about the early part of the night, perhaps up to midnight. It might not be much, but at least this gives us a few more hours to put our plan into place, to try to catch this bastard before he finds that next victim."

"I think Alice's theory has saved us a lot of needless time wasting and manpower sir," Wright added. "This way, we can concentrate our forces in the area surrounding Hastings close, and if our man shows his face, then…wham! We've got him."

"Oh, please, Carl, don't hold me to all of this. It is just a theory after all. I could be entirely wrong. I wouldn't want to be the one responsible for pulling officers away from potential murder sites if you and the inspector here have made arrangements already."

Seeing the worried look on Alice Nickels's face, Mike Holland moved swiftly

"No, it's okay Alice, really. We don't have enough manpower as it is to cover the whole of the town, or even the whole red-light district. This way, thanks to you we have a fighting chance to nab the killer and we can utilise our forces to the best advantage, from our point of view. We had to decide on a centre of operations, a focus for our efforts and I have an idea your theory is absolutely correct. We will indeed be concentrating our effort on Hastings Close and the streets immediately surrounding it. With luck and little bit of patience tomorrow night, we might just have our man in custody by daylight."

"There's something else, sir," Wright interjected, a worried look on his face.

"Go on, Carl," said Holland.

"Well, if we've been clever enough, with Alice's help, to work out where and when the killer is likely to strike again then isn't it safe to assume that he just might know that we've worked out his agenda for the killings? He might assume we're on his track by now and decide to choose a totally different location, even if it conflicts with the original topography of the Ripper crimes."

"You're right, of course," Holland agreed, "but we also have to assume that, like so many murderers before him, our killer is arrogant enough to believe he can't be caught. From what I've learned about the Ripper case, mostly from the two of you I might add, Jack the Ripper also killed with seeming impunity, barely yards from the windows of homes where people were living at the time and yet no-one saw or heard anything, and he was never seen leaving the scene of his crimes even in the case of Liz Stride where, it appears, he must have been almost on the spot when the man who discovered the body came along into the yard where she lay, still warm and bleeding. No, if I'm correct and I pray to God that I am, this bastard feels almost invincible, holds the police in very low esteem and he thinks that he can literally get away with murder. He's going to do it, of that I'm sure, and somehow we have to be there, waiting in the wings in the hope we can stop him before he carries out his next fiendish re-creation."

The two policemen stopped abruptly as Alice Nickels rose from her seat.

"Well, I think you gentlemen have everything in hand," she spoke softly. "I suppose I ought to leave you to plan your course of action."

"Wait, Alice, please," said Holland. "I'd be really grateful if you could manage to stay here in town at least until tomorrow night is over."

"Really?" she replied, smiling at the inspector in a knowing fashion.

"Yes, of course. Who's to say that your help and input in other aspects of the case might not prove invaluable to us over the next twenty four hours or so? Don't you agree, sergeant?"

"What? Oh, yes, of course, sir. We'd appreciate your help, Alice, we really would."

Obviously pleased to be asked, and perhaps as though she'd expected the request from Holland, Alice Nickels took her mobile phone from her handbag, and speed-dialled her office. As she waited for an answer to her call, she turned again to Holland.

"It won't take me a minute to confirm my stay here. My desk is relatively clear and my secretary will be capable of handling any inquiries for the next day or so. I can get a room at the Atlantic down the road. It's a rather nice hotel and I've stayed there a couple of times in the past when I've been down here on business, or for conferences and so on."

Realising that he'd probably been brilliantly 'played' into accepting the presence and the unofficial assistance of the smart, elegant woman who stood at centre stage in his office, Holland could do no more than smile back at her, look at his sergeant who was grinning at him in the style of a proverbial Cheshire cat and exclaim,

"Right, well, that's that then, eh? Settled!"

Chapter 27
A Plan

Holland, Wright and Alice Nickels enjoyed a working lunch of sandwiches and coffee, which Wright procured from the local delicatessen, a few yards down the road from the station. Holland felt more optimistic than he had for days, a feeling that communicated itself to his sergeant. The inspector had sent for a detailed plan of the area of town where Hastings Close was situated and the three of them now closely studied the area where they believed the next intended killing would take place.

"It's a fairly new development, less than ten years old," said Wright. "The homes are all three or four bedroomed detached houses with, for the most part, open plan gardens to the front. There certainly isn't a lot of cover for our murderer anywhere along the length of the street. That's going to make his job harder."

"Ours, too," said Holland. "There won't be too many places for us to secrete our men without them being highly visible to all and sundry."

"What about the back gardens?" asked Alice Nickels.

"Yes, they all have gardens to the rear," Wright replied. "But again, looking at the plans, they're all either walled or fenced in. The walls and fences all appear to be about five feet high, obviously for privacy and security so moving from one to the other wouldn't be an easy task, especially if he has an unwilling young woman in tow."

"Or a body," Holland added, chillingly.

"But, couldn't you hide your men in the rear gardens? Surely if you explained the situation to the householders, they'd be only too willing to cooperate?"

"Alice," Holland sighed. "If we go along and tell the locals what's likely to happen in their street, there'd be a leak the size of the River Thames before you could say Jack the Ripper. News would get out in no time at all and our man would probably go underground or most certainly at the very least, commit the murder elsewhere."

"Even though his plan calls for him to do it in Hastings Close? I thought you said that he'd go ahead no matter what because of his contempt for the police and his belief that he can't be caught?"

"Yes, that's what I said and I still believe it to be true. However, he isn't stupid, as evidenced by the lack of clues and forensic trace at the scenes of his other killings. He won't deliberately put himself in danger of being caught if the word on the street tells him that half the local police force will be lying in wait for him to put in an appearance."

"Then, isn't it safe to assume that he already has a contingency plan in place, just in case his chosen site is unavailable for some reason?"

"Yes, Alice, he probably does, but where that is and what would entice him to use it is anyone's guess. We certainly don't want him to switch his efforts to his secondary site because, let's be honest, we don't have a bloody clue where that might be. We're going along with your theory of Hastings Close because it makes sense, but we still might be way off the mark if we're really unlucky."

All three of them fell silent as the logistical problem of the next day's operation laid heavily on their minds. For want of something to distract the conversation from its current state of lethargy Wright pulled out the two-page document he'd obtained from Mary Kelleher.

"Listen, sir, Mary in Vice provided us with this list of known users of the local prostitute population. Why don't I go through it after lunch and maybe see if any of the names on here correlate to any known sexual offenders in the area? Maybe our man's name is already here in our hands and we just don't know it yet."

"Good idea, Carl, but the more I think about it and based on what Alice here ahs told us, I don't think we're dealing with a local man here at all. Let's check the list, but I think it will serve only to eliminate rather than incriminate any of the names on it."

"You don't? But I thought that with all the local knowledge he seems to have displayed…"

"No. Sorry to interrupt you, but listen. He may appear to have local knowledge, but that doesn't make him a local by default. Anyone could have got hold of maps of the town as we have and then done a bit of homework. It wouldn't have taken him long to do just what Alice has done and mark out his killing grounds based on overlaying one map over the other. Then, all he had to do was scout the area before carrying out each of his murders and make sure he had ways in and out with no chance of being detected. This bastard could have come from anywhere. A couple of weeks to get to know the town and that's all he needed."

"So, my visit to Vice was a waste of time?"

"Maybe, maybe not. It's just that Alice's arrival has given us a new perspective on the case and I'm inclined to believe we're dealing with a very clever sod who's had this planned for a long time. I doubt he'd be some seedy little turd who frequents the local red light district as a customer of the girls. No, this man is a man with a mission and it's our bloody mission to stop him before he kills again. Now, where were we with that plan of Hastings Close?"

A detailed examination of the development confirmed what Holland had already surmised. Concealment was virtually impossible anywhere along the open-plan close. He dammed the use of such wide open spaces by modern planners. It might look good and help to sell houses but it sure as hell was about to make his task so much harder. The only way in and out of Hastings close was from Dorset Street, the main thoroughfare off which the cul-de-sac branched. Alice couldn't help but point out the macabre significance of the fact that Dorset Street had been one of the most crime ridden and run-down streets in the Spitalfields area of Whitechapel during the time of Jack the Ripper. In fact, the body of Mary Kelly, last known victim of the Ripper had been found in her appallingly minute lodgings in Millers Court, just off Dorset Street following her most gruesome murder on 9th November 1888. Carl Wright speculated that perhaps there was some significance in this fact. Maybe, he suggested, the killer had planned the whole series of crimes so that he could commit his next murder in such close vicinity to a road bearing a name that matched one of those linked to the original Whitechapel murders. Both Holland and Alice Nickels agreed that such a possibility couldn't be easily dismissed. Like Millers Court, Hastings Close was situated just off Dorset Street, too much of a coincidence to be ignored. There was no other way to exit the Close, with houses lined along its entire length and breadth, spaciously perhaps but with no other way in or out. If the killer was going to strike in Hastings Close it appeared that he only had only one way open to him. He had to arrive via Dorset Street and he had to leave the same way. Surely, the police could seal off the area and find a means of surveillance that would succeed in preventing him carrying out his next crime.

With lunch over, Alice left the two policemen to formulate their plan of action for the following night. She needed to check in to her hotel and

would return later, she promised. Holland, grateful for her intervention
and assistance promised to buy the attractive solicitor the best lunch in
town if her help did in fact lead to them laying their hands on the beast
who was terrorising the streets of Brighton.

With Alice busy arranging her accommodation for the next two nights,
Holland and Wright set to work. With concealment out of the question
and enlisting local co-operation from the residents of Hastings Close dismissed as too risky, Holland instead decided to concentrate his manpower
on Dorset Street itself. The killer had to approach his intended killing
ground from the street and unlike Hastings Close, Dorset Street was an
older and more cosmopolitan area, with houses of varying sizes and archi-
tecture along its length. There were numerous places where a car could be
parked at the roadside and residents and their visitors would often leave
their cars parked on the street for hours at a time. This would be Holland's
chief means of watching the approaches to Dorset Street. A few well-
placed unmarked police cars containing well-hidden officers or in some
cases a 'courting couple' might just be his best way of being able to spot
the arrival of the killer and his intended victim. They would need to be in
place well before the time that the killer might be expected to arrive and
Holland wanted to err on the side of caution just in case his target decided
to vary his plan for whatever reason. He and Wright would ensure that the
unmarked cars would be in place before midnight, as this would also
cause less local suspicion as they had no desire to alert the locals to their
operation by allowing the arrival of a number of strange cars in the
neighbour hood after midnight with couples kissing and canoodling into
the wee small hours. What would the good citizens of Dorset Street think?
Maybe one of them would call the police, complaining of lewd and lascivious behaviour in the street. That would really screw things up.

No, Holland decided to place all his resources on Dorset Street in
their respective surveillance positions at varying times between ten-thirty
and eleven thirty p.m. again to allay suspicions by either the local residents or, he speculated by the killer himself who just might try reconnoi-
tering the area one more time in order to familiarise himself with his
prospective murder site. Carl Wright suggested the use of the Force's
helicopter. With its thermal imaging array it would be able to spot any
potential suspects approaching from its position high in the sky but again,
as Holland pointed out, the chopper might be seen or heard from the
ground and the killer would know just what it was and perhaps who or

what it was looking for. He did agree to have the helicopter and its crew on standby in case they needed it if their quarry somehow carried out his plan or was interrupted before carrying out the killing and managed to elude the officers on the ground.

By the time Alice Nickels returned from her hotel, having secured a room with a sea view Holland and Wright had fine-tuned their operation as much as they both felt they were able to do. Holland had run it by the chief superintendent who'd approved it wholeheartedly and sanctioned the use of the helicopter as and when it might be required. The team would be assembled and briefed the following morning, so for now there was little they could do. The inquiry would continue, of course, with the officers detailed to the case all working hard either in the station or out on the streets, asking questions, searching for anything that might lead them to the killer without the necessity of the next night's operation. Holland felt in his heart, however, that they were destined to find nothing until such times as the killer showed himself in the flesh. Later events were to prove him correct in his assumption. Meanwhile, he took the opportunity to quiz Alice Nickels on the make-up and purpose of The Whitechapel Society, to which both she and his own sergeant belonged.

"Carl never mentioned it to me before," said Holland. "It's not some kind of secret society is it, like the Masons or such?"

"Of course not," Alice replied, and Wright chuckled as he replied.

"No sir, nothing like that. You've been reading too many of those books I loaned you. I just never thought to mention it to you, that's all. It's something those who study the Jack the Ripper case would be interested in, that's all. I didn't think it would be something you'd be interested in."

"Well, I'm interested now," Holland went on. "Especially after the little bit you told me when you arrived, Alice. I'd really like to know more and even better, I'd like to know who you think Jack the Ripper really was."

Alice Nickels spent the next fifteen minutes happily relating the workings of the society to him. To give it its full title she explained, it is known as *The Whitechapel Society 1888.* As she'd already told him upon her arrival the purpose of the society is to promote the study not only of the Whitechapel Murders of 1888, and the massive social impact that the murders had on the area, but also Victorian and Edwardian life and culture in the East End of London. *The Whitechapel Society,* she went on, is made up of a diverse and eclectic mixture of members drawn from all walks of life and from varied countries around the world. Members range from peers to the ordinary man in the street and is open to anyone with an interest in the subject matters relating to its existence. In short, far from being a 'Secret Society' as Holland may have thought *The Whitechapel Society* is an open forum dedicated to furthering the study of any and all aspects of its remit.

"So you see, Mike, with meetings held every other month in Whitechapel itself and with regular talks and lectures from various members and visitors we have quite a lively and convivial time when we gather to discuss whatever takes our fancy. The Ripper murders are, of course, a part of it, but anything pertaining to life in the period we are interested in is fair game for our members. We also produce our very own magazine, *The Journal of The Whitechapel Society 1888*, and it is distributed to all of our members every three months. As for Jack the Ripper himself, I have my own theories, but none of them lend themselves to me being able to make a positive conclusion as to who he was. His identity is, and I fear will always remain a mystery, my dear Inspector Holland."

"Well, thanks, Alice. I appreciate you filling me in on the Society. I'm impressed. I never knew it existed until today and I must say that you, my dear sergeant, have been hiding your light under a bush for a long time." Holland smiled at Wright as Alice fell silent. "I had no idea you were quite such an intellectual."

"Oh, hardly that, sir. I simply have a great interest in the Jack the Ripper case, as you know and this was a great way to find out more. I've only managed to attend a few meetings over the last three years, but Alice here has always been around and we've always got on rather well. I spend a lot of my spare time studying the case using an internet forum, the Jack the Ripper Forums as well and I must say I've made a lot of damn good friends through doing so."

"Well, I must say I'm impressed," said Holland, smiling at his sergeant. "I have to say that between you and Alice both have given us the best chance yet of cracking the case. I'm glad I have the good fortune to have a... what did you call it? Oh yes, a *ripperologist* on my team."

With Alice having been briefed on what they planned for the following night and she of course pledging to keep everything to herself, the attractive solicitor took her leave of the detectives. It was late afternoon and she decided to return to her hotel and make a few calls to her office. There was nothing more she could do to help the police for now and she agreed to meet Holland and Wright at the police station at ten the following morning.

Holland and Wright meanwhile made sure that they had sufficient copies of the map of the area in which they expected the killer to strike the following night. One would be issued to each of the men and women on the team. Wright was detailed to contact every member of the investigating team, uniformed and plain-clothes, with instructions to attend a briefing at ten-thirty the following day when Holland would introduce Alice Nickels to his team and explain her presence as an expert consultant on the case.

That done, and with little more they could achieve that day Holland gave instructions to the duty sergeant on the desk that he was to be called immediately if there were any further developments in the case overnight, though he expected none at all.

He then ordered Wright to go home as he also intended to do, and to get an early night and be at the station at eight a.m. the next day. As Holland said,

"Tomorrow is going to be a hell of a long day, Carl, and an even longer night."

Walking down the steps of police headquarters, Holland looked up to see a mass of sombre looking dark clouds scudding in over the town, obscuring the weak Autumn sunshine from view. A stiff sea breeze was blowing in towards the town from across the English Channel. As he shivered from the sudden drop in temperatures, Holland knew without a doubt that a storm was on its way. Perhaps, he thought, in more ways than one!

Chapter 28
A Very Private Hell

Jack Reid was in Hell and the Hell in which he found himself held all the ingredients necessary to torment his mind and his soul beyond the capacity for which the human mind was designed. He lay, unsure whether he was alive or dead, his head filled with visions so terrifying, so unworldly that his entire body felt paralyzed with fear.

Twisted amorphous figures, female and yet not female with faces that constantly shifted shape so that they were never more than a blur floated across his line of sight. Their mouths, toothless yet menacing, larger in proportion to their overall size than they should have been, gaped to reveal blood soaked interiors, and the crimson flow of blood suddenly began to well up from deep within their almost transparent shapeless bodies in a rising torrent that spilled forth from their blanched white lips, teeming with waterfall-like grace through the short distance between them and the prone panicking figure on the ground. He tried to twist away, to avoid the cloying, sticky flood that fell towards him but his body couldn't, or wouldn't move. He screamed as the blood sprayed in torrents onto his face, but the scream remained locked within his throat, no sound issued forth. As the flow of blood increased, his eyes, his nose, his mouth began to fill with the vile tasting liquid until he felt he must surely choke to death. He gasped, retched, and suddenly the sound of laugher began to assault his ears, a laughter so demonic, so insane that Jack felt as though he were in the presence of Satan himself. Yet, was there not something familiar about the sound of that maniacal laughter?

And then it came to him. The laugh, the voice, they belonged to the man who'd caused all of this, the faceless man in the room in the house upstairs. He remembered the cellar and yet, if this were the same cellar, where had the harpies that tormented him come from? And who were they, who could they be but the souls of the women he'd killed, if the man were to be believed. Surely if he hadn't killed them they wouldn't be here now, torturing him with their vile rivers of deep red blood. It must be true then. He was a killer. They'd come to haunt him, to taunt him in his helplessness. He felt rather than saw the two forms draw closer to him, their mouths gaping, the blood cascading forth, soaking him from head to foot, until he felt as though he might drown in the torrent.

At last, he heard it, quietly at first, then growing slowly into a crescendo as the harpies let forth a cry so pitiful, so awful in its intensity that his mind virtually cracked and gave way to overwhelming madness there and then. The cries grew to a shrieking sound that filled every cell in his brain. There was no escape, no way to close his ears to the awful keening, the wailing that issued from those terrible gaping mouths. He wanted to shout at them, to implore and beg them to leave him alone, but the more he tried to form the words with his mouth the more blood ran into it. His throat began to fill again with the choking, gagging, sickly sweet nauseating liquid. He retched as he began to choke for what he thought would be the last time before he must surely join the harpies in the Hell to which he'd despatched them. He could take no more. His throat burned and his body, still paralyzed, lay on the verge of finally giving up and allowing the black veil of death to take him.

The harpies moved ever closer and Jack somehow knew that the second those awful gaping mouths came within touching distance, his own life would end. He had no doubts on that score. As the gaping chasm of eternity loomed large before his eyes in the form of those blood sodden lips, those gaping toothless jaws, Jack suddenly felt himself being lifted, carried away from the jaws of death by an unseen strength that seemed to appear from nowhere. It felt as though he were flying, his body felt lighter than air, his body no longer his own, but belonging to someone or something with the power to transport him from this awful place, away from the jaws of death itself, to…where?

He felt himself being carried upward, ever upward until he heard a loud rasping noise which was immediately followed by a blinding flash of light, then something warm and heavy fell across his face, over his head and all was darkness once again. Seconds later he could swear he felt a rush of fresh air, then a metallic clang and the sensation of being lowered onto a hard, cold metallic floor.

Indistinct voices carried in a muffled gabble to him as he lay in the darkness and then he felt the sharp sting of a needle as it was inserted into his neck and the warm flow of something liquid as it surged from the hypodermic into his bloodstream. At that moment, seconds before unconsciousness claimed him once again Jack Reid at least received the confirmation he required. Despite his earlier thoughts to the contrary, and through the drug induced stupor into which he was once more rapidly descending he knew that if it had been necessary for someone to inject him with God knew what, then he could be certain that he was still very much alive.

***

The grubby white delivery van turned the corner into the street, the name 'Harris and Son' clearly signed on its side panels. There was no telephone number beneath the name, and no description of the service provided by the company. The van pulled up gently on the driveway of number six. The driver turned to the man in the passenger seat: "You're sure she'll be in, as you arranged?"

"Don't worry. She'll be here, ready and waiting. I've made sure she's been kept wanting these last couple of days, told her I'd had trouble getting a hold of the stuff. She'll be absolutely gagging for it, man."

"Her parents?"

"Still in France at their place in Normandy. She's alone man, like I promised."

"What about our guest?" asked the driver, gesturing with his eyes towards the cavernous interior of the van, which held only one object, a large white American style refrigerator.

"Ah, you might say he's very much 'on ice' for the moment. I gave him enough to keep him well out of it for as long as we want. When we leave we can give him one of your 'specials' and that should ensure he comes round at just the right time."

"You've done well, I must say. These young girls, eh? Who'd have thought that the daughter of such well-to-do parents would end up a junkie and a prostitute to boot, and at such a young age, fucking old men for a pittance just to raise the cash to feed her ridiculous and filthy little habit? How tragic!"

A mixture of sarcasm and irony emanated from his last words and his companion replied,

"You know as well as I do that drugs are no respecters of age or wealth. Half of my clients are from good homes and good schools. That's where most of 'em get hooked in the first place. You can get almost anything illegal in schools these days."

"As long as one knows the right people of course," said the driver, smiling a demonic smile. His next words were delivered in a flat, chilling monotone. "So, shall we get to work?"

Without another word the two men alighted from the van into the incessant drizzle that had taken the place of the torrential downpour that had accompanied the earlier storm. It was just after six p.m. and there wasn't a soul about in the street as they walked the short distance from the van to the front door, where the younger man reached out and pressed the doorbell.

Within seconds the door was opened from within and a young dark haired teenaged girl, no more than eighteen years old, stood glaring at the two visitors.

"Michael," she screeched as she recognised the younger man. "Where the hell have you been? I'm going out of my mind here. You promised..."

"Yeah, yeah, I know, babe," Michael replied. "Don't sweat it. I got the stuff you need right here." He held out his hand to reveal a small white packet in his palm, manna from heaven to the young drug addict.

"Yeah, but who the hell's the old guy?" she asked as her shaking fingers reached out to snatch the package from Michael, only for him to pull it quickly out of her reach.

"No need for disrespect, Mandy. This here's The Man, you know, the one who gets the stuff for me so I can get it to you, babe. He wanted to come and meet a few of my best customers in person, just so's he'd know where to find you if ever I was out of circulation, like, you know?"

The girl barely appeared to hear his words, so intent was she on obtaining the narcotics contained in that little white packet.

"So, gimme, huh, please, Michael? You know how much I need it."

She held out a trembling hand containing three ten pound notes, and Michael took the proffered cash from the girl.

"So, is there something else you want?" she asked as Michael and the stranger made no attempt to leave. As far as Mandy was concerned, the transaction was over and done with. She wanted to be left alone to sink into her own narcotic nirvana. She certainly didn't need company or an audience, come to that.

"Actually, Mandy, there is something else,.."

It was the first time the elder man had spoken since entering the house.

"Michael has something to show you, don't you, Michael?"

"Yes, it's a new 'product'," said Michael, walking across the hall to a small table that stood against the wall. "Come and take a look at this, Mandy. I think you'll like it. It gives you a real 'high.'"

Mandy followed the young man across to the table where he'd laid a small packet and was making as if to open it. The girl bent forward slightly to get a better look, and never saw the elder man as he produced a long, slender blade from the inside of his jacket, came up behind her and quickly reached around her throat with his right arm. Before she had time to react the blade sliced deeply into her flesh, a spitting torrent of blood cascading forth as a look of shock, pain and horror swept across her face. She tried to scream, but so deep was the wound that no sound issued from her mouth, just a terrible rasping gurgle as her throat filled with blood and the effects of shock instantaneously set in. The man caught her as she fell backwards, supporting the weight of her body as it sagged against him and slowly slithered to the floor, where the gaping wound in her neck continued to pump blood for a few more seconds until death rapidly took the young victim into its waiting embrace, her heart ceased pumping and the flow of blood slowed and finally stopped.

"Bloody hell," said Michael. "That was a smooth job."

"There's no time for self-congratulations," the man replied as he began to set about his next task. Quickly, he lifted the girl's skirt and raised her blouse to reveal her bare abdomen. Taking his time, he worked steadily, recreating the incisions and mutilations that had been inflicted on poor Annie Chapman over a hundred years earlier. Michael had seen him at work before and thought himself immune from the sight of seeing a still-warm body being treated in such a fashion, but even he gagged and had to force himself not to be physically sick when the man slowly and methodically removed a large portion of the girls intestines from the abdominal cavity and draped them over her left shoulder. He arranged certain items upon the floor that he knew would pique the interest of the police and in what seemed to be no time at all completed his macabre task.

Within thirty minutes of having her throat cut and her life so brutally extinguished, Mandy Clark's body now lay in gruesome reminiscence of that of Annie Chapman, certified victim of Jack the Ripper. The man removed his blood stained coat and placed it carefully into a plastic bag which Michael produced from inside his own jacket. He gestured to Michael who, knowing what he had to do, crossed the hall, opened the front door and went out to the van. There was still no-one in the street as the man had predicted. This was a quiet and private cul-de-sac with little in the way of comings and goings outside of the morning and evening rush-hours, now both passed of course.

Opening the side door of the van he pulled out a ramp that was fixed to the inner floor of the van and then slowly and carefully wheeled the large refrigerator out on the trolley on which it had been placed and pushed it quickly into the house.

He and the man again set to work, this time removing the human contents of the fridge before quickly wheeling the device back out to the van where it was soon reloaded and secured in the rear compartment. Before leaving the house the man nodded to Michael, who produced a filled hypodermic from his pocket and swiftly injected it into the neck of the young man who lay on the tiled hall floor just feet from the body of the dead girl. The drug cocktail within it would ensure that Jack Reid remained in a state of unconsciousness for the next thirty six hours, perfect for the man's plan.

After positioning Jack and the body in the required positions and ensuring that the killing blade rested securely in the young man's unconscious hand, the pair left as unobtrusively as they'd arrived. No-one had seen them arrive or leave and though the killing of Mandy Clark had taken place over twenty four hours early in terms of the Jack the Ripper crimes, the man knew that the police would probably be onto his modus operandi by now and he'd felt justified in using a little artistic licence in the execution of his plan.

There just remained the necessity to depart as quickly as possible from his temporary home on the hill and to ensure that Michael was in no position to betray him in the future. That, he knew, would prove to be by far the easiest part of the operation. Getting away would prove to be simplicity itself, and Michael would be an asset for as long as the man needed him, then he would help to seal the perfect end to the whole scenario. It was a pity that he would have to finish his work elsewhere, but he'd always known that things might get a bit too hot to complete his task in one place and his plans allowed for some flexibility.

The man just wished he could see the police's reaction to what they'd eventually find when the time came for them to visit the house on Hastings Close. As he drove through the evening rain, the wipers making a satisfying 'swish, swish' as they swept back and forth across the windscreen he allowed himself a rare smile of anticipation. For now, his work here was done. Fresh pastures lay ahead, presenting new challenges and there was much work to do in order to reach them safely.

Chapter 29
Doctor Ruth Takes Up
the Story Once Again

I suppose this is as good a point as any for me to bring this story back to the present day, to reality as it currently exists for me, for Jack and for the other protagonists in this strange affair. As far as the case of Mandy Clark and the other victims of 'The Brighton Ripper' goes, the facts have been recorded and relayed in court and in psychiatric reports many times.

Following a night-long vigil on the night of 7th/8th September, during which Inspector Mike Holland and Sergeant Carl Wright led their task force in a total surveillance operation in the vicinity of Hastings Close the police had become frustrated and bemused when, by 6.30 on the morning of the 8th there appeared to have been no activity in the neighbourhood that would indicate the killer had so much as approached the area. Bemused, frustrated and just a little fearful that they had somehow tipped their hand and that the killer had caught wind of their presence, at six forty-five a.m the two detectives took a slow walk along the length of Hastings Close, thinking that they might have missed something that had occurred during the long night.

As they neared number six they were amazed to see a young man, his hands and clothing soaked in blood, staggering down the driveway towards them. The door to the house stood gapingly open and the two men knew instantly that they'd overlooked one vital element in the case.

"It's him, sergeant, it has to be. Grab the bastard while I go take a look. We never bloody well thought that he'd kill his next victim indoors. She *has* to be in that house."

Carl Wright quickly caught hold of the young blood-soaked man, who seemed hardly aware of the policeman's presence. He snapped his handcuffs on to the man and turned him around, following the path taken by the inspector. Realising where he was being taken, the handcuffed prisoner suddenly began to panic and resist Wright's pressure on him to approach the house.

"No, please, you can't take me in there. *She's* there, and she's dead!"

"Who's dead?" Wright asked. "Who is she?"

"How should I know?" the man answered. "She's a girl, just a girl."

"Keep going you cold-blooded bastard," said Wright, pushing the man along in front of him. Before they reached the door however, Holland appeared at the entrance to the house and Wright brought himself and his prisoner to a halt.

"Bloody Hell, Carl," Holland gasped, an air of finality and of horror in his voice. "He's done it again and the poor girl's only a kid, still in her teens. Funny thing is, it looks like she's been dead for a day or more. The blood's dry on the floor and on this."

Holland held out his right hand on which he wore a latex glove and held out a long, thin bladed knife of the type used by traditional old-fashioned butchers in their shops. The blood stains on the weapon were evident but, as Holland said, they appeared dry, certainly not fresh, making it appear that the murder had taken place some time before they arrived on the scene.

"He's not much more than a kid himself, sergeant," said Holland as he took a long hard look at the man they now held in custody. "Why'd you do it, son? Why'd you kill these poor girls, eh?"

"I didn't. I mean, did I? I must have done, mustn't I? The man said so, so it must be true. I've got blood on me. Is it hers? She was, just, you know, lying there."

"He's not making a lot of sense, sir," said Wright.

"No, he isn't, is he? Let's get him to the station, sergeant. I'll call it in and get the forensic people here at the double. From the looks of things we've got our man, and if I'm not mistaken he killed her earlier than he planned to throw us off the scent. Somehow though, he stayed here until the time and date the body of Annie Chapman was discovered in Whitechapel. Why, I wonder?"

"If you ask me, sir, he's high on something. Just look at him. I wouldn't be surprised if he was so 'junked up' he killed her without knowing what bloody day it was and then stayed in the house to get junked up on some more and just staggered into our arms by accident when he came around and panicked to find he was still in the house with the body."

At his sergeant's behest, Holland looked closely into the eyes of the young man in the handcuffs. Sure enough, he had the look of a man who had been heavily drugged until a short time ago. The police inspector knew the look of a 'druggie' only too well from his years of experience on the force and this man most definitely looked like a man who was no stranger to the use of illegal drugs.

"I think you're right, sergeant," he agreed. "Get Barnes and Thorne to take him in while we take a closer look at the house."

Wright summoned the two officers Holland had selected from their place in one of the surveillance cars and Jack Reid soon found himself in the back of the unmarked police car and on his way to the police station. He would be held in a cell until Holland and Wright returned to begin Questioning him. The sun rose without apparent warmth for the policemen who now began their tragic investigation into the events that had taken place at the house of death.

***

Number six, Hastings Close resembled a scene of carnage, a charnel house. As they waited for the arrival of the Scenes of Crime officers they did their best to examine the body of Mandy Clark and surrounding blood-soaked hallway. The thing that stood out most to Holland was the fact that, as Wright Quickly pointed out, the killer had arranged the scene to resemble that reported after the murder of Annie Chapman. Close to the body, her killer had arranged a neat pile of the girl's belongings, or perhaps had brought them with him for effect. There was a tissue, neatly folded, two pennies (in Chapman's case it had been two farthings, long discontinued from British coinage), and two combs which forensics would later confirm as having been Mandy's from hair samples clinging to them. This tended to confirm that the killer had remained in the house for some time after the murder and had removed the combs from the bathroom or the girl's bedroom. It was a chilling re-creation of the murder site in Whitechapel back in 1888 and added to Holland's view that the killer had to be in some way deranged to enact so elaborate a copy of the scene.

There was blood on the tiled floor of the hallway and on the table which stood against the wall. Holland assumed correctly that the girl had been standing by the table when she was attacked, perhaps not seeing the knife before it sliced into her neck. The mutilations to her body were what Holland and Wright found so disturbing. Apart from the intestine draped over the girl's shoulder the mutilations to the body were appalling to say the least. Wright pulled a sheet of paper from his inside pocket, and as far as he could see on cursory examination the killer had done his best to copy the exact series of injuries inflicted in Annie Chapman's body so long ago. The later poet-mortem examination of the body of Mandy Clark would confirm that those injuries exactly matched Chapman's. Perhaps the most telling was the fact that Mandy Clarks head been almost severed from her body, the wound to her neck inflicted with great strength and appalling determination. The girl's abdomen had been laid open entirely as in the case of Chapman. The only difference, and Holland assumed this to be because of the drug fuelled state of the young man now in custody was that whereas in Chapman's case certain organs had been removed and taken from the scene by the Ripper, in Mandy Clark's case her uterus, and the upper portion of her vagina had been removed and were found an hour later by a member of the forensic team in the rubbish bin at the rear of the house, another sign that the killer had taken his time over the killing and the subsequent aftermath.

On their way back to the station to commence the questioning of Jack Reid, and despite the fact that they had the man they believed to be the killer in custody, something didn't quite add up in the mind of Carl Wright.

"Something's a bit screwy about this, sir," he said to Holland, a deep frown upon his face.

"Explain, 'screwy' sergeant," the inspector replied.

"Well, so far the first two killings have exactly mirrored the murders of Martha Tabram and Polly Nichols. All of a sudden he deviates from the path. Annie Chapman's organs were never discovered, and if our man was trying to copy her murder, then to be honest we should have found him walking down the road with her organs concealed either on his person or in a bag or something similar, on his way to dispose of them. He had nothing on him at all."

"Because he was influenced too heavily by the drugs, sergeant," Holland surmised. "Look, it's all very well us believing that he set out to re-create the Ripper murders, but we have to bear in mind that with each killing he probably found himself becoming more and more sickened by the actual acts he was perpetrating. That does happen you know."

"Yes, sir, I know it does, but the first two murders were just so cold and calculating. This one seems a bit messy, that's all."

"Good God, they're all messy, sergeant."

"I know, sir, but I think you know what I mean."

"Yes, I do, but let's face it. I think we're dealing with a very sick and highly deranged individual here. I've a suspicion that questioning our suspect might prove to be a very disturbing experience for both of us."

And so it was to prove. Later that day, Mike Holland and Carl Wright sat down in interview room one at the station, with the young Jack Reid seated opposite them, the table and chairs on which they sat being the only furniture present and the hum of the obligatory police tape recorder the only sound in the room apart from the voices of the officers and the suspect.

Chapter 30
Interrogation, Disbelief, and Arraignment

After managing to persuade Jack to identify himself and provide them with his home address, the police arranged for the man's parents to be informed of his arrest. A worried and appalled Tom Reid contacted Holland and informed him that he and his wife would arrive in Brighton the next day.

Meanwhile, under a series of intense interrogations over the next twenty four hours, Jack Reid revealed his amazing, (though preposterous, so the police believed) story. He told of his receiving the strange package bequeathed by his Uncle, Robert Cavendish on his eighteenth birthday, and of how the journal that he found contained within that package and the letters from his uncle and those of his ancestors that accompanied the journal proved beyond a shadow of a doubt that the pages had been written by none other than Jack the Ripper himself. Further, Jack explained, reading the journal had brought about some kind of mental aberration in his mind and he'd set out to discover why and how. He related the story of the untimely death of his uncle and his search for Robert's brother, Mark, in the hope of discovering more about the circumstances of his uncle's death and the events leading up to it. Finally, he'd told of his chance meeting with Michael, of slowly realising he was being drugged against his will and of his meeting with the man at the house on Abbotsford Road and his revelation that Jack was himself a descendant of The Ripper himself and as such, had inherited the genes of the killer and was somehow carrying out the killings in Brighton without being aware of the fact.

The police found all of this quite ludicrous but set about checking the young man's story. Surely, thought Mike Holland, verification of the details surrounding the man named Michael and the man in the house on Abbotsford Road would be simple enough, but that was when the problems began to mount both for the police and for Jack.

First, the address he'd given them for Michael turned out to be a squat, with no official records as to its lawful inhabitant. Of Michael there was no sign and neighbours informed the police that they hadn't seen him for some time. The unlocked flat lay bare and deserted, no clothes, personal belongings or anything to indicate that it had been lived in at all in recent weeks. Despite the police showing a picture of Jack to them, none of the people in the neighbouring flats could ever remember seeing him with Michael, even less remember him actually living there. The only suspicious fact that the police ascertained was that the flat was devoid of fingerprints. It had been wiped clean by its previous inhabitant, giving them no means of establishing whether there was any truth in Jack's story of having stayed there for a number of weeks. In itself, it wasn't enough to corroborate Jack's story, a fact made worse by the police's visit to the house on Abbotsford Road.

Like Michael's flat the house was deserted. Jack had described the appearance of the room in which he'd talked with the man as best he could, allowing for the darkness and the bright lights that shone in his eyes. However, all the police found was a dusty, uninhabited sprawl of a house with a 'For Let' sign standing at a crooked angle in the front garden.

A phone call to the local Estate Agent's office gave them the information that the house had been unoccupied for six months since its owners had left to live abroad, and that they'd had trouble finding a tenant due to the high rent being demanded by the owners, allied with the general dilapidation of the property. Holland even went so far as to have the Electricity Company check to see if any power had been expended in the house in the recent past. Nothing! There had been no electricity used in the house for six months.

Jack's story, weak in the first place, began to look even weaker when the police demanded to see the journal he'd mentioned. Jack reiterated that 'the man' had taken it and that they should get it back from him as it would prove what he'd been telling them. As Holland pointed out to Jack, the fact that 'the man' seemed not to exist lent credence to his own view that the journal was also a figment of Jack's imagination.

As the effects of the drugs wore off, Jack began to think a little more clearly and demanded that he be provided with a solicitor before he said anything further. Mike Holland, fully aware of Jack's rights under the law, had no choice but to suspend his questioning until legal representation could be found for the young man. A short time later, the duty solicitor was found and his first instruction to Jack was to tell his client not to say another word to the police. He would need time and a series of interviews with Jack before he would allow the police to question him further. For now, every question would be met with the same response; "No Comment."

The first piece of good news for Jack came with the arrival of his parents. Tom and Jennifer were at least able to confirm that Jack had indeed received some form of package from his late uncle and that he appeared to have been greatly disturbed by whatever it contained. Sadly, they were unable to confirm the contents of that package, having been prevented from seeing whatever was within the package by Jack himself. Unfortunately, they also had little choice but to reveal Jack's troubled childhood, his fixation with blood and his sporadic outbursts of violence towards other children.

Very slowly the police began to weave together a tapestry of evidence that would show Jack Reid to be a highly disturbed young man with a history of mental illness and a fixation with blood that led in their opinion to the terrible and vicious series of murders that had eventually been perpetrated in Brighton. The fact that he'd appeared to have lied, (or at least fantasised) about Michael and the man in the house on Abbotsford Road only lent further weight to the police theory.

The longer the police inquiry went on the less Jack's story held up. Not one of the so-called 'facts' he'd related to the police could be sufficiently corroborated. Apart from the death of his Uncle Robert and some wild ideas about Robert Cavendish having had nightmares about Jack the Ripper while he lay in a coma some time before his death, confirmed by the man's widow Sarah Cavendish, there was nothing else whatsoever that the police could learn that could confirm any other part of Jack Reid's story. Sarah Cavendish did inform the police that her husband had become susceptible to nightmarish hallucinations in the months leading up to his death, but that information just gave the police more evidence of a degree of insanity or at least some form of mental illness being carried by the Cavendish family, a fact hotly disputed by Tom Reid but nevertheless accepted by those involved in the inquiry.

The one thing that did, however, leave a niggling doubt in the minds of Holland and Wright was the information that Jack provided to them about his Uncle Mark Cavendish, Robert's brother. He'd told them that the mysterious man in the house on Abbotsford Road had told him about the suicide of his uncle in Malta. Police checks wit their counterparts on the Mediterranean island confirmed that fact. How could Jack have known that piece of information? The answer came from the Maltese police inspector who'd handled the investigation into Cavendish's death. Some time before the murders in England had begun, a young man calling himself Jack Reid had telephoned the local police in Valetta, the capital of Malta seeking information on the whereabouts of his uncle. The police officer who took the call had checked the local police records and then informed the young man of the tragic death of his uncle.

Holland was satisfied that they'd got their man, though Carl Wright reserved the right to a niggling doubt, a belief that maybe, just maybe, they'd missed something of importance in the strange and tragic case of 'The Brighton Ripper'.

Following a series of psychological evaluations, a whole battery of further interviews with his solicitor present and no further corroboration of anything in Jack Reid's story, he was committed for trial on the charge of murder, three counts, his trial to commence three months from the date of his arraignment.

Tom and Jennifer Reid hired the best barrister they could afford, Simon Allingham, to represent Jack at his trial, but despite Allingham's best efforts it proved impossible to obtain bail for his client and Jack Reid found himself held in custody until his case came to court. When it did, it would prove to be a short and very decisive affair.

Chapter 31
Trial and Retribution

Just three short months passed before Jack Reid faced the judge and jury at house Crown Court in Brighton's neighbouring town of Hove, in East Sussex. Security was tight on the opening day of the trial and the public gallery filled to overflowing with those who sought a glimpse of the man whom the denizens of the Press had already dubbed 'The Brighton Ripper'. Official opinion of the young man's state of mind had been divided in the run up to the trial. There appeared to have been a fifty-fifty split in the estimations of those learned members of the psychiatric profession, with half of those who'd examined Jack finding him to be a highly disturbed and potentially psychotic individual, the other half reporting that he was as sane as the next man, though with possible homicidal tendencies. Consequently, the defence's submission that he be deemed 'unfit to plead' and automatically detained in a secure psychiatric unit was denied.

Meanwhile, to their credit, Mike Holland and Carl Wright had continued their investigation, under pressure from Wright, in whatever time they could spare to do so. As far as their superiors were concerned they had their man and the case was effectively closed, barring the trial itself. Wright, however, had continued to plead with Holland to delve further into Jack's claims regarding the mystery man and his young accomplice, as something about Jack's tale rang true to the detective sergeant. Holland, not one to ignore the gut feelings of his sergeant had agreed to do whatever they could to try and substantiate or disprove Jack's story completely. Unfortunately, there appeared to be so many holes and inconsistencies in Jack's statement and in his personal recollections of the weeks leading up to his arrest that the two policemen had been forced to abandon any hopes of revealing any fresh evidence before the trial.

So it was that with just three weeks to go to Christmas Day, Jack Reid found himself in the dock. The trial commenced at ten a.m. on one of the coldest December days in recent history. A thick frost had descended upon the south of England that night. White tentacles of ice hung from the branches of trees, decorated bushes and hung from the window ledges of the courthouse itself as Jack was driven to court in a sealed van, and led up the rear steps of the building, to be held in a cell below the court until the time came for him to ascend to the courtroom proper where he would stand in the dock and face his accusers.

Chief amongst those accusers was the Queen's Counsel appointed to prosecute the case on behalf of the The Crown. Ingrid Hewitt Q.C. was in her early forties and rapidly building a reputation as an able and tenacious prosecutor. The Crown Prosecution Service had viewed her as ideal to carry out the prosecution of the Reid trial, as to them it appeared very much an open and shut case, with little chance of an acquittal. No need to wheel out the real 'heavies' then.

Unfortunately for Hewitt and the prosecution case in general, apart from the evidence linking Reid with the murder of Mandy Clark, there was no forensic evidence and certainly no witness evidence to place him at the scenes of the first two murders, a fact that Jack's own barrister Simon Allingham made much of in his attempts to deflect the jury from over emphasis on the Clark murder. This was, said Allingham, in his address to the jury;

"A case where the prosecution would have you believe that the young man who stands before you in the dock committed not one, not two, but three horrific murders. Where, I must ask them is the evidence that might even suggest that Jack Reid carried out the first two killings? There is none. Not one scrap of forensic or other evidence can be presented to link my client with those murders. Why? Because I submit that such evidence cannot exist because Jack Reid did not commit those murders. Also, in the case of the murder of Mandy Clark it is an undisputed fact that Jack was discovered walking along Hastings Close with the victim's blood upon him and that the murder weapon, once discovered, contained his finger-prints. That does not however make him the killer of that young girl. Could he not have been at the house, under the influence of drugs as has been confirmed by the police and the doctors who examined him after his arrest and merely woken to find the girl dead in the house and perhaps panicked when he saw the knife, picked it up and thrown it in the rubbish bin in his haste to depart the scene?"

It was an unlikely scenario and Allingham knew it, but it was his intent to do everything in his power to help Jack Reid. He was good at his job and though his case was weak, almost non-existent in fact, he believed that the prosecution case was equally weak, though of course the evidence such as it was tended to stack up in favour of the prosecution.

The trial itself was short by modern standards, lasting a mere four days. During that time, Jack's parents were called to the witness stand, where they were forced to confirm Jack's history of psychiatric problems as a child, and his strange behaviour upon receiving the odd legacy from his late uncle, Robert Cavendish. Of that legacy, the so-called journal of Jack the Ripper as Jack had described it, and which he'd insisted had caused his latest mental imbalance, no trace had been found, despite extensive police inquiries. Giles Morris appeared on behalf of the family solicitors, Knight, Morris and Campbell, to testify that at no time was any member of the legal firm privy to the contents of the package which had been let in their care until the coming of age of its intended recipient. Under questioning from Ingrid Hewitt he was forced to concede that the package may have contained nothing more disturbing than a family history, or a collection of letters from his uncle, or some such innocent content. Faithful to his clients as always, Morris countered his admission by stating, much to Simon Allingham's relief and no little amusement, that by the same token Miss Hewitt had no proof that the package did not indeed contain the very thing that Jack Reid said it had done. Giles Morris not only saved Allingham from having to ask that very question of him during cross-examination, but in arguing professionally and politely against Hewitt's accusation in the way he did from the witness box, he gave the defence a much-needed assist in their case. The prosecution had traced the girl who Jack had persuaded to impersonate the private investigator in order to try and trace Mark Cavendish. Hewitt made much of the fact that Jack could easily have made such inquiries himself and that the girl, Christine Carter had been an unwitting accomplice in his plan to avoid being identified by the family solicitors in his desire to trace his uncle. The prosecution, however, were unable to explain why, if Jack's tale were false, he would be looking for his uncle. Despite Simon Allingham labouring this point, the jury appeared to ignore the significance of this anomaly completely.

The defence called Sarah Cavendish, who confirmed that her late husband Robert had received a package himself sometime after his father's death, but she was also unable to substantiate what it contained. As for Jack the Ripper, she admitted that her husband had become obsessed with the serial killer after having experienced disturbing dreams and hallucinations during his time in hospital following the car crash that killed his

father and that Robert had continued to have nightmares in the time leading up to his death. She had no idea what Robert had left to Jack, much
less could she hazard a guess as to what such a legacy might have been.
Her evidence, unfortunately, did little to support Jack's case and Hewitt
was able to turn much of her statement against Jack by insisting that his
uncle's own troubled mind showed the family propensity for mental instability, a fact that seemed to swing the jury towards the prosecution case.

Allingham also made the point that in the first two murders the police
had found evidence to suggest that the killer had worn rubber gloves in
order not to leave fingerprints at the scene. Why, he asked would Jack
Reid, if he was indeed the killer have suddenly dispensed with such a
precaution and left his fingerprints not only on the murder weapon, but all
over the house as well? The prosecution merely countered this by suggesting successfully to the jury that Jack was so influenced by the cocktail
of narcotics in his bloodstream that he'd been sloppy in his execution of
his latest crime and the jury, only too willing to come down hard on the
issue of drug abuse linked with murder, agreed with Hewitt's surmise.

In the end, Jack Reid's case foundered on the fact that no corroboration could be found for any part of his story save one. Carl Wright had
traced the taxi driver who had dropped Jack and Michael off at the house
on Abbotsford Road. At least, the driver testified that he dropped them
off somewhere on Abbotsford Road and he couldn't describe the other
man who had been in the cab. To him, they both looked like a pair of
junkies and he took little notice of them apart from ensuring that he received his fare before they 'did a runner' as he put it. He had no idea
where they went when they departed from his cab and the defence were
unable to prove that Jack ever entered the house or that the man with him
was the mysterious 'Michael' who had simply disappeared from his resi-
dence in town. Police inquiries had led them to believe that he'd left town
some time before the murder of Mandy Clark and they'd managed to find
nothing to connect him to Jack Reid, another fact which hampered
Allingham's attempt to defend the young man in the dock.

Finally, the inability of the police to identify or even to substantiate
the existence of 'The Man' as Jack called him weighed heavily against the
defence. Simon Allingham was able to force a leading psychiatrist to admit that, if this man was figment of Jack's imagination it could be taken as
a sign that he was indeed suffering from a psychotic illness whereby his

mind had created an 'alter-ego' a fictional other-self on whom his rational mind could cast blame for his crimes on to.

It was perhaps due to that final admission from the psychiatrist that the jury, when they retired took little over an hour to return with their verdict. Jack Reid was guilty, but they considered him to be insane at the time of the killings and the judge, Chief Justice David Skinner had no choice but to commit Jack to a secure psychiatric unit, a 'special hospital' at Her Majesty's Pleasure. In other words, the young man who stood in the dock would be committed for the rest of his days, or until he was at least no longer considered a threat to society. From what the judge said in his summing up, that time would have appeared a long way off, if at all, to Jack Reid. Thus it was that Jack Reid received his just retribution from the law. His reign of terror was over and the people of Brighton could sleep sound in their beds once more.

As he was led from the dock to be taken to the cells below the court to await transfer to a secure unit, Jack waved to his parents who had sat through every minute of his trial, his face a mask of tears that mirrored those of his mother, Jennifer. Tom Reid tried to appear stoical and strong for his son and gave him a cheery wave in return, mouthing, "we love you" as Jack disappeared down the thirteen steps that led to the corridor housing the cells.

Jack was transferred later that day to Ravenswood, where of course, my story began and where today I spend much of my time in the company of the highly personable and yet, according to the courts, criminally insane young man who so viciously slaughtered three innocent young women during that awful autumn in Brighton.

Under normal circumstances it is highly likely that my tale would end right here and yet recent events which have occurred far from these walls have led to the strangest and most baffling twist in the tale of Jack Reid. They have also led me to believe in the possibility that all may not be quite as it seems in the case of the young man with the fixation for blood and the odd tale of a mystery man in an empty house on a hill. I can only relate the facts to you as they were reported to me and allow you to share with me in the shattering and astounding conclusion to the story of Jack Reid and the case of The Brighton Ripper.

Chapter 32
A Shadow of Doubt

So, here we are, almost back at the point where my recollections of these events began. I say almost, because the greatest mystery of all in the tangled affair surrounding the life and deeds of Jack Thomas Reid only truly began to unravel a few short weeks ago.

My own sessions with Jack had fallen into something of a routine. He would always be polite, deferent almost, as though respecting me a little more than he would someone who wasn't a psychiatrist. He often explained that my position put me on a par with his late uncle Doctor Robert Cavendish and his ancestors who had all practised the art of psychiatry. In some ways I'd begun to feel that Jack virtually hero-worshipped me. He wanted to please me, that much soon became evident in our meetings and he would do all he could to try and put me at my ease while I was with him. He assured me on more than one occasion that what he'd done in the past was literally just that, the past.

"I thought you said at your trial and under interrogation by the police, that you never killed anyone, Jack. Are you now saying that you did?" I asked him one day, following one of his assurances.

"Doctor Ruth," he replied. "I know I said I didn't do it, and I firmly believed that to be the truth, but the police, the jury, the psychiatrists, the prosecution and everyone else says that I did. Even you and Doctor Roper have told me that I can only begin to get better if I can admit to you and to myself that I committed the murders. I'm coming round to the belief that maybe I did do those terrible things, because it was all there, you see, in the journal, just as my uncle Robert warned me and I fell under it's spell and must have done those things while I was under the control of Jack the Ripper, or at least, under the control of the power of his words."

I still believed that the journal was a figment of his imagination, so I found his sudden admission to be a little confusing. Was he still mixing up the truth and the fiction of his situation? That's what I thought at the time, that this was part of Jack's psychosis, his inability to distinguish between the reality and the fiction in his past.

Things began to change quite suddenly one morning, when I received a telephone call from one of the detectives who'd investigated the Brighton murders. Detective Sergeant Carl Wright told me that he'd become aware of some facts that might throw new light on the case, and he and a 'consultant' as he described her, named Alice Nickels, needed to come to Ravenswood to speak to me and if possible, to Jack Reid himself. Wright assured me that he had the full backing and permission of his own superior Detective Inspector Holland, who would be happy to confirm the fact in writing, which I knew would be required in order for Wright to conduct any interrogation of Jack.

I was as anxious as Carl Wright to find out as much as I could about the case and about Jack in particular and I agreed to his request, making arrangements for him to visit me at Ravenswood three days later, allowing time for Mike Holland to send the appropriate paperwork, which duly arrived by first class mail the following morning.

I had the feeling that Sergeant Wright felt there were discrepancies in the case against Jack, not from anything he said directly to me, but simply from the tone of his voice. Call me psychic if you like, but I wasn't far wrong. Warm sunshine bathed the surrounding countryside on the morning of Carl Wright and Alice Nickels's arrival at Ravenswood. Barely a cloud decorated the clear blue sky and the singing of birds in the trees that gave Ravenswood an air of quiet tranquillity allowed for little thought of violent murder and blood lust and yet sadly, such thoughts were never far from the minds of many of the inmates at the facility, a fact that I and many of the staff were forced to face every day of our working lives. Ravenswood may look like a quiet country hotel from the outside, particularly on such days, but it is, after all, a secure hospital and in days gone by the word 'Bedlam' could easily have been applied to my place of work.

Sergeant Wright introduced Miss Nickels as being a leading member of *The Whitechapel Society 1888* at which point I remembered her name being mentioned in one of the police reports that had found its way into Jack's file. She'd also testified at the trial as an 'expert witness.' She had assisted the police in their investigations in Brighton and had been instrumental in piecing together the timetable of events that led them to their eventual apprehension of Jack so close to the scene of the last murder. She was a 'ripperologist', an expert on the Jack the Ripper murders of 1888. She had apparently worked out that Jack had been following the timetable and locations of the original killings by placing a map of Brighton over a grid plan of the original Whitechapel murders, thereby locating the site of what turned out to be the third murder and so to Jack's subsequent arrest. Now, it appeared she had new information that she, Holland and Carl Wright felt should be presented to me, as Jack's physician.

"You must understand, Doctor Truman," she began, "that when I first offered my help to Inspector Holland and Sergeant Wright, I held no pre-conceived ideas as to who the killer may have been. I simply presented what I felt were a series of facts that may have helped them to apprehend the man responsible for those murders. At that time I had no personal axe to grind, or evidence to link anyone, Jack Reid included, to the murders of the three girls."

"Yes, I understand that, Miss Nickels, but what has your visit today got to do with Jack Reid? He's already been convicted of the murders, and there seems little doubt that he did it, or is there?"

"Ah, well, you see, Doctor, that's my problem. At the time we were all so busy congratulating ourselves that the chance of someone else being involved didn't really enter into our minds, despite Jack's insistence that others were responsible for the murders."

"And now you're going to tell me that such a possibility may exist, is that right?"

"Indeed I am. I also have to tell you that Sergeant Wright here and his superior officer, Inspector Holland, both believe that my new information may have some credibility. What we need is to present certain facts to you and to Jack Reid and go on from there if we feel we may have a case of a miscarriage of justice on our hands."

"If that's so, shouldn't Inspector Holland be here himself?" I asked.

"Inspector Holland is in Warsaw," Carl Wright interjected, "following up what we believe may be information that has great relevance to the case."

"Warsaw?" I spoke in surprise.

"Not only that, but Sergeant Wright here is a fellow student of the Jack the Ripper murders and is the ideal man to be present if and when we have the opportunity to speak to Reid," said Nickels.

"Look, will one of you please tell me what this is actually about?" I asked. "What has Warsaw got to do with the case? Why do you think there may be something unsound about Jack's conviction? Do you mean to say there might actually be a grain of truth in his story after all?"

The questions tripped off my tongue. I wanted to know why they were here, and I wanted to know sooner rather than later. I had to get them to come to the point, and quickly. A bright shaft of sunlight poured in through the window like liquid gold, flooding the face of Alice Nickels who raised a hand to shield her eyes from the glare. I rose and closed the blinds a little. Nickels thanked me and then glanced at Carl Wright and on receiving his nod of ascent, she began to relate her tale as I retook my seat behind my desk.

"Well, let's just say that I had certain reservations about Jack Reid's guilt even before the trial."

"You did?"

"Yes. It troubled me that he'd been caught so easily, so sloppily if you like. The first two murders were 'Jack the Ripper' to a tee. There were no witnesses, no forensic evidence, absolutely nothing to link the killer to his victims. Those murders were the work of a cold, calculating, superbly intelligent and highly organised individual who'd gone out of his way to recreate the Ripper murders to the enth degree. In the case of Mandy Clark, however, everything seemed wrong to me. Jack Reid's fingerprints were all over the murder weapon, all over the house and he'd obviously been high on drugs at the time of his arrest. Surely, if copying the original Ripper crimes was so important to him he wouldn't have allowed himself to get into such a state and then leave such a welter of evidence at the scene to incriminate himself. Unfortunately, there was nothing in his story that could be corroborated at the time despite Carl and his boss doing all they could to check out his story. Before you ask why I said nothing of this at the trial, let me tell you that it would have done no good whatsoever. I'm a solicitor by trade, Doctor Truman, and I know the law. If I'd aired my thoughts in court, at best it may have been seen as an attempt to throw doubt on the prosecution case through pure speculation, at worst it would have been instantly rejected by the judge as being nothing more than my own personal conjecture, which to be fair, it was.

"Some weeks after the trial Carl Wright and I met at a meeting of The Whitechapel Society up in London, where we discussed the Reid case. Carl confided in me that he held similar thoughts to my own and together we approached Inspector Holland with a request that we be allowed to delve a little further into investigating Reid's story.

"Inspector Holland pointed out that the case was officially closed and though he agreed to some extent with the scenario that Carl and I pointed out to him, the police couldn't devote their resources to a full investigation. However, he did agree that Carl could liaise with me in his own time and if anything useful came up he'd look into it."

"And something did…come up, I mean?" I said, giving Nickels the chance to draw breath.

"Well, yes, sort of, though at first it was a tenuous link at best, but a link nonetheless. When I thought the whole case through, I thought it unlikely that Jack Reid would build a fictional scenario around a real person. You see, this young man called Michael really existed, that much was confirmed by the police, though he'd disappeared well before the trial. Why, I thought to myself would Reid interweave his story about 'The Man' with one about this Michael unless there was some basis in fact for his story? Please don't say that it could have been part of his psychosis. I know that, but I read all I could on the subject and it would have been far more logical if he'd created a wholly fictional tale. Also, he knew where Michael lived, though of course the police at the time of the investigation said that was probably because Michael had been his drugs supplier.

"Anyway, I decided to focus on Michael and with Carl's help we set about trying to locate the elusive drug pusher."

"And, did you find him?"

"At first it was as though he'd disappeared into thin air. The lack of a surname didn't help, and then Carl, during one of his off-duty expeditions into the seedy side of town found a very old customer of his who remembered him once being known as Devlin."

Carl Wright took over at this point, giving Alice Nickels the opportunity to take a breather.

"The junkie, who's name is Taylor, was one of Michael's earliest 'regulars' and though he couldn't swear that Devlin was actually Michael's name, it was a starting point for me. Anyway, I dug deeper and found that a *James* Michael Devlin had been arrested in Hastings a couple of years ago for small-time drug peddling and that seemed to confirm it. The more I searched, however, the less I found. No-one by the name of James or Michael Devlin had been arrested anywhere in the country as far as records showed, so it was obvious that he wasn't in police custody somewhere unless he'd changed his name. Then, we got a break. Alice had surmised that if the man Reid had spoken of really existed and if he exercised such power and control over Michael, it may have been possible that the man had used Michael to assist in his disappearance from the country and then disposed of him."

The more Wright went on, the more I could see where he was going with their theory. I was becoming enthralled by what he had to say and waited for him to continue, which he did following a short pause.

"I spoke with my boss again, who by then had come around even more to my idea that Reid may have been set up and he authorised a check on possible murder victims or unusual deaths or apparent suicides of young men, not just in the UK, but anywhere in the European Union. We have access to far more information on such things than we used to have and eventually we hit pay dirt."

"You found him, didn't you? You found Michael?" I said, sure now that that was what Wright was about to tell me. "That's why Inspector Holland is in Warsaw, isn't it?"

"Yes," Alice Nickels rejoined the conversation. "Last week Carl received an e-mail from a Polish police detective who'd responded to Holland's request for information. Warsaw, of course, stands on the Vistula River, and it appears that the body of a young man was discovered on the banks of the river a few weeks ago. It was badly decomposed and appeared to have been in the water for some time, but the approximated weight of the victim, the hair colour, and the general description that Holland had circulated made the detective think that the man may have been the one we were looking for, especially when combined with the other news he had to impart."

"Precisely," said Wright. "Listen, Doctor, our chief wouldn't have let Inspector Holland go jetting off to Poland just because they found a body that *might* be the body of one of the men Jack Reid said were really responsible for the murders he was tried for."

"So, why did they let him go?"

"Because of the other bodies," said Alice Nickels.

That was it. They had me and I had to know the rest.

"What other bodies?" I asked impatiently.

Sergeant Wright took up the tale once again.

"It wasn't just the bodies; it was the timing and the locations that did it. At first we were sceptical of the chances of the man being Michael. His clothes, or what remained of them, all had English labels, but that could have been a coincidence. Many Poles live and work in England and he could have been a native of Poland who'd done just that and then gone home. But, as well as the manner of his death, the other bodies confirmed a lot of what Alice and I had suspected."

"What other bodies?" I almost screamed at the policeman in my need to hear what he had to tell me.

"Any chance of some coffee, Doctor?" he asked by way of reply. "I could do with something to wet my whistle before I tell you what we really came to relate."

My frustration was liable to boil over any second, but I managed to retain my air of professional calm as I lifted the phone and asked my secretary to bring in three mugs of coffee.

"Now, sergeant, will you please tell me about these *other bodies?"*

Wright looked at Alice Nickels, who smiled a knowing smile at him, and nodded. As he was about to begin, Tess, my secretary, knocked and entered the office with a tray containing coffee for the three of us plus a thoughtfully well-stacked plate of assorted biscuits. Wright held himself in check as Tess placed the tray on my desk and withdrew from the office. As the door closed quietly behind her, Sergeant Carl Wright took a deep breath and as I looked intently into his eyes, ready to hang on his every word, he began his strange telling of the events in Warsaw that had led him and Alice Nickels to my office that day.

Chapter 33
Alice Nickels Investigates

"I already had my own doubts, as I've told you," Wright began, "and I continued to bug Mike Holland as the weeks after the trial went on. Something about the case just didn't fit in my mind and when I met Alice at the most recent meeting of The Whitechapel Society and we put our heads together, those doubts simply grew until I was sure that Reid's story just might have some truth to it. When I told Mike Holland of Alice's thoughts, he was sympathetic as I've intimated but he wanted more. As I hadn't the time to do it, I asked Alice if she'd like to conduct some research into the affair, which she did, with surprising results."

"And?" I asked impatiently. Wright nodded to Alice Nickels who took up the tale.

"Well, I already believed that whoever was behind the killings was not only clever, but probably severely mentally deranged, as well. Sorry if that's the wrong term to use, Doctor, but it's the way I thought of him. I've already told you that Jack Reid's behaviour after the Mandy Clark killing was just so markedly different from what we expected after the first two killings that I had grave doubts as to his guilt. Now, it follows that if he isn't the killer, so the possibility has to exist that his story is true. My problem was in what way would I go about proving or disproving my theory. Then I had an idea. What, I thought to myself, would I have done if I'd been the real killer and knew that my time in Brighton was up, as the police had caught on to my scheme? The answer, stupid as it may seem, was easy. I'd go somewhere else to complete the series of re-creations."

"But surely," I said, "That would spoil the look of things. I mean the geography of the killings and so on, as you pointed out at the trial?"

"Not if he found a way to stick to the original layout. You see, when I laid the map of Brighton over the plan of Victorian Whitechapel the murder sites matched so, why couldn't the killer have picked a new town or city and done the same thing again, this time adding the other murders by committing them in locations that when added to the earlier killings still produced the same geographical layout as the original Whitechapel mur-

ders? Remember that whoever did this had to be ingeniously and fiend-
ishly clever. Also, his mental state wouldn't have made him think that
perhaps no-one would add two and two together to join the dots and
associate his new murders with the Brighton ones. I've had that confirmed
by a psychiatrist by the way. He assured me that the killer, if there *is*
someone else apart from Jack Reid who is responsible for the crimes, is
probably so fixated on his own 'mission' that he wouldn't care if no-one
else realised the significance of any new killings in a new location. He was
satisfying his own need, a compulsion to complete his re-creation of the
Ripper murders and he would do it in any way he saw fit that would also
enable him to escape detection.

"So, my next step was to try and find out if any murders identical to
those in Brighton had been carried out on the relevant dates relating to
the original Ripper murders. There was nothing in the U.K. That would
have been too easy, I suppose, and would also have been reported in the
press. I began trawling the internet, looking at press reports from around
Europe to begin with. If I'd found nothing, then I would have moved my
search further afield, but I got lucky!"

"The other bodies?" I asked, hoping that the answer was just around
the corner.

"Correct," said Nickels. "I discovered that there'd been a series of
murders in Warsaw, mirroring those of Jack the Ripper, committed on the
correct dates and including a so-called 'double-event' as in the case of Liz
Stride and Cathy Eddowes in Whitechapel. Everything appeared to fit, and
all I needed was to confirm whether the locations would fit with the Brighton
killings in reproducing the locations on the Whitechapel map."

"That's where I came in," said Wright. "Alice brought me her information and Mike Holland was virtually convinced there and then. He contacted the Warsaw police and an Inspector Fabian Kowalski who was in
charge of the Polish investigation, replied by e-mail within a day attaching
a map of the city with the murder sites clearly marked."

"You're going to tell me they matched, aren't you?"

"Yes, they did. When we took the Warsaw map and added the
Whitechapel murder map to it as a template, and then added the Brighton
ones to what we then had, the killings in Poland completed the scenario
perfectly."

"Good God," I exclaimed. "So Jack Reid could really be innocent after
all."

"Wait, Doctor, there's more," said Alice Nickels.

"If we assume that Jack's story is ostensibly true, then we also have to accept that the mysterious journal he spoke of is also genuine."

"You mean the so-called 'Journal of Jack the Ripper?'"

"Exactly. And if the journal exists, and the tale Jack Reid related regarding his own Uncle, Robert Cavendish having been psychologically affected by his perceived family relationship with Jack the Ripper then isn't it also safe to assume that the logical person to have stolen it and who would also have the genetic make-up of the Ripper in his bloodstream and therefore the psychological and deranged motive to carry out these killings must be another direct descendant of the Ripper? Another member of the family, perhaps?"

"But the only other surviving male member of the Cavendish/Reid family is Jack's father," I said, refusing to believe that the mild-mannered Tom Reid could possibly have carried out the killings in Brighton, and anyway, hadn't he been visiting his son regularly here in Ravenswood? Surely I'd have known if he'd left the country for any length of time?"

"Ah, my good Doctor," said Alice Nickels, shaking her head and looking gravely at Sergeant Wright as she did so. "I'm afraid that's not *quite* true. You see, we have discovered that there is another, far more likely candidate for the killings, one who carries just as much, if not more of the Ripper's blood in his veins. That's why Carl's Inspector is now in Warsaw. You see the real prime candidate for the Brighton murders and the man who can clear Jack Reid's name is not only a blood relative of Jack's but also has, or had, extensive business interests in the Polish capital."

"Wait a minute," I said, as the realisation of what Alice Nickels was saying hit home to me. "Are you trying to tell me that the man who did this, the one who killed all those women, drugged and then framed Jack Reid is none other than…"

"By George, I think she's got it," Carl Wright exclaimed before I could finish my sentence.

Over the next few minutes, the theory that the policeman and the solicitor/ripperologist had brought into my office that day began to grow in clarity and conviction until I began to believe, as they did, in the innocence of the young man who currently languished in a locked cell here within the walls of Ravenswood.

Chapter 34
Guilt by Heredity?

"Look," I insisted, "I have Jack Reid's family history here in his file. The only male relatives he had at the time of him receiving the so-called journal were his father and his uncle, Mark Cavendish, Robert's brother, and Mark was later found to have died, probably by committing suicide, in Malta."

"Ah, but that's where things began to get interesting," said Wright. "Mike Holland banged off an e-mail to the police in Valetta, and the Maltese police came back to us with some very interesting information relating to the death of Mark Cavendish. It's true that he was reported as dead but the evidence for that fact was sketchy at best. The police found his clothes on a rocky beach not far from Valetta. His wallet, credit card and money were all intact in the pocket of his jacket. It was assumed he'd been depressed after his brother's death, sold up all of his business interests and eventually ended his life by walking into the sea and drowning himself. A body was washed up on another beach about five miles along the coast three weeks later, but it had been so badly taken apart by the marine life of the area and showed signs of having been struck by the propeller of a ship, leaving it headless, that no positive identification was possible. The police put two and two together, assumed it to be Cavendish, and closed the case."

"But, what about DNA comparisons?" I asked.

"Look, Doctor, far be it from me to cast aspersions on fellow officers, even those from another country, but firstly, the Maltese police had no-one to compare any recoverable DNA with. They would have wanted a nice quick closure to the case so it would have been a lot of trouble for them to have obtained DNA samples from what remained of the corpse and send them to England in the hope that someone here could have traced the man's family and maybe done a comparison test. As far as they were concerned, they had a missing person and a decomposed and badly damaged set of remains that appeared to correspond as far as they could tell, with the missing man. It was only a week ago, after Mike Holland contacted them that they began to have doubts as to the identity of the body. You see, another man was reported as missing some days after Mark Cavendish disappeared and so far he hasn't been found, alive or dead. At the time of Cavendish's so-called suicide, the police wouldn't even have known of the connection between the two men, but it now transpires that the second missing person was at one time a minor business associate of Mark Cavendish who handled some of his interests on the island. If Inspector Holland hadn't asked them to delve deeper into the background of this man, they might never have realised that the two missing men knew each other."

"And you believe that Mark Cavendish killed this man..."

"Guido Bonavita," Wright added, giving the man his name, and therefore a sense of corporeal reality in my mind.

"Right, I think I see what you're getting at. You believe he killed Bonavita and used his disappearance to cover for his own while he came back to England to execute his diabolical plan."

"I do," said Wright, "In the same way that he then cynically used this Michael character as his willing assistant in Brighton, though what hold he had on the man I've no idea, and then took him with him when he did a runner only to dispose of him in Poland, where I presume he thought that Michael would go down as just another unsolved murder. He's clever all right, but I think his mind is reaching a point where his psychosis or whatever it is he suffers from is perhaps beginning to make him take risks."

Alice Nickels spoke again as Wright paused.

"It would also explain why he didn't let Jack see his face and why he disguised his voice. Jack Reid said that there was something vaguely familiar about the man's voice though he couldn't place it. If it was his uncle, he'd have known his face, his voice, everything. It's obvious that Cavendish would want to keep Jack in the dark about his identity."

"But why frame his own nephew?" I asked.

"I'm not sure if that's what he intended to do in the beginning," Wright went on, "but when Jack turned up in Brighton and Michael bumped into him by accident and found the journal in his bag as Jack insists he did, perhaps it gave Cavendish a new side to his plan. For Jack, meeting Michael was a tragic coincidence as he couldn't have known that the man was already in league with his uncle. As far as Cavendish was concerned, what better scapegoat for the killings than another direct descendant of Jack the Ripper? The fact that it was his nephew doesn't seem to have any effect on him at all. I suspect that Mark Cavendish, apart from whatever else ails him, is a classic sociopath. He feels nothing for his victims or for anyone else who he can use to help further his own plans. Cavendish and Michael appear to have used drugs to help control and confuse Jack. I think we'll find that Mark Cavendish has done some serious research into the use and application of various narcotics and he used that knowledge to help him once Jack arrived on the scene and became his unwilling patsy. Having a ready-made suspect with all the right genetic and hereditary background would have been like manna from heaven for Cavendish. All he had to do was leave enough clues for us to find and follow and we'd obviously think we had the right man, and of course that's just what we did.

"The whole preposterous story that Jack told was just too unbelievable to be true, and yet, I believe he told it like it was. Doctor, by the time Inspector Holland returns from Poland, I believe we'll have enough evidence to at least throw doubt on Reid's incarceration here at Ravenswood and maybe re-open the case and prove that Mark Cavendish, not Jack Reid, killed those women. Mike Holland, even now, is working with the Polish police to try and locate Cavendish. You see, Mark Cavendish also had business connections in Poland, all to do with his computer business and he may have a number of friends or acquaintances there who will have information that might help us trace his whereabouts."

"The only problem the police have," said Nickels, "is that without actually catching Cavendish and getting him to confess to the crimes, or at least finding some other evidence such as the journal with which to back up Jack's story, the chances of having him released from here will remain poor to say the very least."

Alice Nickels' last remark set me thinking for a minute and when I spoke it was with an air of resignation and regret as I said,

"But, Sergeant Wright, Miss Nickels, the thing you're forgetting is that whether Jack Reid did or did not kill those women, we are dealing with a severely disturbed young man here. Jack Reid does have a history of psychological disorder, and now exhibits many of the symptoms we've come to associate with a highly dangerous and potentially life threatening individual. He may seem polite, calm and in control, but there are things in that young man's mind which we haven't even begun to unlock yet. Whether we like it or not, Jack Reid is mentally ill and he needs treatment for that illness."

"Agreed, Doctor," said Nickels, "but that doesn't include being branded a pathological psychopathic killer if he isn't one and surely he could receive treatment for his illness without being banged up in the most secure psychiatric facility in the country?"

"I'm sure he could, Miss Nickels, but how would you feel, Sergeant, if he were released, only to go out and harm someone before we'd had a chance to cure him, if a cure is possible?"

"I know where you're coming from, Doctor, and I agree with you for the most part. However, it's my job to uphold the law without fear or favour and if Jack

Red is innocent of the crimes for which he was tried and sentenced to be placed here, then it's my job to right that injustice, as much as it is to catch the real killer. What happens after we present whatever evidence we may find, the decision as to what'll happen to Reid will have to be decided by the courts or whatever relevant authority has the power to deal with what I'm sure will be quite a complex problem."

"Surely you agree that if he's innocent, he mustn't be held here any longer than is necessary?" asked Alice Nickels.

I simply nodded in reply, saying nothing, as I wasn't sure if the news they'd brought me would really help Jack Reid, or society as a whole in the long run. Having presented their evidence such as it was, Carl Wright then asked if they might be able to speak with Jack. I agreed, as long as they understood that I would be present throughout their conversation with my patient. They both readily agreed and a few minutes later, the three of us were sitting in a comfortable consulting room in the company of the young, charming and maybe, just maybe, innocent Jack Reid.

Chapter 35
An Audience with Jack Reid

The consulting rooms at Ravenswood resemble nothing like the name suggests. They are in fact quite luxuriously appointed, each with its own comfortable sofa, armchairs, and even a reclining relaxer for those who prefer such comfort. A long, low coffee table complete with a selection of up-to-date magazines and periodicals sits in the centre of the room, taking the place of the expected physician's desk and doctor and patient sit in the relaxed atmosphere specifically created to ensure a peaceful and tension free environment. The floors are all carpeted with deep pile wool carpets in a variety of designs, the walls decorated in soft pastel colours with landscape prints added as a finishing touch. The only giveaway, the one visible sign that dictates to the visitor that this is indeed a secure hospital and not someone's comfortable lounge in a suburban home, is the presence of the bars that form an inescapable barrier at each window.

Alice Nickels and Carl Wright were waiting for me when I arrived in the consulting room with Jack, the visitors having been escorted there by Tess. Both rose from their seats as I entered and Carl Wright offered his hand to young Jack Reid, who took it and returned his handshake firmly and with confidence.

I carried a small hand-held micro-recorder with which I'd tape the interview as had been agreed with both the visitors and with Jack as I'd walked with him to the room.

"Sergeant Wright," said Jack, smiling. "How nice to see you again. I haven't seen you since the trial. How are you, and Inspector Holland?"

"We're both fine thank you, Jack," Wright replied. "This is Miss Alice Nickels. She's come with me to talk to you about something important."

"I remember you," said Jack, looking at the attractive woman who now sat down in one of the room's two armchairs. "You were at the trial, as well. You gave evidence about the connections of the murders to the crimes of Jack the Ripper."

"That's correct, Jack," said Nickels. "I think you might be interested to hear what the sergeant and I have to tell you today."

"I hope so. I rarely get to hear anything interesting in this place," Jack replied, almost lazily, as though he didn't really care one way or the other what his visitors had to say to him.

It took the policeman and the solicitor almost thirty minutes to relate to Jack the same tale they'd told me in my office such a short time ago. Throughout their telling of the story Jack never spoke once, merely sitting with his head leaning slightly to one side as he often did during our sessions together, listening intently.

I didn't interrupt their relating of their theory, being content to observe Jack, my patient, and his reactions to what they'd come to tell him. Those observations led me to believe that Jack was quite pleased with what they had to say for the most part, but once or twice a quizzical look crossed his face as though he would have liked to argue or at least question something they'd said. Only when they both fell silent and Wright asked Jack if he had anything to say, did the young man finally break his own silence.

"I'm pleased you think I may be innocent, Sergeant. I'm not sure myself anymore, you must understand. My head hurts a lot nowadays and I'm not quite certain what to believe any longer. They all said I did it you see. Even the Man said so, and he couldn't have been my Uncle Mark as you seem to think, because Uncle Mark is dead. The Man told me so himself."

I saw the odd look that Wright and Nickels exchanged at Jack's words. It was as though he hadn't really heard what they'd said, as if he couldn't grasp the possibility that the 'Man' as he called him and his Uncle, Mark Cavendish, might be one and the same person. In Jack's mind, such a possibility didn't seem to exist.

"Jack, didn't you hear what I said? Mark Cavendish set you up. I believe he was the mystery man in the house. He disguised his voice, kept his face hidden from you and kept you drugged to keep you from recognising him thus making it easier for him and Michael to place you at the scenes of the crimes so that you'd come to believe you actually committed the murders. Your uncle used you as a scapegoat, a sacrificial lamb if you like, and then left you to face trial for his crimes. He used Michael, too, and now Michael's dead, Jack. Do you understand me? He's dead, probably killed by your uncle to keep him from ever identifying him or giving his secret away."

"Michael's dead?"

"Yes, Jack. He had his throat cut and his body was dumped in a river in Poland, in Warsaw to be precise."

"Uncle Mark lived in Malta, and Michael's dead in Poland. See, I told you it couldn't have been him."

The strange quizzical look passed between the two visitors once again. It was quite obvious by now that Jack Reid didn't really comprehend their information with true clarity. I had warned them of course, and now they were seeing for the first time the true nature of the disturbances that existed within the otherwise intelligent young man's mind. Whether this had happened as a result of all that had happened to him in Brighton, or due to the influence of the as yet unsubstantiated journal or was linked directly to his childhood problems was something I was yet to ascertain.

"Jack," I said. "The sergeant is trying to tell you that he believes you're innocent and that your uncle faked his death so that he could come to England and commit the murders in the style of Jack the Ripper without anyone suspecting it was him."

My mentioning Jack the Ripper appeared to trigger something in Jack's mind. In a flash he switched from his rather confused state into one of total lucidity. His voice changed, taking on an air of almost benign superiority in a style I'd only heard from him once before, when I'd first interviewed him and he'd told me his whole story with great conviction. That Jack was back!

"The thing none of you is totally convinced of is the existence of the journal," he said. "It was, is, real. I read it from beginning to end and I can assure you it was the journal of Jack the Ripper himself. My Uncle Robert's great-grandfather who I suppose is my great-great grand uncle or something like that, left a number of notes and letters within the journal and he knew everything there was to know about the Ripper. Uncle Robert also placed a few notes in there, which helped me make sense of certain things within it. That journal is evil. It reeks of evil. It emanates from every page and somehow, it has an effect on those that read it, of that I'm sure. When you touch it the pages feel warm as though they have a life of their own. Sounds stupid doesn't it? But it's true, I tell you. You'd have to see it, feel it, read it to know the power that seeps from those old yellow pages. It sent me crazy, you know. Why d'you think I ended up in here?"

He fell silent as quickly as if someone had turned a switch off. Talking of so intense a subject, one that weighed heavily on his mind had obviously tired and distressed him and he sat looking directly at Carl Wright, as though waiting for a response from the police sergeant.

"You ended up here because we, the police, thought you'd committed three murders," said Wright. "The judge and the jury thought so, too, and it was the intervention of a great many medical minds that saw you sent here instead of to a conventional high security prison."

"But don't you see? I *am* a direct descendant of Jack the Ripper. Uncle Robert's great-grandfather confirms that in his notes, as does Uncle Robert in his own annotations. It's logical that if I carry his genes, then I must have carried out those murders, isn't it? I must have done all those things they say I did."

The lucid Jack was beginning to disappear once more. I stepped in to try and help hold him together long enough to conclude the interview.

"Listen to me, Jack. Heredity is a strange thing. If, and I still think it's a big if, you are a descendant of the Ripper then that heritage may not have manifested itself in you. After all, your Uncle Robert didn't go out killing people, did he? Nor did his father, grandfather or great-grandfather. Perhaps the gene that led to the Ripper's being mentally disturbed, if that was his problem, came from his mother not from Robert's great-grandfather, who you say was his father. Just because asthma or cancer or even mental illness runs in a family doesn't mean that the illness will show itself in every generation. You may not even possess the genes that led to the crimes of the Ripper, even if he was an ancestor of yours."

That seemed to give him a psychological lift and he looked at me with what I took to be a form of gratitude for the reassurances I'd given him, though whether he totally believed what I'd just said was another matter entirely. In truth, I wasn't sure that I believed in what I'd just said; such were the complexities surrounding this sad young man and his family history.

"But you're saying that Uncle Mark did?"

"I'm saying that perhaps he believes he does. If he read the journal, which for the sake of argument I'm accepting exists, he may have found it an expedient excuse to launch his own series of murders. It may have nothing to do with being an alleged descendant of Jack the Ripper. It may simply be that a history of mental illness exists within your family that hasn't been fully recognised in the past. Then again, if you're right, he may indeed be something of a reincarnation of the Ripper. Either way, if it can be proved, it would go along way towards helping to prove your innocence in these crimes."

"But if that's the case, why weren't any of the previous three generations affected?"

This question came from Alice Nickels, who'd been listening intently to my conversation with Jack.

"Maybe they were," I replied. "Mental illness doesn't always affect people to the extent that it easily recognised. For all we know, Jack's grandfather, or Uncle Robert, or any of his male descendants could have suffered from an undiagnosed form of mental instability, something that wouldn't necessarily impair their ability to lead a normal life. From what I've heard, Robert Cavendish was certainly a disturbed man towards the end of his life."

"But he'd lost his father, been involved in a horrendous car crash and suffered from appalling hallucinations while in a coma. Surely that would explain his so-called disturbances?"

"Yes, but those disturbances appeared to have spilled over in to his everyday life causing a degree of paranoia, as I understand it. The events you mention may have been the trigger that caused a chemical imbalance in his brain, thus leading to him suffering from a mild form of dementia."

"Hmm, I see," said Nickels. "So, assuming Jack's story to be true, it's likely that Mark Cavendish is indeed mentally disturbed and perhaps his brother's death became the trigger that unleashed his own mental illness?"

"Precisely," I replied.

Jack suddenly spoke again.

"So, did I kill those women or not?" he asked, a confused and almost pitiful look upon his face. He was obviously finding it difficult to come to terms with what he was hearing. He'd begun to believe totally in his own guilt and now that his possible innocence was being discussed he found it hard to accept. Quite often it's easier for a patient in Jack's situation to accept what they're told and let their mind come to terms with what they then see as reality. Any deviation from that reality then becomes a source of confusion for them. In Jack's case his original plea of innocence had been rejected by the police, the courts and the psychiatric services and under the weight of so many opinions and reports telling of his guilt, his mind had found it comfortable to accept those opinions as his own. Changing them would take some time, if such changes became necessary.

"I don't think you did, Jack," said Alice Nickels.

"Neither do I," added Carl Wright.

"And what about you, Doctor Ruth?" asked Jack, a pained and perplexed look appearing on his face, his head leaning to the side once again.

"Jack, after what the sergeant and Miss Nickels have told me today, I have to say that I have some doubts as to your guilt. I don't want to build up your hopes, but if Inspector Holland finds out what he is attempting to discover in Poland, then yes, it may prove that you're innocent of the crimes you were accused of."

"So, will I be able to go home soon?" he asked, in a child-like, innocent manner, as though this had all been a bad dream and he could simply go back to the way things had once been, which I and my visitors all knew would be a virtual impossibility.

"We'll have to wait and see, Jack," I replied. "Time will tell, and you must let the police carry out their investigation first. If they find out that you are indeed innocent I'm sure something will be done to put things right, am I correct, Sergeant Wright?"

"Of course, Doctor," Wright replied. "As you say, time will tell."

By now of course, Wright and Nickels had seen for themselves that, innocent or not, Jack Reid was indeed a disturbed young man, perhaps unsurprisingly after all he'd gone through. What the future held for him even if proved innocent of the Brighton murders would lead to difficult choices being made by those in authority over his case, myself included.

After concluding the interview with Jack and seeing him back to his room, I bade farewell to Carl Wright and Alice Nickels. The police sergeant had promised to keep me updated with whatever progress Inspector Holland made in Warsaw. I walked with the two of them to the sergeant's car, and felt the warmth of the morning sunshine as we walked down the steps that led from the visitors' entrance to the short path to the car park. Birds sang a cheerful refrain in the trees that lined the border of the car park, the daffodils nodded in our direction as they bent their heads quietly in the gentle breeze, and the sky appeared as an almost clear aerial ocean of blue with scarcely a cloud in sight. All seemed well with the world, and I hoped that the policeman and the ripperologist weren't about to open a can of worms that may have disastrous consequences for the young man who once again sat contemplatively in room 404, waiting to hear what the future held for him. In truth, I feared for Jack Reid, for, should he ever be released from his incarceration, I was fairly certain that his instability would one day lead him to further brushes with the law and the psychiatric services. At the moment, he was safe and secure within the artificial cocoon that Ravenswood offered to its patients, its inmates if you prefer. Remove him from that cocoon and things might appear very different to Jack himself, and to those who would come into contact with him.

For now though, like Jack, I would play the waiting game. I had no choice, and as the car carrying Wright and Nickels disappeared down the gravel driveway and stopped at the main entrance to be searched and then released by the security guards, I felt as though a heavy weight had descended upon my own mind. If Mark Cavendish was out there somewhere and he was the real Brighton Ripper, and the police found him it was possible that Jack would be vindicated. If he was I asked myself, would the world be a safer place? I admit that I had my doubts.

Chapter 36
Mike Holland's Polish Odyssey

The 'further information' that Carl Wright had been hoping for as a result of his superior's visit to his Warsaw counterparts arrived much sooner than either he or I expected. A mere three days after Wright and Alice Nickels had paid their visit to Ravenswood I received a telephone call from the inspector himself. Could he, he asked, come down to the hospital to see me in the company of Wright and Miss Nickels?

He assured me that the information he'd gathered in Poland was more than relevant to the Reid case, but he preferred not to discuss it on the phone. I agreed instantly, my own curiosity and the need to know the facts of the case having built up over the previous three days. I arranged with Inspector Holland that he and the others should visit me the very next day, subject to Miss Nickels being able to get away from her own office in order to travel down to Ravenswood. Holland called me back half an hour later to confirm the visit. Alice Nickels appeared to have great leeway with her legal firm. Obtaining time off from her legal practice certainly appeared to present no problems for her.

I'd met with Jack just once since the visit of Wright and Nickels and he'd appeared to have taken in most of what they'd told him, despite his apparent confusion at the time of their interview with him. During our short time together on the day after the visit he'd been lucid and communicative. He assured me that he now knew himself to be innocent of the Brighton murders. Once again he reverted to the story that had been his defence during the original police interrogations and the trial itself. He'd been tricked, drugged and set up by Michael and 'The Man' who he now believed, as Wright had suggested, was his supposed deceased uncle, Mark Cavendish. He expressed his further belief that the police would vindicate him in the course of their current re-investigation of the case. I hoped for his sake that Inspector Mike Holland had found information that would be of help to him. If the police were to discover that Jack was the killer and Mark Cavendish was in fact dead or an innocent man, it could bring about the total mental collapse of my patient. At least, follow-ing Holland's call I knew I wouldn't have long to wait in order to find out.

The day of Holland's visit came soon enough. It was Friday and the end of the working week heralded a break from the humdrum everyday working grind for the majority of the population. Not so for the police or the staff at Ravenswood. Neither crime nor healthcare takes a day off and we at Ravenswood, along with the police forces of the country provide an all-round seven day a week service. Luckily for me this would be my week-end off, when I could enjoy two days of rest and respite from the daily contact with numerous psychopaths, murderers and various other psycho-logically challenged patients within the walls of the high security facility. Every other week I would be on duty over the weekend, with time off during the week which never seemed to carry quite the same restful ambi-ence of the traditional weekend break.

In total contrast to the day of Wright and Nickels's visit, the dawning of that Friday brought with it a thunderous storm. Dark, almost black clouds rolled in from the South carrying with them a torrential downpour, made worse by the winds that began as fierce and soon grew to gale force, causing the rain to slant into cutting icy sheets that stung the face and any other exposed flesh. Though not the best of days for driving, Mike Hol-land and his two companions arrived dead on time at eleven a.m. Holland had picked up Alice Nickels from a hotel en route where she'd stayed the night to make it easier for him and Wright to collect her as they motored to Ravenswood.

There would be no interview with Jack Reid on this occasion, just a report from Holland on the results of his visit to Warsaw. I couldn't wait to hear what he'd discovered and after greeting my visitors at the main en-trance and ushering them along the corridors that led to my office, I ea-gerly awaited Holland's discourse. Firstly, however, I arranged for coffee and biscuits to be served, Tess once again the willing deliverer of the refreshments. I'd told my secretary what had transpired three days previ-ously and she was as interested as I in the outcome of this further visit. Tess, however, would have to wait until Holland and the others left before I could fill her in on what may or may not be the future dispensation of our most celebrated patient.

"A foul day, Doctor," Holland began.

"Indeed it is, Inspector. I'm surprised you weren't late in arriving what with the rain and the gales."

"I pride myself on never being late for an important appointment. When I saw the weather first thing this morning I called Sergeant Wright and Miss Nickels and had them be ready thirty minutes sooner than expected so that we might make an early start in order to be here on time, and it worked, as you can see."

"I'm impressed, Inspector Holland. Now, please, you have something important to tell me?"

"Yes, I have. I'll ask you to allow me to complete my story before you voice your opinion, as it may sound a little rambling as I go along, but I want to tell it to you as it happened and you will then be better informed as to what we may have to do in the future."

"Agreed," I said. "Please go on, Inspector."

Before beginning his story Mike Holland nodded to Carl Wright and the sergeant passed him the black attaché case he'd carried in to the room. Holland opened it and withdrew a brown cardboard file, which appeared to contain a number of loose papers and a small collection of photographs. Though Holland held the file in his hands, he said nothing of its contents at first.

I switched on my recorder, sat back in my chair and together with Carl Wright and Alice Nickels, listened as Inspector Mike Holland began to relate to us the results of his investigation though, of course, I knew that Wright would already be aware of the contents of the report. Even so, he appeared to be as attentive as any of us. I had a feeling this was going to be some tale, and as it transpired, I wasn't disappointed.

"Let me say first of all," Holland began, "that if it hadn't been for Sergeant Wright's constant nagging at me that he felt there was something wrong with the case against Reid, and for Miss Nickels's intuitive and quite extraordinary research and investigative skills I wouldn't have been sitting here today telling you what I'm about to. You, Alice, could have been a police officer. You are a quite extraordinary woman."

Alice Nickels smiled, nodded, but said nothing, not wanting to interrupt the inspector.

"When Sergeant Wright kept nagging at me about the case and I personally reviewed all the evidence and the trial transcripts and looked back on everything we'd been through in bringing Jack Reid to trial, I had to admit that there did appear to be flaws and discrepancies in the whole affair. Obviously, as the case was effectively closed when Reid was sent here there wasn't a lot I could do to actively re-open the investigation, but my sergeant and Miss Nickels, convinced that there'd been a serious miscarriage of justice, refused to let the matter drop. How on earth Alice came up with the idea of seeking information about murders outside the UK, I'd no idea at the time, though she's since explained her reasons to me and they were, of course, perfectly sound. Why would our killer, if it wasn't Reid, place himself in danger of capture by continuing his crimes here in England when owing to his deranged mindset anywhere would have done? All he had to do was plan his locations to overlay those in Brighton and Whitechapel and his means would be served. The brilliance of the criminally insane is often far greater than that of your average criminal and in this case, perhaps even more so."

I saw Holland was looking intently at me as he mouthed the last sentence and I nodded my assent to his belief. It is indeed true that the criminally insane quite often display a genius, though often a warped version of that trait, in the quite brilliant execution of their crimes, fuelled by the intense and often very frightening psychoses that exist within their minds. The inspector went on.

"When these two redoubtable experts in the history of the crimes of Jack the Ripper laid their final batch of facts and beliefs before me I had little choice but to take them seriously. The more I looked at it, the more it looked as though Jack Reid had been set up to take the blame for the Brighton killings while the real killer, or killers, made their escape. The messy scene at the house of Mandy Clark confirmed what Alice believed, though I'd never have thought of it myself. I was too pleased to have caught the man who I believed had carried out the murders and to his credit, my sergeant here was generous enough to admit that at the time he felt exactly as I did. It was only later, when the doubts began to creep in that he and Alice started to seriously bombard me with their beliefs, and I was eventually forced to take a close look at the case when the Polish connection came along. Of course, I couldn't do much about it on my own authority, but the Chief Superintendent was wholly behind me when I presented Alice and Wright's theory to him. Once the sergeant received that e-mail from Warsaw and we'd made contact with the Warsaw police and got a few facts from them, it appeared more and more as though the 'Warsaw Connection' could hold the answer to what Alice and Wright, and by then, I believed. The Chief Super authorised my visit to Warsaw as there wasn't a lot I could do simply on the basis of telephone calls and emails between here and Poland, so off I went.

"On my arrival in Warsaw I was wonderfully looked after by Inspector Kowalski. He met me at Frederic Chopin Airport, escorted me by car to my hotel, and left me to get settled on my first night in Poland. Funny thing is, I thought Poland would be a really cold country and yet the temperatures were much the same as here. So much for taking my winter thermals.

"Anyway, we began work together the following day and Fabian and I became good friends in a very short space of time. He's a little older than I am, though he looks younger, damn him, and has been a police officer for over twenty-five years. He says that his wife tells him that he loves the police force more than he does her. He laughs about it, but I suspect there may be some truth in those words. He loves his job, is fanatical about catching the bad guys, and yet I saw him change when I showed him some of the stuff I'd taken to Poland with me.

"He was intrigued by the potential connection between the Polish murders and those in England. There isn't a policeman in the world who hasn't heard of Jack the Ripper and the possible connection between the murders and those in Whitechapel over a century ago had him drooling at the mouth, in an investigative sense, of course.

Anyway, before taking me to view the actual murder sites in Warsaw he gave me a thorough run through of the sequence of events. On the night of 30th September both Anna Adamczyk and Florentyna Jaworski were killed less than a mile from one another, their bodies posed in death much as the bodies of Elizabeth Stride and Cathy Eddowes had been in 1888. In the case of Adamczyk, the wounds mirrored those of Stride's with little mutilation having taken place, but in Jaworski's murder, the killer had removed her uterus and one of her kidneys and had slashed and mutilated her face as Jack the Ripper had done with Cathy Eddowes. He'd also laid out the few possessions she'd carried in her clutch bag beside her body, another Ripper re-creation as I understand it. Fabian showed me the crime scene photographs and believe me, if it weren't for the fact that they were in colour and the girls dressed in modern clothes, I could have been looking at the photos of Stride and Eddowes that the sergeant gave me to take to Poland for comparison. In these two cases the Polish police drew a blank. There were no witnesses, no trace evidence left at the scenes and no-one in the area heard a sound. Oh yes, I should mention that both girls were known to the police as being working prostitutes, though I suspect you'd already worked that out, Doctor."

I nodded, and gasped with revulsion as Holland at last took something from the file on his lap. Two photographs of the murdered girls as the police discovered them. It was as he said, horrific and bloody and all the hallmarks of a series of Ripper-style murders. I said not a word, as I'd promised and he continued.

"Despite channelling a lot of resources and manpower into the investigation, the Warsaw Police drew a blank due to the lack of evidence and witnesses. In fact, they were almost on the verge of declaring the two murders as unsolved and scaling down their investigation when, on the 9th November, the most horrific murder that Fabian had experienced in his time on the force occurred. A young twenty year-old prostitute by the name of Maria Kaminski was literally butchered in her apartment. Whoever killed her had taken their time and made sure that the crime scene resembled that in the case of Mary Kelly in Millers Court in Whitechapel. Fabian admitted to me that he'd been violently sick when he'd seen the body as he entered the apartment. Never had that happened to him before and he confessed that if he ever came across such a horrendous sight once more in his career he would probably resign from the police force that very day."

Once again Mike Holland reached into his case and passed me the crime scene photos without saying a word. He didn't have to. They were as he'd intimated, literally horrendous. Any right thinking human being could only take some comfort from the fact that the poor girl was already dead when her body had been virtually torn limb from limb by the crazed knife of the butcher who'd perpetrated the vile and unspeakable horror. In all my years in the business of dealing with and treating those unfortunate souls whose minds had become affected by numerous psychological disorders, even I baulked at the thought that one human being, no matter how mentally afflicted, could have inflicted such vile and despicable mutilations on another. Still, I remained silent as Holland continued his tale of the macabre and chilling results of his visit to Poland.

"Of course," he went on, "there was still nothing at that stage to connect the killings to Mark Cavendish, assuming he was still alive, or to any other individual. The Warsaw police had, by the time of my arrival, made a connection between the murders of the two girls and the young man who we now believe to have been James Michael Devlin. Fabian had been astute enough, although the cases at first appeared unconnected, to compare the wounds on the girls with those described by the pathologist who'd carried out the post-mortem on Michael. The wounds on the bodies, and the throats specifically, matched. The same knife had in all probability been used to cut the throats of all the victims. Unfortunately, by the time I arrived on the scene all the bodies had been cremated so there was no chance of my either viewing the remains or obtaining DNA samples for any future comparisons. There were just too many coincidences present for there to be no foundation to Alice's theory. Everything seemed to fit, right down to the overlaying of the maps to produce a near-perfect representation of the geography of the Whitechapel murders. The only thing that Fabian and I had to do, or so it appeared, was to find proof that Mark Cavendish was alive and well and committing murders in Poland when he'd supposedly died by drowning in the warm waters of the Mediterranean. Fabian took me to the murder sites, which gave me the creeps but produced no results, naturally, and he circulated a description of Cavendish together with copies of a photograph that I'd obtained from his brother's widow, with instructions to all forces within Poland's borders to be on the lookout for the man in connection with the Warsaw murders. Detectives and uniformed officers were showing copies of Cavendish's photo to hotel and guest house receptionists and proprietors all over the country, without much success I must say.

"The evidence we were seeking, when it finally presented itself, came in the most unusual fashion and I was fortunate to be there just a few days ago when it appeared. Fabian and I were in his office when he received a phone call from the head of the police department in the city of Lublin. Having received Fabian's circularised plea for information on any suspicious foreigners in their areas and also the photo and information about Cavendish, the head of the Lublin force had something very interesting to report to my new friend. Lublin is about one hundred and seventy miles from Warsaw and the city is divided in two by the Bystrzyca River. It appeared that there'd been a fatal car accident on the outskirts of the town, when a hired car had gone out of control due to what was subsequently discovered to be a completely accidental brake failure caused by poor maintenance. The vehicle had gone over the low parapet of a bridge and plunged down into the river below. Unfortunately, there were a number of large rocks waiting to cushion the car's fall and one of them must have punctured the petrol tank which ignited and the whole vehicle was quickly consumed by flames, the driver included. When the police arrived on the scene it was too late for them to do anything for the driver who was burned beyond recognition, and must have died a terrible death and only the fact that enough of the car remained to identify it and trace it back to the car hire company allowed the police to obtain the name of the man who'd hired it. He'd given his name as Joseph Barnett from London, having produced a passport with that name on it when completing the documentation. As I now know from all the knowledge I've gained on the Ripper case, Joseph Barnett was the boyfriend of Mary Kelly and was at one time interviewed by the police investigating the Jack the Ripper killings. It seemed to me that the man in the car had to have been Cavendish. Using the name of Barnett just added to his own twisted little game. Inspector Dabrowski in Lublin informed Fabian that there was simply not enough left of the driver of the car to even attempt an identification based on the photograph or description that had been circulated, but there was something else that was found, something that clinched it for me, at any rate."

Inspector Mike Holland now reached in to the file on his lap once again and withdrew a sheaf of what appeared to be old and weathered pages from a large book. He passed them to me. As I took them from him I realised they were copies of the originals which must still be in the hands of the Polish police. As I began to read the topmost page however, it became immediately obvious as to what I was reading.

"The journal," I gasped in incredulity. "It's real, it exists."

The copied page showed that the original had been damaged and it began,

"*I*st *October 1888*

Two in one night! A glorious if unintended double. Tracked one whore, and tempted the bitch with grapes. What whore can afford grapes? She could not resist my gift, and I should have had great sport with her carcass but for interruption. I slit her easy enough, though in the dark used the shorter knife, not so quick or sharp, and saw the blood spurt in a copious river from her neck. Then, damnation, couldn't begin to gut the whore. Heard sounds outside the yard, and horses footsteps on the stones. Had to flee, and quick, kept close to the wall as a horse and cart came close by and slipped away before the man raised the alarm. Had no blood upon me, so slipped into the nearest tunnel and kept invisible, rising soon in Mitre Square. God Bless Mr. Bazalgette! Another whore soon made herself available to me, and this time I made no mistake. This one bled as a stuck pig would, and the blood gurgled as it left her gashed throat. I ripped her face apart, and gutted her as easy as you like. The street was stained fair red;

even in the dark I saw it. I could swear she moved as I sliced her innards, poor bloody little whore! Maybe not. Took no time at all, and this time sliced the ear as promised. Used the whores' own apron to… the page was torn here.

There were other pages, damaged and in places obliterated, but they were there all right and I gazed in wonder at what I now held in my own hands and at what they signified. There was even the remains of what must have been a letter from Cavendish's great-grandfather to his own son, telling him of the sad tale of the journal and how he came to possess it.

"It's real enough, Doctor," Holland resumed his story. "The police in Lublin found these and a few more pages of the decrepit looking journal floating in the river, where they appeared to have fallen from a briefcase that the driver had been carrying in the vehicle, and which must have snapped open and discharged its contents as the car hit the water. After reading Fabian's information and request for help, Dabrowski had no doubt that the man in the car was the one Fabian was looking for."

By now, I was so convinced by Holland's story that I had to ask the question that had been forming in my mind for some time as I'd listened to his telling of the events in Poland. "So, Jack Reid is innocent, then? The journal is real, so his story must be true, or how else did the man in the car come by it? It had to be Cavendish and he had to have stolen it from Jack."

"I know it all appears to support Jack Reid's story," Holland replied. "None of the things I've mentioned either by themselves or collectively actually clear Jack Reid or prove the guilt of Mark Cavendish, despite what we may believe, and in fact, know in our hearts to be the truth."

I really thought for a moment that Holland was about to leave it there, that he'd all but proved Jack Reid's innocence and his uncle's guilt but had failed to produce the solid evidence required by the courts in England to overturn Jack's conviction. Then, like a conjuror who'd saved the best of his tricks until the end of his performance, Mike Holland reached into the file once more.

"These, however, might just convince the courts that Mark Cavendish was the killer and Jack Reid nothing more than a dupe."

Holland reached across and handed me a tiny collection of photographs. I took them from him, barely able to prevent my own hand from shaking as I did so. There, in colour, was the evidence that proved that Mark Cavendish, aided and abetted by Michael, had been the true killer.

The photographs, obviously taken by Michael, showed Mark Cavendish in the midst of his hideous and gruesome mutilation of his victims. Lying to one side on the ground in each case, was Jack Reid, appearing to be insensible and presumably in a drugged state. Another set of pictures showed Jack posed as though he were the killer, still drugged I presumed, but in a semi-conscious state, making it easy for Cavendish and Michael to control him. They would have been the photos that Jack insisted 'The Man' had showed him to prove that he'd killed the young women. It had been a fiendish plan and one that could only have been devised and executed by a seriously deranged individual.

I was about to speak when Mike Holland produced one last surprise. He reached across to where Carl Wright had been holding a canvas-wrapped package throughout our conversation, or rather through Holland's virtual monologue. Wright passed the package to his inspector who proceeded to unfasten the brown string that held the canvas wrapping closed. As the package fell open he revealed its contents. There, before my eyes was a black-handled, long bladed gleaming knife, of the type used by butchers in an old-fashioned traditional butchers shop to slice their way through the bones and sinews of the animal carcasses that would hang on their hooks.

"This," said Holland "was the clincher. It still bears traces of blood, and tests have already identified that blood as being from all three of the victims."

He smiled at me as he relaxed in his chair. Carl Wright and Alice Nickels also appeared to relax, as though they'd been holding their breath throughout Holland's long delivery of his evidence. Both exhaled simultaneously as if to confirm that they, and indeed Jack Reid, may just have reached the end of a long, hard road and were about to emerge from a tunnel into the light of day once more.

"Jack Reid never hurt anyone in Brighton," said Alice Nickels. "I presume that with this evidence to back up an appeal, you will support any campaign for his early release from Ravenswood, Doctor?"

"As I said the other day, Miss Nickels, Jack is still a seriously disturbed young man. He does suffer from a psychological disorder and could yet prove to be danger to himself and to others. Any decision to release him would have to take that fact into account."

"But he *is* innocent," she went on. "How can you justify keeping someone locked up who hasn't done anything, simply on the grounds that he *might* one day do something? Surely that goes against the whole system of British justice."

In essence, she was correct of course, though it would take a lot of hard work and effort by his lawyers to try and get Jack Reid released, presuming that the courts upheld the appeal which would now surely follow when the police informed his solicitors of the new evidence they'd obtained.

The interview with the two policemen and the solicitor/ripperologist took place in my office a little over six months ago. The course of British justice, though one of the fairest and most respected in the world, does have a habit of running about as fast as the proverbial slow boat to China. The appeal process took longer than any of us expected before reaching the panel of judges who would finally decide Jack Reid's future. I myself was called upon to give evidence in court, and yet I have to say that I was surprised at the end result of the learned judges' deliberations.

Chapter 37
The Judgement

The three judges who sat to hear the appeal lodged by Jack Reid's legal team produced what I saw as a rather extraordinary final judgement in the case of the so-called Brighton Ripper. Jack's barrister Simon Allingham once more conducted a spirited and expertly constructed defence of his client, this time backed up by the information obtained through the diligence of the police officers who had originally investigated the case.

Jack's parents sat solemn faced throughout the proceedings, hoping that this would be the end of their own nightmare and that their son would be returned to them, mentally damaged and scarred perhaps, but physically fit and healthy nonetheless, ready to start a new life in the bosom of his family.

Alice Geraldine Nickels was called to give her evidence and the solicitor, at home as ever in the legal environment, delivered her own statement of the facts surrounding her involvement in the post-trail investigation into the case. She never wavered once, even when questioned deeply by one of the appeal judges, His Honour, Lord Chief Justice Roland Hume about her motives for becoming involved in the case.

"Justice, your honour," was her simple reply. "Everything about the original case against Reid seemed wrong to me. I knew the police had done their best but as someone who knows the original Whitechapel murders intimately you might say from my years of research into the case, the murder of Mandy Clark simply didn't add up. Reid was captured too easily and the Ripper, if that's who he was copying would never have allowed himself to become so sloppy in his execution of his crimes, especially when, in his mind, there was still 'work' to do in the guise of at least three more murders."

Mike Holland took to the stand and was quite blunt and succinct in his retelling of the original investigation, the doubts raised by his sergeant after the trial and his own subsequent belief in the possibility of Reid being an innocent man. He re-told the details of his visit to Warsaw almost word-for-word as he had to me in my office at Ravenswood and, of course, all the photographic evidence, the fragments of the journal and the knife used in the murders were all produced in evidence to support the case for clearing Jack Reid's name and laying the blame firmly at the feet of his uncle, Mark Cavendish.

Sergeant Wright basically backed up his inspector's evidence and spent the shortest time in the witness box of all the witnesses.

I was eventually called to the stand, but instead of being asked immediately to give my professional opinion on the state of Jack Reid's mind I was surprised when I was asked by Lord Hume to give my professional insights and conjectures on the reasons why the killer had carried out the murders and attempted to implicate Jack Reid as his means of escaping detection.

"Your honour," I began. "I'm a professional psychiatrist and conjecture about the state of mind of an individual I've never met, let alone had the chance to interview or form an opinion on, would be highly unethical of me."

"I understand your reticence, Doctor, but please, just for once, indulge me. If you were to be asked how you view the state of mind of the type of man who could have committed these crimes, in a hypothetical scenario of course, how would you reply?"

"Well, when you put it that way, I would have to say that we are dealing with a highly motivated, very intelligent but psychologically flawed individual. This man, if he was indeed related to Jack Reid, obviously had no compunction about attempting to lay the blame for his own crimes firmly at the feet of his nephew. That would indicate to me that he was probably a sociopath, one with no sense of responsibility or feelings of guilt regarding his actions. The condition known as Sociopathy is also known as Antisocial Personality Disorder and individuals with this disorder invariably have little regard for the feelings or the welfare of others. That would go some way to explaining this man's total disregard for the consequences of his own actions and the effect they would have on others, including his family. As a clinical diagnosis it's normally limited to those over the age of eighteen. Vary rarely it can be diagnosed in younger people if they commit isolated antisocial acts and show no signs of other psychological disorders. I should also mention that the condition is chronic and once begun, lasts throughout adulthood."

"And what would the symptoms be, Doctor? Are there any outward signs, things which are visible to the casual onlooker or at least to a trained psychiatrist such as yourself?"

"The usual symptoms, some of which could be detected in a psychological consultation include not learning from experience, the person having no sense of responsibility, an inability to form meaningful relationships or control their impulses, a lack of moral sense, chronically antisocial behaviour, emotional immaturity, a complete lack of any feeling of guilt and, of course, no change in behaviour after punishment."

"I see, and if you were asked to make a diagnosis, purely hypothetically, of course, on the man whom the police believe to be the real killer of those poor unfortunate women in Brighton based on what you know of him from the information they've supplied you with, what would that diagnosis be?"

"Well, if the man was Mark Cavendish as has been suggested by the police I would say this. If we begin with emotional immaturity, perhaps that showed in a small way in the fact that he ran a company which produced video and computer games, toys in fact, though highly technological, but toys nonetheless. He had no roots as such, no wife, no close friends and shunned the limelight throughout his life, classic antisocial behaviour. He was very much a reclusive type of man from what I've learned from his family and certainly disappeared further into his shell after the death of his brother. Speaking hypothetically, I suspect that Robert Cavendish, being a psychiatrist himself, knew of his brother's condition and was perhaps the only man who helped Mark stay on the straight and narrow for as long as he did. Once Robert was gone, Mark was 'released' and felt free to do as he wished. I've already mentioned the lack of guilt that would be experienced in implicating his nephew, so I would say that, yes, Mark Cavendish, or at least the man who killed those women in Brighton, almost definitely suffered from the disorder."

"I see. Thank you, Doctor."

The judge turned to his fellow learned colleagues and the three appeal judges sat in close whispered consultation with his colleagues for a minute before turning back to me.

"One last question, Doctor. In your time spent in the treatment of Jack Reid, do you believe that he, too, suffers from this, ah, Sociopathy?"

"Jack Reid is a disturbed young man, your honour, of that I have no doubt. As to whether he is a sociopath, I would have to be honest and say no, not at this stage, though it is possible he might develop those tendencies in the next year or two. He certainly suffers from a psychopathic personality disorder and exhibits great confusion at times, and is easily open to suggestion. Those are not, however, the symptoms of Sociopathy, so my answer to your question, I repeat is no. I would, however, like to caution your honours against releasing him from my care at this stage as he is without doubt..."

Judge Hume interrupted me before I could finish my sentence.

"Yes, yes, thank you, Doctor Truman. We have your complete written report on Reid's condition here," Hume held it up so that I could see he was indeed holding the fourteen page report on Jack that I'd written in response to request from the court. "We have taken advice from a number of leading psychiatrists in this case, your good self amongst them and we will now retire to consider our verdict on the appeal of Jack Reid."

I was shocked to be so summarily dismissed from the witness box, but short of exposing myself to a charge of contempt of court by protesting to the appeal court judges, there was little I could do. Together with the police officers and other witnesses I could only leave the court and await the trio of learned judges' decision. Quite often the results of appeals are not revealed for some time after the court sits, but in this case, the three appeal judges arrived at their decision that very day.

As everyone will know, back in 1888 Jack the Ripper carried out his murderous spree with apparent impunity, never, so it seems, coming close to being either named or apprehended. In a judgement that certainly surprised those who'd been involved in the case of Jack Reid and I must admit, almost took my breath away the three judges of the Court of appeal decided thus:

"In the case of the appeal in the case of The Crown versus Jack Thomas Reid, we find as following: There being sufficient evidence as to cast reasonable doubt on the conviction and subsequent sentencing of detention at Her Majesty's Pleasure in a secure psychiatric unit, we hereby overturn the original sentence, and find that the aforementioned Jack Thomas Reid is, in point of law innocent of the crimes for which he was originally tried. There being insufficient evidence to establish the identity of the man who perpetrated the crimes, despite overwhelming physical evidence having been found to establish that someone other than Reid *did* in fact commit the murders in Brighton on the given dates, we find no reason to name a potentially innocent man in connection with the crimes. Had the police been able to establish the identity of the man in Poland by either fingerprint, DNA, or visual identification this decision may have been different but the law will not permit us to name and vilify a man who has not been positively identified and we instruct that the case be placed on the 'open' file once more and the police are at liberty to re-open their investigations into the murders in the hope that they will establish and perhaps eventually positively identify the perpetrator of these heinous crimes. The fragments of the journal that the police uncovered go a long way towards establishing the innocence of Jack Reid as do the knife that was used in the killings, but they alone neither identify the writer of the journal nor the man who carried it with him at the time of his death. We accept, as is included in Doctor Truman's report that the killer, in his deranged state of mind assumed himself to be a descendant of Jack the Ripper, and for that reason embarked upon his crime spree using Reid as a dupe to throw the police authorities off his own trail, but again, no evidence actually exists to prove the identity of the man concerned.

"As for Jack Thomas Reid, it is the finding of this court that he be immediately released from the secure unit at the Ravenswood Psychiatric facility and placed in the out-patient care of his local Area Health Authority with instructions that he be regularly examined and interviewed by a consultant psychiatrist from said Health Authority, who will have responsibility for his well-being under the Care in the Community Programme."

I couldn't believe it. They were not only refusing to name the killer even though everyone, which I'm sure included the three appeal judges knew to be Mark Cavendish, but they were simply going to release my patient into the community out of some sense of responsibility to the political correctness that has all but taken over the establishment in the UK in every one of its many facets. Jack Reid was potentially dangerous. I knew it, they knew it, everyone in the court knew it, but because he'd been cleared of the murders and hadn't harmed anyone so far as any of us was aware, he was to be released despite my professional recommendations and simply trusted to appear on a regular basis for consultations with a psychiatrist at his local hospital.

As I left the court that day, I was caught up as I walked down the steps towards the road by Inspector Holland, Sergeant Wright, and Alice Nickels.

"You all right, Doc?" asked Inspector Holland as he saw the look on my face, one of shock and worry I'm sure, as they were the two emotions I was feeling most strongly at that time.

"I can't believe it," I replied "Any of it. First they let Jack go, just like that, and then they fail to even name Cavendish as the killer. It's as though he's got away with it. It's just like Jack the Ripper. No-one will ever know who really killed those women, but this time it's due to a legal technicality, the lack of a positive ID of the man you almost caught up with in Poland."

"I know, Doctor," Holland replied. "I was shocked myself at that part of the judgement, but I never really expected them to keep Jack in Ravenswood once it was established that he was innocent of the crimes he was convicted of."

"It's terrible," Alice Nickels said. "We went through all of that to clear Jack, and now we can't even tell anyone who really did it."

"Maybe one day we will be able to," Carl Wright added. "We won't give up, and there's a chance that the Polish police might yet turn something up."

"Do you really thing that's going to happen?" I asked with a note of cynicism in my voice.

Neither policeman answered.

"No, neither do I. As for Jack the Ripper, you even managed to establish the existence of his journal, but that was so badly damaged and almost destroyed in the car crash in Lublin that we still can't even establish who the Whitechapel Murderer was, can we?"

In the silence that followed we reached the last of the steps that led to the wide pavement. As we stepped onto the broad expanse of flagstone I turned and looked back at the towering court building behind us, the statue of Justice atop the domed roof, her eyes firmly blindfolded and her scales held aloft, glinting in the afternoon sunshine.

"It's not right you know, " I said, looking into the eyes of the man who had first arrested and then finally been instrumental in helping to clear the name of my patient, who would be released from his incarceration in Ravenswood upon my return.

"Jack may not have killed those women but that's not to say he's safe to be allowed to roam the streets as though he's the same as the rest of us, because he isn't."

"I know what you mean, Doc, but after all, and despite what you may think of him, Jack Reid is an innocent man."

"Yes, he is," I replied, "but for how long…?"

Epilogue
From the Pen of Jack Thomas Reid

I suppose by now you've all spoken to Doctor Ruth. She'll have told you the whole sorry tale of how I came to be in that awful place. I have to say though, that she was always as nice as she could be in the times we spent in her office or in the consulting rooms at Ravenswood. I tried to be as polite and as courteous in return as I was brought up that way. She's a nice person, Doctor Ruth.

I must admit that she was sad to see me go. When she came back to Ravenswood that day after the appeal and told me the news of my impending release I was so happy I could have cried. Well, in fact, I did cry, just a little. Doctor Ruth did tell me that she was a little unhappy at me being released so soon and without what she called 'proper' safeguards for my future being put in place. I wasn't sure what she meant until the next day when my barrister Mr. Allingham arrived at Ravenswood with my parents. Mr. Allingham and the doctor had a bit of an argument when she told him that she was worried that I wouldn't receive the constant care she thought I needed once I was released. Mr. Allingham told her that I was no longer her responsibility and that she should be pleased that an innocent man would no longer be unjustly locked up in a psychiatric hospital without due cause. Doctor Ruth told him that there was plenty of due cause for me to be in Ravenswood but that she had been overruled by the courts. I wasn't angry with her for her attitude towards me. After all, in her own way she was concerned for me, even if I felt such concern was no longer warranted. After all, I *was* innocent, wasn't I?

I soon settled into life back home with Mum and Dad. Finding work wasn't easy because of my notoriety and the fact that everyone in town seemed to know who I was and where I'd been. One man who didn't care about my past was Dave Longbridge, the owner of the small car repair shop a few streets from home. It was well-known that he'd done time in prison for assault and battery in his younger days so perhaps he took pity on me. He offered me a job valeting cars, and though it was quite menial and boring, it was a job after all and I accepted it with good grace and in time I've grown to enjoy the work.

I attend the local hospital once very two weeks where I have a consultation with Doctor Bill Redman, a nice psychiatrist who encourages me to talk about my past and my hopes for the future. He thinks I'm doing okay. He assures me that any connection my family had with Jack the Ripper is all in my mind, that the journal may have been real but there's no reason to suppose I'm a descendant of the Ripper or that his murderous genes could possibly be inherited by me, or by any member of my family. Doctor Ruth used to say that, before she became a believer. But then, what do the so-called experts know of genetics, heredity and such? They think themselves so superior and knowledgeable, but they know so little when all is said and done. Only those of us who have the gift know the real truth.

So, as for Doctor Redman, I haven't told him about the dreams of course. Why should I? They're my dreams and they're private, aren't they? He wouldn't understand anyway and if he did he'd try to have me put away again. They always start the same way, with the pages of the journal of Jack the Ripper swimming before my eyes, the words unclear but the voice that follows the pages being as clear as day. It's odd really. I remember reading the journal when Uncle Robert first left it to me, but don't really recall the details that were contained in the pages, not word for word anyway, though I do recall much of the meaning of what the Ripper said in them. That voice keeps me awake much of the night. At least, I think I'm awake, especially when I see the shape of the man who almost ghosts his way through my bedroom window and stands before my bed, waiting, just waiting. It's as if he knows exactly what I'm thinking and what I'm going to do with my life, as though he is a part of that life, which, of course, he is.

Tomorrow is the first day of August, and there's just under a week to go. The seventh is an important anniversary and I have new work to begin, work that only I can do! You know, all the time I was under the influence of my Uncle Mark and of Michael, and through the trial and everything else, none of them knew that I'd left one page of the journal at home when I left. I didn't know either until I was released from Ravenswood and I came home to live with my parents. I found it one day, lodged under the wardrobe where it must have floated down and found itself alone, there in that dark place when I left home in such haste. Mum would never have thought to move the wardrobe to look for it. Why should she? No-one knew of its existence did they, least of all the police? They denied that the journal even existed until the end. Would you like to read it? Here it is, for this is my destiny, my legacy, my future.

Blood, beautiful, thick, rich, red, venous blood.
Its' colour fills my eyes, its' scent assaults my nostrils,
Its' taste hangs sweetly on my lips.
Last night once more the voices called to me,
And I did venture forth, their bidding, their unholy quest to under-
take.
Through mean, gas lit, fog shrouded streets, I wandered in the night,
selected, struck, with flashing blade,
And oh, how the blood did run, pouring out upon the street, soaking
through the cobbled cracks, spurting, like a fountain of pure red.
Viscera leaking from ripped red gut, my clothes assumed the smell of
freshly butchered meat. The squalid, dark, street shadows beckoned,
and under leaning darkened eaves, like a wraith I disappeared once
more into the cheerless night,
The bloodlust of the voices again fulfilled, for a while...........
They will call again, and I once more will prowl the streets upon the
night,
The blood will flow like a river once again.
Beware all those who would stand against the call,
I shall not be stopped or taken, no, not I.
Sleep fair city, while you can, while the voices within are still,
I am resting, but my time shall come again. I shall rise in a glorious
bloodfest,
I shall taste again the fear as the blade slices sharply through yielding
flesh,
when the voices raise the clarion call, and my time shall come again.
So I say again, good citizens, sleep, for there will be a next time...........

So you see, as I told you, I have important work to do, and I don't have much time to prepare. If you should see Doctor Ruth, please say hello from me.

Jack

A Study in Red – The Secret Journal of Jack the Ripper
Winner of The Preditors & Editors Best Thriller of 2008 Award
and Coming soon in motion picture from Thunderball Films LLC

A Study in Red - The Secret Journal of Jack the Ripper by Brian L Porter tells the story of Robert Cavendish, a modern day psychiatrist who is bequeathed a strange set of papers which purport to be the journal of the long-dead infamous Whitechapel Murderer whose crimes gripped the hearts and minds and instilled terror on the streets of Victorian London. As he begins to read the journal, Robert becomes convinced of its authenticity and finds that the words of the Ripper have a strange and compelling effect on him. Unable to cast the pages aside he finds himself being drawn into the dark and sinister world of the killer until he is unable to distinguish what is fact and what is fantasy. In short, Robert Cavendish begins to feel as though he is being taken over in some way by the soul of the long-dead Ripper. What happens as he progresses through the journal will disturb and shock the reader as the close dividing line between sanity and madness is explored to the full.

Available in paperback, e-book and audio editions from
Double Dragon Publishing Inc

http://www.double-dragon-ebooks.com
http://www.double-dragon-publishing.com
And from Amazon.com and all good retailers

"A Study in Red' Is A BLOCKBUSTER Of A NOVEL" – Barbara Watkins, author, Amazon.com

"A Study in Red is seductive; it pulls you in, it draws you closer, it whispers in your ear. You cannot leave it, you cannot put it down – not until the very end – and by then it is far too late; it has you, mind, body and soul." - Graeme S. Houston, Mythica Publishing.

The Author

Brian L Porter is a member of The Whitechapel Society 1888, which is a real organisation and is featured within the pages of 'Legacy of the Ripper'. He also belongs to The American Authors Association and The Military Writers Society of America. In addition to winning The Preditors & Editors Best Thriller Award of 2008 for A Study in Red – The Secret Journal of Jack the Ripper, he also won the Best Poet of 2008 Award in the same awards poll under his pseudonym of Juan Pablo Jalisco. In addition to his writing the author is also the Mystery/Thriller Consultant Editor for a Scottish Publishing House, and Science Fiction Conceptual Consultant to a U.S. Publisher. He lives with his wife, two step-daughters and eight rescued dogs.

Printed in the United Kingdom by
Lightning Source UK Ltd., Milton Keynes
141152UK00001B/66/P